MR. MUO'S TRAVELLING COUCH

Mr. Muo's Travelling Couch

Dai Sijie

Translated from the French by Ina Rilke

Alfred A. Knopf New York 2005

THIS IS A BORZOI BOOK
PUBLISHED BY ALFRED A. KNOPF

www.aaknopf.com

Originally published in France as Le complexe de Di by Gallimard, Paris, in 2003.
Copyright © 2003 by Editions Gallimard

ISBN 0-7394-6483-3

Manufactured in the United States of America

CONTENTS

CONTENTS

PART THREE
LITTLE ROAD

PART ONE

TRAJECTORY OF THE SPIRIT OF CHIVALRY

1. A DISCIPLE OF FREUD

The metal chain sheathed in transparent pink plastic is reflected, like a gleaming snake, in the window of the railway carriage, beyond which the signals fade to pinpoints of emerald and ruby before being swallowed up in the mist of a sultry night in July.

(Only a short while ago, in the squalid restaurant of a little station near the Yellow Mountain, this same chain had been looped around the leg of a fake-mahogany table and the retractable chrome-plated handle of a pale blue Delsey suitcase on wheels belonging to one Mr. Muo, a Chinese-born apprentice in psychoanalysis recently returned from France.)

For a man so bereft of charm and good looks, thin and scrawny, a scant five foot three, with an unruly shock of hair and bulging eyes slightly squinty behind thick lenses, Mr. Muo moves with surprising assurance: he takes off his French-made shoes, revealing red socks (the left one with a hole, through which pokes a bony toe, pale as skimmed milk), then climbs up on the wooden seat (a sort of banquette deprived of padding) to stow his Delsey on the luggage rack; he attaches the chain by passing the hoop of a small padlock through the links on either end, and rises up on tiptoe to confirm that the lock is secure.

Having settled on the bench, he stashes his shoes under the seat, dons a pair of white flip-flops, wipes his glasses, and, lighting a small cigar, uncaps his pen and gets to work—that is to say, he begins noting down dreams in a school exercise book purchased in France, this discipline being part of his self-imposed training as a psychoanalyst. Hardly has the train gathered speed when the hard-seat carriage (the only one for which tickets were still available) is bustling with peasant women carrying large baskets and bamboo panniers, plying their modest trade between stations, lurching up and down the aisles, some with hard-boiled eggs and sweet dumplings, others with fruit, cigarettes, cans of cola, Chinese mineral water, and even bottles of Evian. Uniformed railway staff work their way down the crowded carriage pushing trolleys laden with spicy ducks' feet, peppered spare ribs, newspapers and scandal sheets. An urchin of no more than ten is sitting on the floor, vigorously applying polish to the stiletto heel of a woman of some mystery, remarkable on this night train for her oversized, dark blue sunglasses. No one notices Mr. Muo or the maniacal attention he accords his Delsey 2000. But once he becomes engrossed in his writing, he is oblivious to the world. Travelling on a day train a few days ago—likewise in a carriage with hard seats—he had just completed his daily entries with a resounding quote from Lacan when looking up he observed a trio of passengers so intrigued by his security measures that they had mounted the bench for a better look. They were gesturing dramatically in double time, as in a silent movie.

Tonight, his right-hand neighbour on the three-seater bench, a dapper fifty-year-old with sagging shoulders and a long, swarthy face, keeps glancing at the exercise book, covertly at first, but then quite brazenly.

"Mr. Four Eyes," he enquires, in a tone more obsequious than his rude address would imply, "is that English you're writing?" Then: "May I trouble you for some advice? My son, a secondary-school pupil, is utterly hopeless—hopeless—at English."

"By all means," Muo replies with a serious air, not in the least offended by the moniker. "Let me tell you about Voltaire, a French eighteenth-century philosopher. One day Boswell asked him, 'Do you speak English?' and Voltaire replied, 'Speaking English requires placing the tip of the tongue against the front teeth. Me, I am too old for that; I have no teeth left.' Do you follow? He was referring to the way the *th* is pronounced. The same goes for me: my teeth aren't long enough for the language of globalisation, although there are certain English writers whom I revere, and also one or two Americans. However, what I am writing, sir, is French."

Initially awed by this reply, his neighbour quickly composes himself and fixes Muo with a look of profound loathing. Like all workers of the revolutionary period, he can't abide those whose learning surpasses his own and who, by virtue of superior knowledge, symbolise enormous power. Thinking to give Muo a lesson in modesty, he draws a game of Chinese checkers from his bag and invites him to play.

"So sorry," says Muo, in all earnestness, "I don't play. But I do know exactly how the game originated. I know where it came from and when it was invented . . ."

Now completely nonplussed, the man asks, before settling down to sleep, "Is it true that you are writing in French?"

"Indeed it is."

"Ah, French!" he intones several times, his words echoing in the silence of the night train, the tone of satisfied comprehension belying the complete bewilderment on the face of this solid family man.

For the past eleven years Muo has been living in Paris, a seventh-floor flat, that is to say, a converted maid's room (a walk-up, with the red carpet on the stairs stopping at the sixth floor), a damp place with cracks all over the ceiling and the walls. He spends every night from eleven till six in the morning noting down dreams—first his own, then those of others, too. He composes his notes in French, using a Larousse dictionary to check each word he is unsure of. And how many exercise books he has filled already! He keeps them all in shoe boxes secured with rubber bands, stacked on a metal étagère—dust-covered boxes, like those in which the French invariably keep their utility bills, pay stubs, tax forms, bank statements, insurance policies, schedules of instalment plan payments, and builders' receipts: in other words, the type of boxes that contain the records of a lifetime. (He himself has just turned forty—the age of lucidity, according to the old sage Confucius.)

In the decade since his arrival in Paris in 1989 Muo had been recording these dreams in a French mined painstakingly from Larousse, when suddenly he found himself changed—changed no less than his wire-framed spectacles (like those of the last emperor in Bertolucci's film), stained with yellow grease, clouded with sweat, and so twisted that they no longer fit in any spectacle case. "I wonder if my head has changed shape, too," he noted in his exercise book after the Chinese New Year celebrations of the year 2000. That day, tying an apron around his waist and rolling up his sleeves, he resolved to tidy his garret. He was doing the dishes, which had been stacked in the sink for days (such a bad bachelor's habit), a solemn mass jutting iceberg-like from the soapy surface, when his glasses slipped from his nose—*plop!*—into the murky water, on which floated tea leaves and food scraps, above the reefs of crockery. He groped for them blindly under the suds, fishing out chopsticks, rusty saucepans encrusted with rice, tea cups, a glass ashtray, rinds of sugar melon and watermelon, moldy bowls, chipped plates, spoons, and a couple of forks so greasy they slipped from his grasp and clattered to the floor. At last, he found his spectacles. He carefully wiped off the suds and polished the lenses before holding them up for inspection: there were fine new scratches among the old ones, and the sides, already bent, were now a sculpture twisted beyond recognition. But all in all they were fine.

Tonight, as this Chinese train pursues its inexorable journey, neither the hardness of the seat nor the press of his fellow passengers seems to bother him. Nor is he distracted by the alluring passenger in oversized sunglasses (a showbiz wannabe travelling incognito, perhaps?), sitting by the opposite window beside a young couple and across from three elderly women. She is graciously tilting her head in his direction while resting her elbow on the folding table. But no indeed, neither train nor intriguing stranger can offer our Mr. Muo such transport as he finds this moment in words and writing, the language of a distant land and especially of his dreams, which he records and analyses with professional rigour and zeal, not to say loving tenderness.

Now and then his face lights up with pleasure, especially as he recalls or applies a phrase, perhaps even an entire paragraph, of Freud or Lacan, the two masters for whom his esteem is boundless. As though recognising a long-lost friend, he smiles and moves his lips with childish glee. His expression, so severe just a moment ago, softens like parched earth under a shower; his facial muscles slacken; his eyes grow moist and limpid. Freed from the constraints of classical calligraphy, his writing has become a confident Western scrawl, with strokes growing bolder and bolder and loops ranging from dainty to tall, undulating, and harmonious. This is a sign of his entry into another world, a world ever in motion, ever fascinating, ever new.

When a change in the train's speed interrupts his writing, he lifts his head (his true Chinese head, always on guard) and casts a cautious eye overhead to make sure his suitcase is still attached to the luggage rack. In the same reflex, and still in a state of alert, he feels inside his jacket for his Chinese passport, his French residency permit, and his credit card in the zippered pocket. Then, more discreetly, he moves his hand to the back of his trousers and runs his fingertips over the bump produced by the stash in his underpants, where he has secreted the not-inconsiderable sum of ten thousand dollars, cash.

Toward midnight the strip lights are switched off. Everyone in the packed carriage is asleep, except for three or four card players squatting by the door of the toilet. Bills continually change hands amid the feverish bets. Under the naked bulb of the night-light, whose weak blue glow casts violet shadows across their faces, the players hold cards fanned close to their chests as an empty beer can rolls this way and that. Muo recaps his pen, places his exercise book on the folding table, and observes the attractive lady who, in the semidarkness, has removed her wraparound sunglasses and is smearing a bluish cream on her face. *How vain she is,* he reflects. *How China has changed!* At regular intervals the woman turns to the window to behold her reflection, before removing the bluish unguent and starting all over again. It has to be said, the mask gives her the sphinxlike aspect of a femme fatale as she studies her face in the glass. But when a passing train flashes a succession of lights on the window, Muo observes that she is crying. Tears stream down on either side of her nose, defining wonderful, sinuous pathways in the thick, bluish mask.

The stark, imposing mountains and interminable tunnels give way to sombre rice fields and slumbering villages scattered on a vast plain. A windowless brick edifice (a warehouse, perhaps, or a watchtower in ruins) appears on a vacant lot with lamps all around. In theatrical solitude, it looms majestically, and on its blind, whitewashed wall is an advertisement consisting of a few gigantic black ideograms: GUARANTEED CURE FOR STAMMERING. The absurdity of the slogan is punctuated by the vertical stripe of a rusty metal ladder propped up against the wall in the centre of the inscription. As the train draws level with the tower the ideograms swell up until one of them fills the whole carriage window as though trying to get inside, with Mr. Muo only a hair's breadth away from the rusty ladder. Quite apart from the dangers inherent in their height and instability, ladders have, as every analyst knows, special significance, for they exert a dark, sexual fascination in the most purely Freudian terms.

At this moment, in his hard-seat carriage, Muo is seized by the same vertigo he felt twenty years earlier (on 15 February 1980, to be precise) in a room measuring six square metres, with tiered bunks shared by eight students. It was a damp and chilly room, where the air smelled of greasy water, instant noodles, and accumulated trash that stung the eyes—an atmosphere that still pervades the dormitories of Chinese universities. It was past midnight (a strict lights-out at 11 p.m.), and the dormitories, five identical nine-storey buildings, three for boys and two for girls, were plunged into obedient darkness and silence. For the first time in his life, young Muo, then aged twenty and a student of classical Chinese literature, was holding in his hand a book by Freud titled *The Interpretation of Dreams.* (It had been given to him by a white-haired Canadian historian for whom he had translated inscriptions on ancient steles into modern Mandarin during his winter holidays and from whom he received no other compensation for his labours.) Lying on a top bunk under the coverlet, he read the book by the tremulous yellow beam of his flashlight, poring over the foreign words, tracing one line after another, pausing frequently to focus on some abstraction and then losing himself all over again in a long, labyrinthine passage before reaching a period or even a comma. When he came upon Freud's commentary about a staircase in a dream, it was as if a brick had been hurled through the window and hit him in the head. Pulling tight the coverlet, stained with sweat and other nocturnal emissions, he wondered whether Freud had penetrated the meanderings of Muo's own brain to witness one of its recurrent spectacles, or indeed whether he wasn't by astonishing coincidence dreaming the very dreams that Freud had dreamt before him, in another place. That night, Freud ignited a joyful flame in the spirit of this disciple-to-be. Muo threw down his sorry blanket, switched on an overhead lamp, and, despite his roommates' groaning chorus of complaint, entered into a state of beatitude produced by his communion with a living god, reading and rereading the mystical sentences out loud, on and on, until the burly, one-eyed proctor stormed in and confiscated the book amid curses and threats. The nickname coined by his bunkmates, "Freud-Muo," stuck with him thereafter.

He now thinks back to the sign he inked on the distempered wall next to his bunk at the end of that revelatory night: the ideogram for *dream*. He wonders about the fate of his youthful graffito. He had not employed the simplified form of modern Chinese script, nor the more complicated form of classical Chinese, but the primitive writing used on tortoise-shell inscriptions dating from thirty-six hundred years ago, when *dream* was a binary ideogram: the left half a bed, represented graphically, the right a flowing line reminiscent of a Cocteau drawing, symbolising a sleep-

ing eye, crossed by three slanting strokes—the eyelashes—
with a thumb pointing down at it as if to say, "The eye
sees even as it sleeps: beware!"

MUO ARRIVED IN PARIS in the early nineties; he'd
won a gruelling competition in China and received a
stipend from the French government to complete his
doctoral thesis, which learned disquisition concerned
one of the many alphabetic languages that had been
spoken along the Silk Road before these all disappeared
into the sands of the Taklamakan Desert, the Desert of
Death. This stipend, by no means ungenerous (two
thousand francs per month), was accorded to him for
four years, during which time he presented himself
thrice a week (Monday, Wednesday, and Saturday
mornings) at the home of Michel Nivat, a Lacanian
psychoanalyst who had a mahogany couch on which
Muo was invited to recline. Throughout the lengthy
confessional sessions Muo's eyes would fix on the elegant wrought-iron spiral staircase in the centre of the
room, leading up to his mentor's private quarters.

Mr. Nivat was the uncle of a student Muo had met in
a Sorbonne lecture hall. Neither handsome nor ugly,
neither fat nor thin, he had attained such a cultivated
asexuality that it was some time before Muo, having
presented his letter of introduction, could even make
out the analyst's gender. His shock of hair with silvery
highlights, which stood out against an abstract painting
of almost monochromal stripes on the facing wall,
seemed neither masculine nor feminine, and his voice,
perhaps a fraction coarse for a woman, could hardly be
thought manly. As for his clothing, it was not merely

sexless but ageless as well, befitting as easily a young scholar as a learned elder.

The mentor paced the room with an agitated limp that recalled Muo's grandmother. During the four years of Muo's schooling, Mr. Nivat received Muo free of charge with the easy patience of a Christian missionary lending a forgiving ear to the fantasies and secrets of a convert newly touched by the grace of God.

Having no French at first, Muo spoke Chinese, of which his psychoanalyst understood not a word; even if he had, he would have been hard put to cope with the dialect of Sechuan, the province from which Muo hailed. At times, in the middle of a long monologue, Muo's superego would get the better of him, casting his memory back to the Cultural Revolution, whereupon, lest another emotion overwhelm him, he would laugh and laugh until the tears streamed down his cheeks, obliging him to remove his glasses to wipe them under the watchful eye of the mentor. The latter seemed unperturbed even while suspecting, deep down, that the joke was on him.

OUTSIDE THE CARRIAGE the rain continues to pour down, as it has since the train departed. Muo nods off, but his sleep is light, stirred by recollections of his Paris years, the muffled sound of a little cough somewhere in the car, the theme of a TV soap hummed by a card player enjoying some luck, and the thought of his precious suitcase overhead . . . His drooling neighbour, the father of the hopeless pupil of English, slumps to one side, straightens up, and slumps again, until his head comes to rest on Muo's shoulder just as the train is crossing an illuminated bridge over a murky river. For a moment Muo has the sense of being assaulted by a succession of lights aimed directly at his face, a punctual, luminous scrutiny. He opens his eyes.

Without his glasses he can't see much, but he has the impression of a stick or rod waving in front of his nose, first from front to back, then from side to side, in a continuous movement.

Rousing himself, he discovers the rod to be the handle of a long broom, wielded by a girl, of whom he can make out little more than a blurry outline as she moves about, bending over him to clean the floor under his seat with wide, rhythmic sweeps.

The train lurches again, then stops almost at once. In the jolt, Muo's twisted glasses fall off the folding table next to the girl with the broom. She reaches for them, but he bends down at the same time and receives a blow to the head from the broom handle. As she replaces them on the table, Muo has a fleeting contact with the girl, whom he can barely see, and catches from her hair the familiar fragrance of Eagle Soap, a cheap product scented with bergamot. In the old days his mother and grandmother would wash their hair with it down in the courtyard of their apartment block. Little Muo would draw cold water from the communal tap and mix it with hot water from a thermos jug to rinse his mother's silky black hair (and sometimes the silvery hair of his grandmother), pouring steaming waterfalls from an enamel mug decorated with a picture of Mao in a halo of red rays. Crouching on the ground before a basin (enamel, too, but decorated with huge red peonies, symbolizing the great revolutionary spring), his mother would rub her scalp with a bar of Eagle, smelling pleasantly of bergamot and genteel poverty, as iridescent bubbles formed between her fingers to drift off in the air.

"Tell me, my dear, why are you sweeping the floor at this hour?" Muo enquires.

She sniggers and continues cleaning. With the aid of his glasses Muo identifies what she is wearing as a man's undershirt. One thing is clear: she is not a member of the railway staff. In baggy shorts to her knees, mud-encrusted, cheap rubber shoes, and a grimy, patched cloth bag—the shoulder strap cruelly emphasizing the flatness of her chest—she is the picture of material want. Muo notes the black tufts in her armpits, the source of the acrid aroma mixing with the bergamot of her hair.

"Excuse me," she says, "may I move your shoes?"

"Of course."

She bends down and lifts them delicately, her fingers respectfully curled.

"Oh my, Western shoes! Even the soles are lovely. I've never seen such lovely soles!"

"How can you tell they are Western? They seem pretty ordinary, my poor shoes; nondescript, actually."

"My father used to shine shoes for a living," she says, smiling.

She puts the shoes down again, sliding them into a corner under the bench, against the side of the carriage. "He always used to say, 'Western shoes last much longer and never lose their shape.' "

"You have just washed your hair. I can tell by the fragrance. It's bergamot, which comes from a tree in South America, probably Brazil. First imported into China in the seventeenth century, roughly at the same time as tobacco."

"I washed my hair because I'm going home. I've been

gone a whole year, slaving away in Pingxiang, a dump of a town a couple of stations back."

"What sort of work do you do?"

"I sell clothes. The shop went bust all of a sudden, so I took the opportunity to celebrate my father's birthday at home."

"Have you bought him a gift? Do forgive me for being so inquisitive, but, to be honest, my work consists in large part of studying the relations between children and their parents. I am a psychoanalyst."

"What's that?"

"It is a matter of analysis . . . How shall I explain? I do not work in a hospital, but soon I shall have my own private practice."

"You're a doctor, then?"

"No. I interpret dreams. People with problems tell me their dreams, and I try to help them understand what they mean."

"You don't look like a fortune-teller," she chuckles.

"I beg your pardon?"

Without giving Muo a chance to address the misconception, she continues, pointing to a cardboard box in the luggage rack. "That's my present, up there," she says, "a 'Rainbow,' twenty-eight-centimetre screen, made in China. My father would have liked a bigger Japanese TV because of that rotten cataract of his, but it cost too much."

While Muo raises his eyes to take in the cardboard box, holding that token of filial devotion rumbling along on the luggage rack to the rhythm of the moving train, the girl drops her broom, takes a bamboo mat from her bag, and spreads it out under his bench. Then, yawning discourteously, she takes off her rubber shoes and, placing them next to Muo's, crouches down, and in a slow, fluid, feline movement, slides out of view under the seat. (To judge by the lack of even a toe poking out, she must have drawn up her knees, and by the silence that settles over the darkened carriage, fallen asleep the moment her head touched the patched cloth bag serving as her pillow.)

The ingenuity of this sleeping arrangement leaves Muo openmouthed. His heart goes out to her, almost as if he is falling in love, and with a welling of tears in his nearsighted eyes, a mist spreads across his glasses, almost obscuring the appearance of the girl's bare feet when they emerge at last from under the seat. It is a hypnotic sight, those feet crossing and recrossing, languidly rubbing together to fend off invisible mosquitoes. He is charmed by the delicacy of the ankles, and—despite the vanity it betokens—even the hint of coral varnish on the nails of her big toes. The next instant, in a rapid flexing of the knees, the girl's feet, none too clean on closer inspection, disappear again, but the sight of them, crossing and recrossing, remains in Muo's mind for as long as it takes him to complete his mental picture of the reclining figure in the dark: the scabby knees, the twisted shorts, the man's clammy undershirt, the dust clinging like a sad little collar to the moist, gleaming skin of her nape.

He rises from his seat and, apologising to his sleeping neighbours, picks his way through the passengers sitting in the corridor to get to the toilet. But when he returns he finds that his precious seat—that tiny paradise, one third of the hard bench—has been claimed by the father of the hopeless student of English, the man's head resting so soundly on the folding table one would think he had received a bullet to the temple. Leaning against the family man's shoulder is another usurper, likewise a drooler, while the seat on the aisle is occupied by a peasant woman with an unbuttoned blouse who is suckling an infant at her swollen left breast. Muo bitterly accepts the loss of his place and settles down on the floor at her feet.

In the faint light he notices that the infant's head is almost lost in a red bonnet. *Why cover the poor child's head in this hellish heat?* Muo thinks to himself. *Is there something wrong with it? Is the mother not aware that a celebrated psychoanalyst once pointed out that in European folktales, a red bonnet symbolises the menstrual flow?*

At that instant a spark is ignited, either by the red bonnet or by the idea of menstruation, and his brain is set ablaze.

Could the girl with the broom be a virgin?

A thunderclap resounds in his head. His pen falls off the folding table and bounces on the floor before skittering away to the end of the aisle. But with his eyes fixed on the baby's red bonnet, Muo can think of nothing but the question that has entered his head.

The infant begins to howl, and Muo in startled pain averts his eyes to follow the shadows shifting from one face to the next in the carriage, the lights flitting past outside the window—an empty service station, a street lined with shuttered shops, construction sites with unfinished apartment blocks in bamboo scaffolding.

The infant in the red bonnet, silent now, leans over and thrusts its puny fist into Muo's face. Its mother is too drowsy to restrain it. Muo receives this little battering without flinching, and watches as the empty beer can rolls past the card players and crosses a puddle of indeterminate fluid. He can feel a tickle of warm air. Twisting around, he sees the baby leaning out from its mother's arms to bury its nose in his neck as though seeking out some particular scent. It gives Muo a wary, almost hostile look before flaring its tiny nostrils and resuming its olfactory exploration. It sneezes and begins to cry again.

This time, the screams are earsplitting. Muo shivers as he meets the stern, accusatory gaze of the infant, which speaks complete understanding of what is lurking in his mind—the extraordinary fancy, or rather extraordinary thrill, at the thought of having happened on his secret quarry, of having arrived at the end of his journey.

But not a moment later, Muo turns his back on the child, remembering that such a thought can only defeat his resolve as a healer of souls.

Choosing the only path away from the screaming infant, he gets down on all fours. Diving into the dense gloom beneath the seat, he has the sensation of being struck blind. In the overpowering stench he has to hold his nose to avoid gagging, and yet for the next few seconds certain errant smells return to him from long ago, when he was a boy at the start of the Cultural Revolution. An airless basement where his grandfather, a Christian pastor, was being held along with his grandmother and several other prisoners in a stink of urine, faeces, sweat, damp, and dead rats, which lay rotting on the narrow steps and tripped little Muo as he descended. He can scarcely imagine what it would be like under the bench now had the salesgirl from Pingxiang not swept the floor underneath so vigorously before settling down.

Geographically speaking, the underfoot microcosm is not as small as he'd imagined. The unsuspected depth more than compensates for the lack of height, the equivalent of two benches. Though only the scantest light enters dimly from left and right, he can sense the presence of the sleeping beauty curled up on the floor like a heap of rags.

Pity, he left his matches on the folding table and his lighter in the Delsey, bound to the luggage rack. Still, the darkness enfolding him feels welcoming, sensual, even romantic. He imagines himself navigating secret passages of pyramids or blocked Roman sewers that ultimately lead to treasures.

Before crawling all the way under, he again checks, by sheer force of compulsion, for the wad of bills in his underpants and the French residency permit in the inside pocket of his jacket.

He creeps forward diagonally, thinking he might turn his temporary blindness to his advantage. Suddenly something hard—the girl's bony knee?—hits him in the face, smashing his glasses into the bridge of his nose. The pain makes him cry out in the gloom, but does not provoke the least response from the sleeping beauty.

"Listen here, young lady," he says, his voice in the dark low and sincere, as befits the grandson of a pastor, "there's no need to be afraid. It's only me, the psychoanalyst you were talking to earlier. You interest me. I would like you to tell me one of your dreams, if you can remember any. If not, you could draw me a tree— no matter what kind, big or small, with or without leaves . . . I can interpret your drawing for you and tell you whether or not you have lost your virginity."

Still on all fours, he pauses, waiting for the girl to respond. Thinking over what he has just said, he is quite pleased with his peremptory authority in broaching the subject; and he believes he has concealed his own inexperience in sexual matters quite well.

But there is no response from the girl. In the darkness his fingers come into tremulous contact with one of her bare feet, and his exultant heart leaps into his throat.

"I know you're listening," he continues. "From your silence, I gather my proposition has upset you. Perfectly understandable. Let me explain: interpreting drawings is not some charlatan's trick, nor is it something of my own invention. I learnt the technique in France, in Paris to be precise, at a conference for teachers of traumatised children, a conference organized by the French Ministry of Education. I clearly remember the trees drawn by a boy and two girls younger than you, victims of sexual abuse. Gloomy trees they were, moist, with huge, spreading branches like the threatening, hairy arms of an ogre."

As he speaks he feels his worst enemy—his own subconscious or his superego—rising up uncontrollably and running riot in his head. It does not, however, restrain his hand from fondling the invisible foot, which feels cool but silky. His fingertips explore its dainty outline, tracing the bony instep, which seems to tremble at his touch. Finally, he curls his hand around the slender, fragile ankle, sensing a delicate vibration of cartilage, and his member hardens.

In the near-total darkness, this foot, which he cannot see, takes on another dimension. The more he fondles it the more it is transformed, and little by little its essence, its nature, becomes that of another foot, encountered by Muo the Saviour twenty years earlier and so often mentioned to his psychoanalyst since (although the French mentor would persist in neglecting this train of association in favor of one rooted in childhood.

IT WAS A SPRING DAY in the early eighties, the setting a dimly lit, noisy canteen teeming with university students armed with enamel bowls and chopsticks. The loudspeaker was blaring poems glorifying the government's new policy. There were long lines at each of the twenty filthy windows; endless rows of good-tempered, dark-haired youngsters jostled in the steamy air. Glancing around furtively to make sure no one was watching, Muo dropped his meal voucher, which was tinged with soy sauce, grease, and soup. In the ensuing hubbub the voucher whirled away, landing "accidentally" at the feet of a female student whose shoes caught the light of a sunbeam filtering through the cracked glass of a barred window. The black velvet shoes with their paper-thin soles set off the curve of her white-socked insteps. His heart pounding like a thief's, Muo crouched down to retrieve the fallen meal voucher and in so doing he touched the velvet shoes with his fingertips, thrilling to the warmth perceptible from the white ankle socks.

As he lifted his head, through the vapours of the cafeteria he noted that the girl was looking at him not with curiosity or surprise or reproach, but with a tender smile of indulgence.

It was his classmate H.C., like him a budding specialist in the study of classical texts. (H is her family name, composed of an ideogram whose left part signifies *ancient* or *old*, whose right part signifies *moon*. Her given name, C, is likewise composed of two parts, the left representing *fire*, the right *mountain*. Together they make the loneliest name imaginable—Volcano of the Old Moon—but it is also most pleasing to the eye when written and no less magically melodious when spoken. Even today, Muo melts the moment his mouth shapes the words.)

NOW, IN THE SEMIDARKNESS of the railway carriage, just as the clanking subsides and the grinding wheels begin to slow, he is overcome at the memory of those delicate velvet shoes and at the touch of the cold, bare foot in the space beneath the seat. He lets out a little groan, half ecstatic, half pained and then shameful, as a scalding jet spurts from his groin, blooming over his underpants and trousers, fortuitously sparing his precious wallet.

The train stops. From the platform, bundles of shimmering light partially illuminate the space beneath the bench. Muo discovers that the foot he has been fondling, the cause of his humiliation, is nothing but the handle of a broom, discarded under the seat.

With his eyes shut and his hands covering his face, he lies back and prays for the train to depart again so that the evidence of his shame will be concealed by the night, but an eerie silence hangs about the stationary carriage. Under the bench, a voice suddenly booms out.

"Where are we?"

At this, Muo turns over onto his stomach as quickly as he can to hide the front of his trousers, in the process dislodging his glasses.

"Who are you? And where is the girl from Pingxiang, the one who sells clothes?"

"She's gone. Sold me her place for three yuan."

Muo realises that during his brief trip to the toilet, the population beneath the seat has changed dramatically, and not in his favour. Was it then that the girl had made off? Anxious to know, he edges toward the slumberous father of the poor student of English and discovers that the girl's rubber shoes are gone. But it takes several minutes to discover that his own Western shoes, sturdy and shape-retaining, have vanished, too.

Covered in dust, his trousers stained, his face grimy, he twists himself around in frantic apprehension to look up at the luggage rack, where in the glow of the station lamps a length of metal chain, severed who knows when or how, dangles in midair.

He dashes to the exit and bounds onto the platform. Half blinded by the fine drizzle wrapping the station in a dense shroud, he runs up and down the platform, shouting like a madman, but his voice is lost among the gleaming rails, passengers hurrying on and off, the railway staff chatting idly by the carriage doors or squatting on the platform to slurp their instant noodles or playing billiards in the station master's office, recently converted into a makeshift karaoke bar floodlit like a stage.

"THE TRAIN WAS ALREADY pulling out of the station by the time I found a policeman," Muo writes in the new notebook with a pearl-grey cover he acquired the morning after his suitcase was stolen, along with a boxy black suitcase—this one without wheels—a more formidable chain, and a mobile phone. "I ran after it, but couldn't catch up. For a long time I trudged on through the rain, along the tracks stretching away as far as the eye could see, calling out the name of my beloved H.C., Volcano of the Old Moon, beauty and wisdom incarnate, and I prayed for her to come to my aid."

Having written these words in his room in a small hotel, he begins to make a list of the contents of the stolen suitcase, item by item, followed by the price in French francs and then converted into yuan at a reasonable rate. As he adds his shoes, exercise books, and thermos, all for the eventual claim to be filed with Chinese Railways, he stops, convulsing with laughter. "Anyone would say I've been gone too long from the great fatherland," he chuckles to himself. He tears up his list and scatters the confetti out the window.

2. THE PRENUPTIAL DRAMA OF AN EMBALMER

"Tell me, when did you first hear the word *homosexual*?"

"Let me think . . . I must have been about twenty-five."

"Are you sure? Twenty-five? That old?"

"You haven't changed a bit, Muo. Still got that nasty

way of opening old wounds. You know it's a sore point for me, like it is for every woman of forty."

"Well, I believe that if an old wound hasn't healed, then at least I can analyse the pain. Forget that I'm nearly a thousand kilometres away and consider this conversation a free therapy session . . ."

"You can stop right there, Muo. You call to wish me a happy birthday, and that's very sweet of you. But we're not classmates anymore, and I'm too old for games. I am a widow and, moreover, an embalmer by trade."

"Such a wonderful word—*embalmer*! I don't know the least thing about your work, but I've fallen in love with the word. A bit like falling in love with a flower before you've even seen it."

"So?"

"Why so prickly? You know I'll keep anything you tell me strictly to myself. Psychoanalysts are like priests—they never reveal the secrets of the confessional. A matter of professional ethics. Trust me, talking will do you good. Go on, give it a try."

"The first time I heard about it, you mean."

"Yes, *homosexuality*. One would think you were scared of the word."

"Before I was twenty-five, I'd never even heard it spoken aloud."

"Do you remember the first time?"

"Yes, I do. It was about two years before Jian and I got married, although we were already engaged by then. He was teaching English at a secondary school. It was a Saturday—still a workday at that time. He came to pick me up at the mortuary, at around six p.m. I was riding pillion, as usual. And as he pedalled away . . ."

"PEDALLED AWAY." PEDAL. On the other end of the line, Muo muses about the word in French, *pédale,* slang for *pederast.* He had often seen her round-shouldered, bookish young man, with his thin face and carefully combed, squeaky-clean long hair, pedalling his way toward the grey concrete building where Muo and the young Embalmer lived with their respective families. He would slow down and remain motionless on his bike for several seconds, balancing like an acrobat, before placing his feet on the ground almost nonchalantly. He always dismounted some distance away, as though afraid his property would go missing in the dark jumble of bicycles parked around the entrance.

"AS USUAL, WE TOOK the road alongside the music academy, then past the confectioner's and the tire factory."

"By the way, I have a little question for you at this point—somewhat personal, perhaps, but highly significant for the purposes of Freudian understanding. It's about the chimney of the tire factory. You know, that tall stack thrusting up to the sky? Does it appear in your dreams at all?"

"No, never. I loathe that chimney, belching black smoke into the sky, day in, day out. Soot and grime raining into the street, onto every roof and treetop. Worst of all is when the air is very heavy just before a downpour and the thick smoke wraps around your head and suffocates you. Awful. What I do like, though, is going past the confectioner's. It smells so good. Do you remember that?"

"I certainly do. When we were kids in the sixties there was that wonderful smell of milk mixed with vanilla—I adored those sweets and never found anything like them again. Go on, tell me more. You were on the back of Jian's bike, in the black smoke of the tire factory."

"All right, then. It was already getting dark, and once we were past the Sechuan Opera House, Jian took a shortcut."

"I know the one you mean—that narrow dirt alley that runs by the open sewer that was always full of stinking muck. With all those bumps, you can't have been very comfortable sitting on the back of Jian's bike."

"No, not really. In fact, hardly anyone used the alley because it was so badly rutted. Anyway, halfway down there was a sort of shed—you remember?"

"You mean the men's public toilet?"

"Public toilet? You must be joking. Nothing but a shithole, that's all it was."

"True. A brick building, as I recall, very run-down and with holes in the tiled roof that let in the light. Thick with flies. No electric lighting. Puddles all over the place. The floor was never dry, even in good weather. You can imagine what it was like when it rained, couldn't set foot inside. Everyone just pissed from the entrance. It was like the Olympics sometimes, to see who could piss the farthest."

"Well, that day the public toilet, as you call it, was quite a scene. At first all I could make out were some shadowy figures moving around the shed. Then, as we drew near, I saw that they had guns. The alley was strangely quiet, but soon the place was crawling with police in uniform. They arrested about a dozen men, some young and some not so young. I couldn't really tell. Their faces were cast down as they filed out of the building. Jian and I continued on foot. I asked my future husband who these poor men were. He said, 'They're the homosexuals.' First time in my life I heard that word. And I was twenty-five years old."

"What were they doing in the shed?"

"Jian explained that it was their meeting place. They were led, cowering, past us to a police van with barred windows. They looked like broken animals. Even the police looked at them with a kind of astonishment. The silence was terrible. You could hear the telegraph wires humming in the wind, the effluent in the sewer trickling against the sides. I could even hear my empty stomach rumbling. Jian just sat there stunned, staring at the mud splattered on the front wheel of his bike. When we got on the bike again I put my cheek against his back and it was drenched in cold sweat. We never took that short-cut again."

"Did he often pick you up after work?"

"Almost every day."

"That was nice of him. Even if I were madly in love I couldn't do that. I'm scared of the dead."

"Jian wasn't."

"You don't mean to say he was fascinated by death, do you? That's a mind-set prevalent in the West. Most intriguing. A pity I didn't get a chance to analyse your young man."

"Come to think of it, d'you know where we actually met, Jian and me? In the mortuary in the very room where I still work today."

"I'm listening."

"It was in the early eighties. It's been almost twenty years—I can't even picture what he was wearing that day."

"Go on, try. It'll come back to you."

"No, I'm tired. Let's pick it up tomorrow, all right?"

"But I really want to know how you two met! Go on, humor me."

"Tomorrow."

"IT WAS GOING ON FIVE in the afternoon. My boss and colleagues had left for a friendly basketball game against the fire-brigade team. In the ceremonial room I found Jian standing by a body on a gurney. I remember that his hair was neatly combed, but it was so long it brushed his collar. I remember his sad, drawn face, his hollow eyes, and especially his smell! You know how rare it was back then, in the early eighties, to get a whiff of anything like perfume, even rich people didn't have any. As soon as I stepped into the room I knew it was the real thing—geranium with a hint of rose, a subtle, musky, exotic fragrance. In his hand he held a long necklace, which he fingered, mechanically, like a monk with his rosary. It wasn't until much later that I would discover he owed those stubby, swollen fingers to his reeducation in a remote mountain village. And his right hand was badly scarred in two places, also thanks to the Cultural Revolution."

"What were you wearing on that day?"

"My work coat and gloves."

"A white coat?"

"Of course. I always keep my coat clean and smelling

fresh from the laundry. You should see the others—they don't even bother to wash their coats."

"I see. Jian must have appreciated your fastidiousness."

"Well, at the time, he didn't even look at me. He was staring at a bluish discolouration on the side of his mother's head. It's usually the first sign of decomposition. He presented me with a letter he had obtained who knows how from the mortuary director, giving him permission to attend the embalming as a discreet observer. I wasn't yet licensed. The devil only knows what came over me, but instead of telling him that, I just dressed the hair and said that we ought to wait for my boss before getting to work."

"How often did you have spectators?"

"Very rarely."

"You know, listening to you, my heart goes out to your poor Jian. The perfume must have been his mother's; the necklace, too."

"Such powers of deduction, my dear French psychoanalyst! But does the good doctor understand himself? Tell me, why aren't you married yet? Still carrying a torch for that girl at university, Volcano something, the one who wouldn't give you the time of day?"

"Volcano of the Old Moon. I won't have you mocking her. Anyway, you're undermining the analysis."

"Okay, where was I?"

"You were going to embalm his mother."

IN HIS SHABBY LODGINGS, the psychoanalyst is disturbed by a sudden burst of noise from upstairs: water

gurgling in the pipes, a man's voice singing in the
shower, and a toilet being flushed, bringing the roar of
a waterfall right overhead. The sheer force of the din
causes chalk pellets to fly out of the old cracks in the
ceiling like old wounds reopening. Muo manages
nevertheless to remain focussed on his telephonic psychoanalysis, until he hears the calmer trickle of the cis-
tern filling up again, followed by the throb of a washing
machine, a sound that like an old song transports him
back to a spring Sunday long ago—more than twenty
years, in fact. In his mind's eye he can see the communal faucet in the packed courtyard, where the
Embalmer and her fiancé stood side by side, proudly
admiring their brand-new washing machine. It was
their first joint purchase before getting married. Back
then there were no taxis in that city of eight million,
and the couple had brought the great East Wind—a local
product—home on Jian's bike, secured with ropes of
plaited straw, he doing the pulling and she the pushing.
It was a momentous occasion, worthy of note in the
annals of this courtyard, which was home to several
hundred medical families. When they arrived, a mass of
children and adults, including doctors young and old,
swarmed around the machine. They proclaimed astonishment and peppered the couple with questions about
its price and operation. The call for a public demonstration was irresistible. The Embalmer ran inside to
fetch her dirty laundry, while her fiancé connected the
machine to the tap. To Muo the event seemed like the
launch of a spacecraft. When Jian pushed the start button, red and green lights started flashing above the
round window, behind which the clothes slopped and
tumbled in the flux and reflux of water, accompanied

by the murmur of a stream and myriad bubbles bursting into multicoloured stars in the spring sunshine. Linking arms with Jian, the Embalmer patted the obedient machine approvingly. Soon, however, the white shell began to shake more and more violently, at last reaching the pitch of an aeroplane just before takeoff.

After several minutes of these convulsions, the demonstration reached its climax. The door was ceremoniously opened in full view of the crowd. Kneeling before the machine, the couple reverentially removed the clothes: clean, but shredded beyond recognition, having been blown about for less than ten minutes by the pitiless East Wind.

"HIS MOTHER WAS NOT a pretty sight, even for a corpse, let me tell you. It wasn't the loss of colour—I was already used to that. What shocked me were her features, which were so twisted that I could only imagine she had been consumed by hatred when she died. Her facial muscles were frozen in a howl, wide open, her mouth contorted, gums bared like a horse under gunfire, whinnying in a world of grey, black, and white. She was a linguist, Jian told me, still weeping, his voice barely audible. She had died suddenly on the Sino-Burmese border, where she had been researching the language of a primitive matriarchal tribe, in the effort to prove that most of the words of this vernacular derived from the ancient Chinese spoken in the era of the Warring States, before the first emperor. Apparently she had been holding forth in this unknown language on her deathbed at the local hospital. They weren't even real words, just the roots of words, strings of strange syllables and unheard-of isolated vowels and intervocalic plosives."

"But aside from these linguistic indications, what did the autopsy report say?"

"That she died either from some obscure tropical disease or from food poisoning caused by a toxic plant or mushroom; the proof was that her liver had crumbled to dust at the medical examiner's touch. Jian was devastated and had to take care of the funeral arrangements. He was all alone, poor thing."

"What about his father? Wasn't he a linguist, too?"

"His father works in Peking. His parents divorced in the late sixties, and he was raised by his mother. He was desperate for her to look beautiful in death, whatever the cost. He wanted her to wear an expression befitting a great scholar, not that horrible grimace. But the body had been repatriated by plane and, as I said, it had started decomposing. When I closed her eyes—my immediate professional impulse—I noticed the bluish stains on her temples and neck. I told Jian there was not a minute to lose—we needed to lay her on a bed of ice in the embalming hall. Since the staff had gone off with the boss to play basketball, they had padlocked the freight elevators, so we had to carry his mother up to the first floor ourselves. We wrapped her in a blanket to lift her rigid body. I took the shoulders and Jian took the feet. He did not speak. His face was utterly blank. His walking was stiff and jerky, as if he had wooden legs. He was in a very bad way. To free his hands he had slipped the necklace around his neck, and then it was clear that he was crying. The staircase wasn't far, but with each step the body seemed to get heavier and to slip lower and lower until it almost touched the stairs. I had to stop several times to catch my breath. When we paused I sank down onto my haunches, and with my back against the wall, his mother's head resting on my knees, I sat gasping, inhaling his perfume. I shut my eyes and didn't move. Jian was there, very close to me, but I couldn't see him. I couldn't hear him breathing or even speaking; I just smelled his scent, a sun-scorched geranium with a hint of rose, and soon I was inhaling it greedily, that fragrance now more familiar and pleasant, and it took possession of me. It was like a dream. There I sat, with my eyes shut and his mother's head resting on my knees, feasting on the smell of geranium until I had the sensation of turning into a long seed pod. Ever seen a geranium seed? It looks something like the beak of a white stork, sleek and beautiful."

"So how did you make it up the stairs?"

"It was a concrete staircase, steep and very narrow. When we reached the foot of it he said it would be better for him to carry her up on his own. First he tried gathering her up in his arms, the way a man in a film would sweep up his young bride before bounding up the stairs two at a time. But Jian couldn't do it. Finally, he asked me to help him heave his mother onto his back. The dead woman's cheeks were even more hollow and her skin even greyer than I had realised, which meant that the muscles were beginning to slacken and that her jaw would soon drop, causing me enormous trouble later on, when I would have to shape the death mask. I tried to secure her jaw with a cloth tied around her head. In the glow of the bare bulb hanging in the stairwell, I saw that her eyes had opened again, but now the look in them was different—less rage, less hatred, but so much sadness, such despair, that I had to turn away. As Jian struggled upward manfully, step by step, it seemed there could be nothing heavier than the body of his dead mother. His calves quivered, and it seemed the sharp bones of his ankles might pierce his skin. But he persevered until the necklace hanging from his neck apparently caught on something and snapped. Watching incredulously as one after another of the beads cascaded down the narrow steps, bouncing off the concrete, before falling and leaping again with a piercing, crystalline sound, I held out my hands as if trying to catch them in midair, like a hapless infant trying to catch a fly. Then a burst of untimely laughter rang out above me and I very nearly jumped out of my skin. Raising my head, I saw Jian looking over his shoulder, still laughing. He apologised for his hysterical fit of mirth before resuming his ascent of the concrete stairs, each staggering step scattering more beads to patter and dance before my eyes. And I no longer tried to restrain them."

THE GURGLE OF PIPES, a sound less crystalline than that of beads striking concrete, plays in Muo's head: the sloshing of water in a washing machine, when much to the delight of the Embalmer and her fiancé, Jian, they once again filled the courtyard to capacity on the Sunday following the drama of the first trial. Having taken the defective East Wind back to the East Wind factory, they had returned seven days later, trundling a new washing machine on the back of the bicycle, Jian once again guiding the handlebars and the Embalmer pushing from behind. Dusk had already fallen, but their arrival in the courtyard provoked an even greater commotion than it had the week before. A doctor who lived on the ground floor—known for his bad temper and nervous tics, which were said to manifest themselves five or six thousand times a day—passed a lead out of his window to power a five-hundred-watt lightbulb suspended over the communal tap. The new East Wind stood in readiness. There was not only the ardent crowd milling around the machine, but also curious neighbours hanging out of their open windows as if they were in the dress circle of a theatre. Boys threw lit firecrackers, and girls, glad of a chance to get out of the house, came running, still holding their supper bowls and picking with their chopsticks at each other's remaining portions, eager to join in the laughing, chatting, and flirting. As the Embalmer had destroyed a good deal of her dirty laundry in the first trial, she was obliged to load the new machine with clean clothes, which she did, smiling graciously, in full view of everyone. The young couple stood hand in hand, gazing into the window behind which blue jackets and jeans frothed and swirled among flowered shirts, printed poplin skirts, a pair of flared trousers that no one had ever seen either of them wear, and several promotional T-shirts from the mortuary.

Little by little, like the swelling tones in the closing movement of a symphony, the new machine rumbled toward its finale, in the proper time allotted to the wash cycle, a gratifying show of efficiency following the nightmarish roar that had nearly caused its predecessor to take flight. When the last of the daylight was gone, the five-hundred-watt lightbulb swung rhythmically in the breeze, casting a shadow play of yellow, crimson, and grey across the faces of the spectators, all of whom fixed their eyes on the anxious owners of the East Wind, whose own eyes dared not stray from the machine's porthole, now opaque with steam and water droplets.

Still throbbing with a regular, mechanical, well-oiled baritone, the machine, to the general relief of the crowd, seemed to be on the verge of coming to a rest when it apparently decided to prove its kinship with its unruly predecessor. The specified duration of the rinse cycle had been exceeded, but the machine, stubborn as an ass, refused to stop. Ten minutes went by, then twenty, and still the new East Wind showed no sign of relenting. Some of the onlookers wandered off, grumbling their impatience, before one joked that the factory had sold the couple the first machine a second time. Muo saw that the girl, flushed scarlet with mortification, was trying hard to laugh along with everyone else. But soon a great flood of mockery deafened the Embalmer and her fiancé as they stood with bowed heads, their shoulders sagging as a fine drizzle began to assault them in the yellow glare.

Moments later, the courtyard was empty. True to his miserly nature, the ground-floor doctor with the tic-ridden face collected his lightbulb, grumbling that he should never have lent it in the first place and insisting that the Embalmer refund him the expense of the electricity.

Now lashed by the rain, the machine careened on in the semidarkness as though intent on prolonging its hateful solitary mayhem ad infinitum. Muo stood on the porch of the building opposite, peering through the rain at the ghostly twinkle of ruby and emerald lights. There stood the cold robot, a hard, inexorable monster indifferently doing exactly as it pleased, singing in the rain, but now the baritone had risen to a strident mega-lomaniacal tenor.

Soon the swags of talk drifting down from the dress circle turned into jibes, jealous taunts aimed at the Embalmer and her fiancé, who were still standing by the communal tap under a black umbrella held by Jian, gazing dully at the rain, the stubborn machine, and the flooded courtyard.

If only they'd known for sure what was to come when the hatch was finally opened with a metallic click and the clothes were removed by the flickering light of a torch, they might have come in from the rain rather than waiting to collect their second heap of shredded rags.

"YOU REMEMBER I TOLD YOU that I wasn't yet a qualified embalmer? At the time, I was still assigned the hairdressing, never having prepared a body, properly speaking, or even done any cosmetic work. Not owning up at the start to being only an embalmer-in-training got me into quite a fix. Once his mother was laid out on the refrigerated slab, I started combing her hair very slowly in the hope that my boss and the others would soon get back from their game. Despite her age, she had wonderful hair, streaked with grey and not very thick, but incredibly silky. I washed it, dried it, and brushed it strand by strand, and then I tied it back in a knot. Jian had told me she used to put her hair up for special occasions: birthdays, new year's celebrations, and so on. Apparently she used to admire the sight of her long, elegant neck and her youthful, smooth skin in the mirror. When I finished fixing her hair, I must say it

looked very nice. She looked intellectual, even aristo-
cratic. But, of course, the hairdo could do nothing to
alter the expression on her face, in all its silent anguish.
That's when I decided I could not wait for the boss and
would simply have to take the plunge."

"Do you think you had fallen in love with him?"

"I don't deny it. Don't you think we've done enough
talking for today?"

"No. Tell me what you did with his mother. Briefly,
if you like; just tell me some little professional secrets."

"Though I had never done it myself, I knew the procedure for injecting the formaldehyde-based fluid into
the veins of the deceased. It's nothing like a blood
transfusion. You make an incision in the leg, into
which you insert a catheter; the fluid is then pumped
through the body and out again. No one but the boss
himself was allowed to make that incision. I would stand
beside him sometimes, to help reposition the body or to
pass him instruments, but for some reason I could
never bear to look. Something repelled me. It wasn't
the corpses per se; I was used to them. It was more the
boss. He had such ghoulish white hands, and he kept his
fingernails very long and rather pointed, like something you'd see in a horror movie. But even worse was
his breath, always reeking of alcohol. Mind you, I like
the odd drink myself, to accompany a good meal or
some festive occasion, but embalming a person's mortal
remains . . . That's the last token of goodness to be
bestowed on a human being on this Earth. Well, anyway, the boss's breath was so sickening, even a faint
whiff of it, that I could never bear getting in close
enough to watch him make the cut. So you can imagine

my dread as I laid out the instruments, the fluid, and the slightly rusted pump, before getting to work on Jian's mother. I turned up the left trouser leg to expose the calf, which was slender and icy but misshapen, no doubt because she had been left lying in an awkward position for too long. I took the scalpel and made a cross in two clumsy strokes. A thick liquid seeped out, like mash mixed with blood. Jian was paler than a corpse himself, and kept his eyes shut tight. Suddenly I thought I heard someone on the ground floor. As I listened for the boss's footsteps down the corridor, my heart jumped as I imagined that my rescue was at hand! I ran out to greet him. I was so ashamed of my deception, so terrified of making a mistake, that I thought nothing of the consequences of confessing to him this intrusion into his professional domain. I flew down the stairs, but when I entered the half lit corridor to the entrance, there was no one there. And so with daylight fading, the heat dissipating in the evening breeze, and me feeling as icy as Jian's mother's leg, I made my way back along the fake marble hallway, hearing nothing but my own steps, seeing only my ghostly reflection in the floor, and shaking with terror all over again. I was tempted to run and find my alcoholic boss at the basketball court, but I turned around and climbed the stairs again, not knowing what I would do next. Back in the embalming hall I asked Jian if he could just help me reposition the body for the final cut and insertion of the catheter. He asked if it was all right for him to recite a poem in English for his mother. He told me that she had taught him English when he was a boy, and he was now studying it at university, spending every waking hour improving his command of the language, which was his sole passion. He told me these things so humbly that I couldn't possibly say no. He began to recite the poem in a loud voice, which was pleasant, if a little effeminate. You know I don't understand a word of English, but it sounded beautiful. Beautiful and sad. My hand stopped shaking and obeyed my commands, making a neat cut. The poem he recited was an old Irish song he had come across in a novel by James Joyce. I asked him what it meant, so he translated it for me, and I liked it so much that I copied it down. I can still recite it:

> *Ding dong, the Castle bell!*
> *Farewell my mother!*
> *Bury me in the old churchyard*
> *Beside my eldest brother.*
> *My coffin shall be black*
> *Six angels at my back,*
> *Two to sing and two to pray*
> *And two to carry my soul away . . .*

"Miraculously, his mother's face gradually regained its pinkish colour, thanks to the fluid filling her veins, propelled by the rusty pump, operated by Jian. I set about brushing her teeth, and that's when I noticed that she had the same little gap in her front uppers as her son. In less than an hour her muscles relaxed, first in her jaw, then in her hands. The hard grimace softened until her face was as calm as the sky after a storm. The linguist's serenity was restored; she was relieved of the torment of that Sino-Burmese tribal dialect. In fact, she looked rather good, and Jian was so encouraged that

he said it would be a shame not to take the extra trouble
of applying a little makeup. He went off to fetch her
makeup case, leaving me alone with the corpse. I sat
looking at it for some time before dozing off. When I
woke, it was raining. I don't know what happened while
I was asleep, but something inside me had changed.
Everything seemed sweet and gentle; even the patter of
the rain sounded like music. I had an urge to sing
a mourning song, a very ancient dirge that floated
into my mind, filling my head and parting my lips.
You see, in my line of work, you get to hear plenty of
laments for the dead. I know quite a few. I sang it until
Jian returned. He said he liked my song very much
and asked me to sing some more, which I did as he
opened the patent-leather case, from which he took her
eyeliner and traced a light accent, fluid like a caress,
upon his mother's eyelids. I then smeared her lips with
glossy coral and brushed her lashes with French mascara. Finally, he placed a gold necklace set with a sap-
phire around her neck. She was smiling, and in her way
beautiful."

"I expect that was when he fell head over heels in love
with you."

"Well, that's what I thought, too. But when it comes
down to it, Mr. Psychoanalyst, you know as well as I do
that a homosexual can't make love to a woman. If he
could, he wouldn't have thrown himself out the window
on our wedding night, and I wouldn't be a widow and a
virgin to this day."

"Perhaps."

"Otherwise the drama would make no sense."

3. GAMES OF MAH-JONGG

The session of telephonic psychoanalysis ends at midnight. Muo had feared that his months crisscrossing the vast province of southwestern China might be in vain. His sinister encounters with crooks and prostitutes disguised as innocent maidens and the successive theft of his Delsey suitcase on the night train, his cigarette case in a market, his watch in a small hotel, and his jacket at a karaoke club had all made him feel as if he were in some endless tunnel. But now, talking with his former girl-next-door, with the Embalmer's unlikely admission of being still a virgin, Muo can see a bit of light.

Having put the receiver down, he takes a joyful little skip backward. Buoyed on a happy cloud, he throws himself on the bed, but his insouciance turns to sharp pain upon impact with something hard lying on the mattress: the porcelain teapot he had bought earlier in the day, now shattered. Determined nonetheless to preserve his good mood, he considers the example of his asexual psychoanalyst Michel, who like any Frenchman in a film would go down to the corner bistro and buy a round of drinks whenever there was something to celebrate. So, despite the late hour, Muo gets dressed to go out. A Serge Gainsbourg tune he is whistling merrily rings out in the windowless stairwell of his hotel. "*Vive l'amour,"* he murmurs as he pauses at the front desk to deposit his key with the room number carved into the wooden fob. He blows the receptionist a mischievous kiss and darts out.

(Nights and weekends, the reception is manned by a student who makes the rounds at eleven p.m., offering to procure prostitutes. His imitation Nikes can be heard coming to a squeaky halt by each room in the corridor just before his fingers tap the door lightly and precisely, like a computer keyboard, and his youthful voice calls with mechanical hospitality: "Anyone for love?" He is in fact the most cultured but least effective of all the native guides Muo has engaged in his painstaking quest for a virgin.)

Muo turns into the shadowy main street; the public lighting, for reasons of economy, isn't switched on in this city. Yet the hairdressing salons with their raw neon signs spread a glow of blue and pink, and the shops are alive with "hairdressers," who lounge in doorways or sprawl languidly in armchairs, watching TV in nothing but their bras, panties, and heavy makeup. They call out to Muo as he passes, inviting him in with their quaint provincial accents and lascivious poses. Also open for business are a restaurant and two pharmacies specialising in aphrodisiacs, with cunningly lit window displays of live, writhing snakes, counterfeit antlers and rhinoceros horns, dried crabs, and weird-looking plants, including the long-haired ginseng root. At the end of the street, beyond some more hairdressers, with similar personnel and lighting, loom the furnaces of a privately owned brick kiln, which has prospered in the recent construction boom. The light of the moon shows up the silhouettes of stooping night-shift workers, loading and unloading bricks, antlike, emerging from the deep maw of the furnaces trundling barrows and then pausing to catch their breath before retracing their steps along the thin, dark lane, only to be engulfed once more in the smoke belching from the fires.

Muo steps into a teahouse opposite the kiln. He has been here before, a week ago, accompanied by another local guide. He liked the pitched, tiled roof; the little open courtyard; the low wooden tables; the bamboo chairs, creaking comfortably; the dark floor of beaten earth, damp and littered with peanut shells, sunflower seeds, and cigarette butts: a sweet, familiar smell reminiscent of his boyhood. Best of all on that first visit was when the waiter brought the tea in a brass kettle with a fine spout one metre long, through which he poured a jet of boiling water, the arc descending as if from the sky, straight into the porcelain bowl on its iron saucer, filling it without loss of the smallest drop before the waiter delicately placed a white porcelain lid over the hot tea. But since Muo's first visit, the teahouse has been transformed; today it's a vast, smokey billiard hall, teeming with players, leaning along the darkened walls, bending over the green baize to gauge the trajectory of the colliding ivory balls, all in the glare of the lamps with heavy milk-glass shades that are suspended above the tables. The scene reminds Muo of a saloon in some bad American Western. He swaggers to the bar, feeling like Clint Eastwood. For once he's eager to play the big spender, to raise a glass, perhaps not to his own success but, let's say, to "American imperialism." He asks what drinks cost. The price of hard liquor, while not unreasonable, is higher than he expected, and so he asks about the local beer as he attempts to do a head count of the billiard players. Overcome by the arithmetic, and before the bartender has time to reply, he beats his retreat without having drunk a drop.

"My dear Volcano of the Old Moon, for your sake I shall be sensible and thrifty," he vows aloud. Thirsty and with an empty stomach, he heads out of the city to the beach, picking his way carefully between mounds of wet trash.

He crosses a bridge and follows the bank of the murky, sluggish river beneath the silver disc of the moon in an anthracite sky. The Bay of Crabs is not yet in sight, but already he can smell the sea. It is a cold smell, at once strange and familiar, a feminine breath borne on gusts of nippy air. To one side are the shacks on stilts used by the crab fishers, who come in from poor villages. In the distance he hears a baby crying, and the doleful barking of stray dogs. The breeze softens, and Muo hears a moth fluttering helplessly in a tangle of fishing nets hung out to dry on the shingle. He approaches the nets, drops to his knees, and crawls underneath to rescue the delicate, terror-stricken creature, helplessly batting its purple wings marbled with grey, its spindly body convulsing in the mesh.

"My poor friend, have no fear," Muo says. "A few hours ago I was in just the same predicament. I, too, had to extricate myself from an exceedingly tangled web, no less expertly knotted, namely the Chinese justice system."

He frees the moth and watches contentedly as it disappears with a faint whirr, like a miniature helicopter.

"Several thousand kilometres from here," he reflects, "another delicate creature sleeps in a prison cell. How do you manage, my beloved Volcano of the

Old Moon? You always had trouble sleeping. Do you have a straw mattress? Do you sleep in striped prison clothes?"

The blood rises to his cheeks and throbs in his head as he stoops to take off his shoes. His feet are boiling, too. He digs them into the cool, grainy sand, then paddles in a sheet of greyish water near where the river flows into the sea. He splashes his face with the lukewarm water. He turns back to the shore, where he proceeds to undress, not forgetting to take off his new watch, which he wraps in a sock, tucking it into one of his shoes. Then, scooping up the clothes in his skinny arms, he heads toward a rocky outcrop. The streamers of dark emerald seaweed on the sand crackle underfoot; sharp pebbles prickle his feet. The buffeting sea wind makes him stagger and almost whips his glasses off, but it cools the fire in his veins nonetheless. He walks gingerly. He knows the crabs are there, monstrous and invisible, armed with mandibles and huge pincers, prized for the whiteness of their meat and its aphrodisiac properties. They are there, lurking at the bottom of the pools, submerged in the sticky sand, hiding among the pebbles, lying in wait for his toes, stalking him among the low rocks and in the tidal pools, and he can almost hear the conspiratorial whispers of an imminent attack.

Despite the crustacean menace, he vows to come back one day with Volcano of the Old Moon, when she is released from prison. "I'll sit her on a big inflated inner tube and push it from behind so the crabs can't reach her feet. Her bare feet, so noble and shapely, with grains of sand and shell clinging to them in a delicate crust." Hearing her cries of delight resounding in the surf, he imagines the joy of watching her savour freedom as she rides the black rubber ring, dipping and rising in the surge of the foamy tide. "Naturally, she will bring her camera," he thinks aloud, "to take pictures of the fishermen, of their toil and their poverty, the poorest in China, if not the whole world. As for me, I will record the dreams dreamt by everyone and their children. And when I reveal Freud's theories, especially—most important—that of the oedipal complex, then we'll have a good laugh watching them shake their swarthy heads in disbelief."

He thinks he sees glowworms dotting the surface of the sea, drifting languidly on the current. But they are fishing craft, small wooden dinghies with room only for two, each darker than the night but for an acetylene lamp hanging over the oarsman, whose partner casts the nets into the water. Their shapes alternately blur and sharpen with the choppy swell and the tranquillity that follows. When calm prevails, the water laps and murmurs. It is time for the fishermen to pull in their nets.

On land, at Muo's back, the roar of an engine draws near. A tourist coach spills out its passengers, the express purpose of whom is no doubt to feast on freshly caught, libido-building crab. Speaking for all, a man shouts out that he wants the smallest ones, the ones with the whitest meat. Is he the guide? Are these people from Japan? From Taiwan? Perhaps Hong Kong? An open-air restaurant lights up in the darkness. In no time, tables and chairs of moulded plastic are set up facing the sea, beneath a string of brightly coloured lightbulbs. A few waiters, probably assistant cooks, go to the water's edge and call out orders to the fishermen. As the midnight visitors take their seats, he sees a game beginning immediately at every table, and Muo decides they must be Chinese. The empire of mah-jongg holds sway over a billion aficionados. Waiting for a meal of fresh steamed crab presents them a perfect opportunity to play, fending off even the spectre of a moment's boredom! Muo is proved right when the driver squats near the empty coach and on his harmonica plays a revolutionary song from the sixties.

IN THE PRISON, harmonicas are banned. Crabmeat does not exist, just a few weekly thumbnail slivers of pork, buried under slimy cabbage leaves on Wednesday and floating forlornly on the surface of cabbage soup on Saturdays. Cabbage, day in, day out. Boiled cabbage, stir-fried, seasoned, marinated, rotten, worm-eaten, cabbage with sand, and cabbage with hairs from goodness knows who or what. Cabbage with rusty nails. Cabbage without end. Mah-jongg does not exist in her prison, either. During one of his visits there she told him of the only game they could play in her cell: "Madam Tang's Weewee," named for one inmate, a doctor's wife, condemned for involuntary manslaughter. She had difficulty urinating due to a venereal infection. Each time she squatted over the communal bucket her cellmates would make sport of anticipating the amber-tinged, malodorous discharge from her poisoned bladder, placing bets on the cooperativeness of her urethra that day, with any remaining morsels of their precious pork rations as the stakes. If, after a tense silence, Madame Tang was unable to pass any urine, the triumphant would dance with voluptuous greed. As for the others, those who had bet affirmatively, they would rise up and encircle Madam Tang, urging her on like a woman in labor: "Push! Relax! Now push!" Sometimes after a piercing cry a few droplets would fall into the bucket, a sound barely audible but enough to announce that God had changed sides that day. It was on that first visit, when approaching the prison, that Muo had looked up to see those terrifying, immense, black characters daubed on the very long white wall, which was surmounted by barbed wire: WHO ARE YOU? WHERE ARE YOU? WHY ARE YOU HERE? ("You are my Volcano of the Old Moon," he'd said to himself. "Thirty-six years old, unmarried, a photographer who took pictures of people being tortured by the police and gave them to the European press. You are in the women's jail of Chengdu. You are awaiting the outcome of your trial.")

THE SEA, TRANQUIL NOW, beckons to Muo, who clambers down from the rocky outcrop and steps gingerly into the water. Bothered by his glasses, he turns back to put them away in the pocket of his trousers, which he has left up on his rock. He'd like to dive in from there, but doesn't dare, so he inches down and jumps in with a big splash from the shore. It takes him some time to reach the middle of the bay. He swims at a slow, studied pace, not sporty in the least. In typical Muosian fashion, his arms move in the gentle, ceremonious rhythm of t'ai chi, pointing forward and flexing by turns, his legs barely spread, following the cadences of an ancient poem of the Tang Dynasty, gathering momentum in the violet night sky with timeless stars and murmuring tide, slow and mysterious, and he is reminded of the Schubert sonata that he couldn't abide on account of all those repetitious chords until he heard it played by a Russian pianist by the name of Richter. That is the kind of magic that delights the young disciple of Freud. Suddenly there is a cry in the night, slightly muffled, possibly female, but he is not sure.

SHE USED TO LAUGH at him during swimming instruction at the university pool. Just two or three long, calculated strokes and she would shoot past him, like a giant frog, before turning around to say: "How do you manage to swim so slowly? You're like an old woman with bound feet!" She would get out of the pool and, from the edge, in front of everybody, offer an exaggerated imitation of Muo's technique. The water would drip from her slender body, slithering down the delightful scattering of faint little chicken-pox scars. Then, seated on the edge, she would kick and kick with her dazzling limbs in the greenish-brown water. Muo would swim over to stammer that in his own repertoire he had only one plausible imitation: that of a monkey, which likeness he had honed during his years of reeducation in the mountains, where monkeys abounded. "But you, my proud, keen-eyed Volcano of the Old Moon, you made no reply, but just cocked your sceptical head before diving in to speed away."

THE SOMBRE, MURKY TIDE complicates Muo's efforts to swim eastward across the bay. Those faint cries, drifting in the air above the open sea, call to him still. After several minutes of a vigorous breaststroke he discerns a glimmer of light, vacillating and becoming larger as he approaches. A lamp belonging to some crab-catchers, he supposes. The cries fall silent. He can sense that there is something different about this fishing craft, but he can't put his finger on it. For one thing, the sway of the lamp above the waves is strange: a remarkably irregular cadence, juddering wildly, as if the boat were about to capsize in a raging storm, leaning over the water within a hair's breadth of extinguishing itself before righting itself again, even though the sea is tranquil. Although he is close enough to see the net rippling on the surface of the water, he can't see anyone on the craft tossing madly on the waves. A mirage? A vessel in distress? He imagines the woman having succumbed after her final cry for help. A female crab-catcher, perhaps; the lone survivor of a shipwreck; a clandestine emigrant; a victim of sharks, of pirates, or of murder. All his senses pricked, his courage stirred by ideals of citizenship and chivalry and the Napoleonic code, Muo approaches the craft to investigate. Drawing a heaving breath, he makes to climb over the side, but upon identifying at last the succession of muffled cries rising from the interior, he freezes. He hears not only a woman's voice, but a man's, not cries now as much as vocalized heaving breaths and groans in tandem. Muo's cheeks are burning with shame and he withdraws as discreetly as he can before a would-be knight-errant can be branded a Peeping Tom.

He recalls the invisible, muscular fingers of the pianist Richter flying nimbly over the keys as Schubert's sonata rings in his head, accompanying the creaking of the craft as it strains to contain its load of lust and eternal conjugations. A sonata in honour of the copulating crab-catcher, the naked prince of the sea, and his unseen partner, perhaps in rags and smelling of fish, but for now queen of the sombre tide.

ONE EVENING LAST SUMMER in Paris, his room was wreathed in peppery, spicy vapours rising from two hot plates bearing pans of steaming broth, into which his Chinese guests—all exiles of various kinds: political, economic, even cultural—ritually dipped their chopsticks to capture shrimp, thinly sliced beef, vegetables, tofu, bamboo shoots, cabbage, or scented mushrooms. As usual, at least in this company of political refugees, students, and street artists, Muo and a blind poet were engaged in heated debate. Passions had reached a climax when, suddenly, the steamy air sizzled with a spray of blue electrical sparks. No one took any notice. The sparks kept coming. Then, in a fit of exasperation, the blind poet rose, took two hundred-franc notes from his wallet, and waved them under Muo's nose, exclaiming: "How can you discuss psychoanalysis if you've never made love?"

At this, everyone lapsed into silence. The blind man continued: "Here, take a cab straight to the rue Saint-Denis and find yourself a whore. Get yourself laid, *then* come tell me all about Freud and Lacan."

He meant to slap the money down on the table, but the bills fluttered away in the steamy air, landing together in one of the saucepans, where they floated briefly before being engulfed in the red, oily broth. Retrieving the money gave rise to an indescribable commotion, which was further exacerbated when the fuses blew and the room was plunged into utter darkness.

MUO, WITH HIS NEARSIGHTED SQUINT, gropes
his way up to the rocky outcrop where he left his clothes
and lies down flat on his back. The breeze has softened,
and over the lapping of the tide he can make out the
rattle of mah-jongg tiles and the strains of the harmonica. The banquet of white-meat crab has yet to
be served in the restaurant. He hears a song from a
Chinese opera, hardly suited to the instrument but
performed ably enough by the driver, who gives it a
jaunty swing. Muo joins in, first whistling a few bars,
then singing along until the driver launches into a
saccharine love song from Hong Kong. Whenever he
can recall the refrain of each old ditty the driver plays,
Muo whistles along and sings. His solo act culminates
in a rendition of "The Mah-jongg Player," which Muo
performs with such infectious enthusiasm that the
entire company in the open-air restaurant joins in the
chorus:

> Were it not for mah-jongg
> Our nights would be too long
> Ah mah-jongg!
> Ah mah-jongg!
> Although I haven't a penny
> Joy comes from being many
> It's wonderful
> It's marvellous.

As in a Hollywood musical, the choral surge is no more
out of place than the dozens of mah-jongg games in the
impromptu beach restaurant, or the orange glow of the

dangling lightbulbs over the somnolent, murmuring, white-capped tide. A cloud slides slowly across the moon, deepening the marine hue of the bay. A shiver runs down Muo's spine at the recollection of a remark made by Judge Di, who shares his name with a fictional judge of the Tang Dynasty invented by the mystery writer Robert van Gulik, a westerner well known for his erudition regarding the sexual habits of ancient China. Said the Judge, "Ah, the pretty little mah-jongg tiles, what exquisite freshness, as exquisite as the ivory hand of a young virgin."

The aroma of steamed crabs wafts his way: a swirl of cloves, finely chopped ginger, basil, mountain herbs, and white cinnamon, a fragrance heightened by the gusty, salty sea air. Brusquely swept into little heaps, the mah-jongg tiles give way to steaming dishes, bowls of rice, and glasses brimming with Chinese liquor, imitation French wine, and counterfeit Mexican beer.

Reclining on his rock, Muo mulls over Judge Di's remark: "As exquisite as the ivory hand of a young virgin."

IT WAS BACK IN MAY, two months before his suitcase was stolen on the night train and four and a half months before this wakeful night under the baroque stars of the Bay of Crabs, that he pled her case before Judge Di. His argument rested mainly on ten thousand dollars in cash.

The judge's full name was Di Jiangui. He was of working-class background, Jiangui, his given name, being very common among males whose date of birth coincides with that of the Communist Republic in

1949; it means "Construction of the Fatherland," a phrase from the solemn vow pronounced on Tiananmen Square in the somewhat reedy counter-tenor of Chairman Mao. In the early seventies, Di Jiangui had joined the police. He gave fifteen years to that pillar of the proletariat's dictatorship, becoming a member of the elite firing squads before his appointment in 1985 to the tribunal of Chengdu. It was more than his due as a good communist. In a city of eight million during the heyday of economic reform, the position was among the most privileged and sought after. It operated according to the rules of most government affairs, especially those involving the law, and Di had been the first to establish a fee of one thousand dollars for his pardon of a criminal offence, an astronomic sum at the time. Subsequently, and in step with the rising cost of living, his price had increased tenfold, which was just when Volcano of the Old Moon was arrested and fell into his clutches. That, as they say, is politics.

Although our psychoanalyst had been born and bred to the bone in this land so dear to his heart, and had gained his own experience of the Cultural Revolution and its ensuing innovations, and although he had often told his friends "The only true saying in Mao's Little Red Book is the one that goes 'the Chinese Communist Party makes miracles happen,' " the miraculous power of judicial bribery still came as a shock. He heard it explained by the lawyer assigned to his sweetheart, Volcano of the Old Moon. Although officially independent, the lawyer was appointed by the tribunal and was besides, although somewhat less overtly, a member of Judge Di's chambers. (Yet another miracle, no less astonishing to Muo.) This lawyer had a reputation for dressing exclusively in black Pierre Cardin suits and bright red neckties, the latter taste having been famously remarked upon in an outburst by an illiterate salesgirl accused of theft by her employer, who was represented by this same lawyer. The girl had thrust her chin in his direction and sneered: "Why don't you take a look in the mirror, you scumbag! You're wearing your wife's sanitary napkin around your neck!" The lawyer was in great demand, not merely for his bulging address book and his warm relations with judges, but also for his skill at organizing pretrial banquets in private salons or behind fake antique lacquer screens in five-star restaurants (at the Holiday Inn, for example). The judges and alleged murderers could thus negotiate the term that the former would administer to the latter while both savored an array of delicacies such as abalone (also known as ormer), a gastropod from South Africa; or bear's paws imported from Siberia; or the dish called "Three Cries" (the preparation includes live baby mice, whose squeals are meant to evoke those of a newborn infant; the first cry comes when they are pinched between the jade chopsticks; the second when they are dipped into a sauce of vinegar and ginger; the third when they land in the gourmet's mouth, among the yellow teeth of a judge, perhaps, or the dazzling dentures of a lawyer, his red tie slightly stained with grease).

The dossier on Volcano of the Old Moon proved both complicated and tortuous, concerning as it did politics as well as national reputation; the lawyer was unequivocal in his counsel that no conceivable banquet, however expensive, could possibly smooth things over, and that indeed it was necessary to proceed with the utmost caution, method, and patience, as the slightest misstep could be fatal.

At the home of Muo's parents, the lawyer sat amid the kitchen clutter of saucepans, unfolding his ingenious plan, at its kernel his inside knowledge of Judge Di's weekly run. From the outset of his career as a magistrate, Judge Di was in the habit of "recharging his batteries" with a solitary run every Sunday morning. His course was a stretch of wasteland that was then, as now, the scene of all executions by firing squad, whether of individuals or of groups. The site, so familiar and dear to this former elite marksman, lay to the north of the city, at the foot of Mill Hill. It was the lawyer's scheme that Muo should go there, presenting himself not as a psychoanalyst but as a law professor from a major Chinese university charged with surveying execution grounds in connection with the government's plans to draft new legislation. The encounter was to appear fortuitous. The judge would naturally launch into a sentimental account of his experiences, to which Muo would respond so effusively with cries of admiration and surprise that the judge—and here was the trick—would accept an invitation to take tea with him afterward. At their ensuing tête-à-tête in the private room of a teahouse Muo would have a suitable opportunity to mention the plight of Volcano of the Old Moon and petition for her release, in consideration for which judgement he would offer the ten thousand dollars.

The following Sunday morning Muo put on one of his father's old suits and gulped down a bowl of instant noodles served with an egg by his mother (his parents, both low-ranking assistants in the department of Western medicine, would otherwise keep a discreet and prudent distance from this caper). He took a taxi across the city to Mill Hill, arriving around 7:30 a.m., soon after daybreak. The fading chorus of toads, frogs, and crickets and the general terrain called to mind the hillside where, as a twelve-year-old, he had spent the summer helping the revolutionary peasants with their work. He walked along a footpath he took to be a shortcut, almost losing his balance several times, not because of any irregularity underfoot but because whenever some apparently human shape crossed his path, he would take it, regardless of gender, to be Judge Di. Each time, the phony professor's cheeks would flush, as if his blood had turned viscous and black. At one point, just when the path seemed deserted and he thought he was lost among the multitude of paths forking across the slope, he came upon a vast burial ground with the graves of the firing-squad victims. Some had convex tombstones, and others—perhaps those whose families were too poor or too fearful to claim the bodies—were no more than mounds of bare earth, unmarked and nameless.

A water buffalo with a bell around its neck appeared at the end of the misty path winding among the graves. Muo, now seeing Judge Di in every form, nearly jumped out of his skin when the bell clanged. Gathering his wits, he saw that there were two figures following the buffalo: a young peasant in a Western-style jacket and jeans rolled up to his knees, carrying a heavy wooden plough on his shoulder, and a girl in a skirt and rubber-soled shoes with high, square heels, trundling a bicycle. This modern-looking pair seemed not the least surprised to see him; they matter-of-factly pointed him in the right direction and, without interrupting their lively chatter, moved on, as in a pastoral poem, to the dulcet tones of the buffalo's bell. Muo marvelled: "Such harmony in the morning hours! How wonderful my socialist homeland is, and how deserving of tributes from this errant son!"

It was nothing like he remembered it; this setting of supreme terror now seemed unremarkable. Gone were the tall yellow grasses, eerily swaying, the soil, which was sodden with tears shed in begging for mercy, yellowed, too, like old men's spittle; so too the drifts of pale mushrooms, fleshy and brooding in the damp undergrowth, and the vultures winging darkly overhead. Nothing but a featureless wasteland, devoid of colour, sound, and direction, stonily indifferent to suffering. Once Muo's eyes adapted to the surroundings, he spotted two figures in the distance, soundlessly digging a hole with their spades.

The face of a long-forgotten boyhood friend floated into his mind, causing him to shake with fright. It was Chen, nicknamed White Hair, the only one of his friends to have struck it rich in the early eighties. He had married the daughter of someone big, the director of a company listed on the stock exchange and the city's mayor to boot, only to end up sentenced to death for trafficking in foreign vehicles. Could it have been here, at the foot of the hill, that he had been made to kneel and was shot by an anonymous gun from behind? Muo had heard it said that much importance was attached to the way the condemned's hands were tied behind him; the hands had to be pulled painfully high so that the elite marksman could aim precisely for the small gap between thumb and forefinger, through which the bullet could enter the heart.

The men with spades were dressed in plain military uniforms without officer's epaulets. Neither of them could be Judge Di. The heat drained from Muo's face. As one of them thrust his muddy boot against the edge of his spade to drive it into the ground, his oversized helmet—decorated with a red star—slipped off and tumbled into the hole at his feet. Bending down to retrieve it, he was much amused to discover a green-and-brown striped earthworm wriggling on the smooth metal dome. He shook the creature off and, with his spade, hacked it to pieces, each splattering blow eliciting rowdy laughter from the twosome.

Muo's assumed identity suited him very well, and he was amazed at his knack for improvisation. The lies poured from his lips with poetic ardour. "Oh, naked flower of my lips," as the poet Mallarmé was wont to say. Imitating perfectly the earnest, vaguely academic tones of a law professor from Beijing, Muo duly impressed the two soldiers with the importance of his government mission. He enquired after the purpose of the holes they were digging.

"Without them," explained the worm-killer, "the bodies just roll away, spilling blood all over the place."

"Criminals are executed on their knees," added the other man, who seemed slightly more intelligent. "A bullet through the heart. They keel over right into the hole. If they twitch a lot in their death throes, the loose earth settles nicely around them. Next the doctors come to remove the organs. You could get a special permit, if you're interested, for tomorrow. Then you can see for yourself what the procedure is."

Muo cast a glance at the gaping, dark holes and felt himself turn cold.

"Your information has been most helpful," he said, pretending to take officious notes in his exercise book.

"He's the philosopher of our gang," said the worm-killer, indicating his companion.

Almost cowering with respect, the soldiers were about to take their leave when Muo caught sight of a man of about fifty running toward them, in what appeared to be a pyjama top—white with blue stripes, and with two buttons missing.

"That must be Judge Di on his daily run," observed Muo in a voice tremulous with excitement.

"Judge Di? Who's he?" the worm-killer asked the philosopher. "Take a look at that shirt—isn't it what they make retards wear?"

"Haven't you read any of the Dutchman's stories?" replied the philosopher. "Judge Di is a renowned detective. That thing he's wearing is the robe worn by the famous judge of the Tang Dynasty."

A gleam of triumph in his eyes, he grinned and shook Muo's hand, after which he and his fellow digger walked away. Muo hurried after them.

"The man I am waiting for is the top judge of the district, a man with the power to sentence anyone to death. Is that him?" he asked.

"Sure it is," affirmed the philosopher, winking discreetly at his companion.

"Yeah, the famous Judge Di of Chengdu, king of the criminals' hell," added the worm-killer.

A few moments later, sitting on the ground in the middle of the wasteland, Muo followed the runner's circular path with his eyes. Muo did not dare approach

him yet, so he waited until a vehicle honking in the dis
tance made the judge presumptive freeze theatrically in
his tracks to listen. Muo hesitated. He let another
minute pass, but there was no further honking. The
runner took a deep breath and carried on, like an ant
struggling with its load. At last Muo rose and screwed
up his courage to approach the runner.

"Judge Di, I presume?"

The man eyed him in silence. Muo thought he saw a
muscle twitch in his eye. With an awe born of both fear
and contempt, he studied the man's pale, gaunt face.
He was extremely thin, and the white shirt with the blue
stripes flapped around his frame as if on a hanger. With
his dishevelled hair and the dark pouches spread under
his eyes, he suddenly seemed to Muo nothing but a poor
fellow suffering mental anguish, haunted no doubt by
the ghosts of his victims—and now, indeed, a lost soul
himself. Muo extended his hand, forgetting all about
the subterfuge he had prepared.

"My name is Muo. I am a psychoanalyst, recently
returned from a spell in Paris. It is my belief, Your
Honour, that I can be of assistance to you."

"Of assistance to me?"

"Yes. It is clear that you would benefit from psychoanalysis, as propounded by Freud and Lacan, on whose
theories . . ."

"Freud?" barked the gangly man, and before Muo
could utter another word he landed a punch of such
ferocity that it embedded Muo's twisted glasses into his
face. Howling with pain, Muo heard a loud buzz in his
head before everything went dark. He could scarcely
believe he was lying sprawled on the ground, but managed instinctively to peel off his glasses before passing

out from the violent blows raining on his skull, lower abdomen, kidneys, and liver.

The judge made off. But on second thought he halted and retraced his steps. Bending over the body lying unconscious on the ground, he stripped Muo of his jacket and coolly traded it for his own white shirt with blue stripes. He seemed especially pleased to be able to button all the buttons, and he stood for a moment, preening, before he was startled by the sound of a horn. As he fled, an ambulance hove into view, sirens wailing. It rolled onto the wasteland and circled around Muo before stopping to let out two hulking medics. The men advanced cautiously, one of them carrying a photograph.

Muo woke to see two stooping giants staring him in the face. At the same time he noticed that he was wearing his assailant's striped shirt, of which he could only say, "Gosh this shirt stinks," before passing out again.

Even without his glasses, Muo's face was impossible to recognise on account of the large purple bruises and the blood seeping from his nostrils, but after due deliberation and careful comparison the men decided that he was indeed the man in the photograph, the madman who had escaped from the hospital through the main sewer leading from the latrines. (After searching without luck for two days, they had been alerted to his whereabouts by a telephone call from a young peasant couple.) They tried rousing him by slapping his face, but to no avail. Lights flashing, the ambulance speeded away across the execution ground, with Muo handcuffed in the back.

As for Judge Di, the real one, he had been unable to recharge his batteries that particular Sunday, having

been felled by a cold caught while staying up all night
two days earlier, playing mah-jongg, that irresistible
game.

WHAT IF YOU SUDDENLY
TURNED INTO SOMEONE ELSE?

(Chengdu, from our special correspondent.) A week ago
Mr. Ma Jin, recently escaped from Chengdu
Psychiatric Institute, was found in a coma,
his face battered and bruised, on the execution ground at the foot of Mill Hill. Having apparently suffered a mild concussion, he
was transported back to the Institute where,
upon regaining consciousness, he manifested
delusional symptoms of paranoia, claiming
to be a psychoanalyst returned from France,
where he had worked mainly as a follower of
Freud (though he found Lacan to be "intellec-
tually interesting, blessed with a strong personality, capable of persuading his Paris
clientele to pay high fees for private sessions
that never lasted more than five minutes"). Dr.
Wang Yu-sheng, one of China's most eminent
psychiatrists and deputy director of the Centre
for the Treatment of Mental Illness at Beijing,
and Mr. Qiu, titular professor of French at the
University of Shanghai, were called upon for
their consultation in this most extraordinary
case. They subjected the patient to a series of
tests, in the course of which the aforemen-
tioned Ma Jin recited, in a clear voice and

apparently in perfect French, entire passages of
Freud, as well as various phrases known to be
from Lacan, Foucault, and Derrida, and also
the opening lines of a poem by the poet Paul
Valéry. The patient, who insisted his name was
not Ma but Muo, further astonished the clini-
cians by reeling off the names of a street where
he claimed to have lived in Paris, his metro station, the corner tobacconist (called *Le chien qui
fume*), the café on the ground floor of his
building, and a bistro across the street. He
invited his examiners to savour the beauty of
the French word *amour* as well as the richness
and untranslatable complexity of the word
hélas. But despite his inexplicable Francophone
abilities and rote recitation, the patient, who
by his account had been attacked and robbed by
a jogger, now seemed unable to recall the reason for his presence at the execution site, an
amnesia attributed together with his other
symptoms to the blows he sustained to the
head.

The two eminent experts issued a formal
report of their findings, noting that the case
was among the most perplexing in the annals
of psychiatry, a conclusion that caused an
immediate stir among the intellectuals of
Chengdu. Professors, researchers, journalists,
students of literature, and especially students of philosophy—some of whom expressed
long-held ambitions of one day becoming psychoanalysts themselves—flocked to the asylum,
where the room of the mysterious French-

speaking madman was, during visiting hours, overrun with gawkers, and at all other times monitored through a peephole by a special nurse assigned to stand guard. When this reporter paid him a visit, he was being interviewed by a researcher in Chinese mythology, who took copious notes, simultaneously recording the exchange on tape. The researcher's aim was to establish a link between the persona of Ma Jin—Muo and that of the famous immortal cripple of yore. (According to legend, the soul of a monk returned from a spiritual journey to discover that one of his disciples had mistakenly burnt his body, which had lain inanimate for seven days. The God of Mercy took pity and wrought a miracle, enabling the errant soul to slip unnoticed into the body of a crippled beggar who had been dead only a short while. The lifeless body suddenly resuscitated and miraculously rose up, giving a triumphant laugh and making his limping way toward the temple in the hope of saving the now-traumatised disciple from suicidal despair.) Among the offerings piled high around the patient's hospital bed, I came across a little magazine put together and printed by some local students, containing an article proposing a different hypothesis, according to which the escapee was in fact the reincarnation of a translator from the French who had been shot long ago. Sources within the clinic confirmed another remarkable fact: this patient, unlike all the others, regardless of affliction, never complained about the food or the strict hygienic discipline. And having for weeks maintained his delusional claims with some vehemence and agitation, he had lately evinced signs of having grown content with his situation. Without a hint of mockery, he would occasionally declare the asylum to be the world's best university. The former raving madman became quite a gentle and considerate soul whose solicitude respecting his fellow patients extended to enquiring about everything from their hysterical cries in the night to the after-effects of their electroshock therapy, and even their dreams, which he noted down assiduously. Despite a heavy regimen of sedatives administered morning and night, he regaled me with many smutty and not-so-smutty stories, both Chinese and foreign, and in return he asked of me only that I bring him more writing paper. The use he made of this made him seem, in the words of his guard-nurse, rather "a romantic type," for he wrote a succession of very long love letters, which he surely knew were never to be delivered, to a woman prisoner whose name he said was most strange and unforgettable, though honour constrained him from divulging it.

To end the story, yesterday Ma Jin's wife, a former opera singer, was finally located and summoned by the asylum administrators. On first sight of him she seemed shocked. She had not seen her husband, a convert to Buddhism, since he left her to take up residence in a temple three years ago, and in the conversion he had apparently changed almost beyond recognition. She expressed a wish to speak to him in private, which she was permitted to do, and at the end of their chat she confirmed that he was indeed her husband, Ma Jin. She filled out the forms for his release and took him home. But that was not the end of it. That very evening, while pretending to take a shower, Ma Jin escaped again, this time through the window, with the aid of a long rope made of towels and nightshirts knotted together. He has not been seen since.

This morning, the former opera singer Mme. Ma told reporters: "I sincerely hope he will be found. We had barely a chance to become reacquainted."

4. A MINIATURE AEROPLANE

The third drawer of Judge Di's writing cabinet was open a crack, just as Volcano of the Old Moon's lawyer had predicted. This discreet aperture, barely noticeable, was the secret sign that an offering would be accepted. The convention was that the petitioner would slip a red envelope containing the offering into the drawer, and the beneficiary would pretend not to notice.

From behind his miraculously intact spectacles, Muo's bleary, dark-ringed eyes fastened onto the minute opening of the drawer, much as a secret agent in a spy film would recognise his counterpart in a stranger by some prearranged signal. His heart in his throat, he felt a magical wine rise to his head. The judge's assistant had left him alone in the office, seated on a leather sofa from which emanated a lingering, musty smell. He slipped his hand into his briefcase and ran his finger-tips over the envelope, which bulged voluptuously with one hundred brand-new hundred-dollar bills, secured by a thin elastic band stretched to its limit.

Muo got up from the couch and sidled toward the writing cabinet. The heat steamed up his glasses, and made him light-headed. It was the closest he had yet come to happiness. Before him stood the radiant article of furniture in a brilliant halo, as though Volcano of the Old Moon herself might spring from the third drawer at any moment. In that resplendent crack he had finally discovered a chink in the armour of the prole-tariat's dictatorship, and he feasted his eyes.

In a flash it dawned on him: this famous third drawer was never otherwise arranged. It was a permanent green light, a message addressed to all and sundry, not just him. How many times had the cabinet's owner opened the drawer to retrieve the red envelopes, without the least regard for the name of the donor or the reason for his donation?

Sobered by his insight, he saw the desk for what it was: a polished wooden cabinet with a dusty marble slab on top, upon which rested a framed photograph of two smiling girls (the judge's daughters?) and a television, itself a pedestal for a strange-looking object. Glinting in the light coming through the venetian blinds was the only item in the office that could be said to have any artistic merit: a scale model of a fighter plane made entirely of spent cartridges, whose coppery sheen gave it a sequined aspect—hundreds upon hundreds of cartridges, each minutely engraved.

Muo heard footsteps on the marble threshold and then on the wooden floor. His gaze left the fighter plane to meet that of the elderly man in the navy-blue uniform with the red emblem of the Republic of China and the word *magistrate* embroidered on the sleeve.

"Good day," murmured Muo. "Are you Mr. Di?"

"Judge Di," corrected the old man with the thin moustache as he posted himself beside the writing cabinet.

He had a desiccated air about him. He was no taller than Muo, despite the thick black heels on his shoes. His hair was thinning, too. How old would he be? Fifty-five? Sixty? One thing was certain: he bore not the slightest resemblance to the psychotic fugitive Muo had encountered on the execution ground. The old man standing before him could never have dealt all those blows. His violence was of a different order.

Judge Di's eyes were small, the left one almost permanently closed. He opened the first drawer and took out several small bottles, from which he poured a number of tablets and pills onto the marble cabinet top. He lined them up, counting as he went, and then took a large bowl of tea and swallowed all ten pills. While Muo introduced himself as the editor of a scientific publishing house in Peking, the judge fixed his right eye on him and narrowed the crepey eyelid to a slit, by which gesture one could recognise the former elite marksman, coolly appraising his target.

Hardly had Muo begun explaining his purpose—stammering, his eyes rolling, as he tried desperately to recall the exact words the lawyer had instructed him to use—when he was cut short by the sound of the judge's mobile phone.

The call was news of the Olympic Games that were taking pace in Sydney. China had just won a twentieth gold medal, in women's judo, and was now one place behind the United States but ahead of Russia. Exultant, the judge switched on the television. Two young women of impressive size were rolling across the screen, panting and grunting in slow motion. The judge's left eye opened, moistened at the heartwarming success of the fatherland, and his right eye flickered with emotion. Still talking on the phone, he stepped up close to Muo, much to his visitor's distress, for Muo had no idea how to interpret this extraordinary breach of protocol. He wondered whether the judge would embrace him. Judge Di was radiant. He raised his arm with the red emblem of China embroidered above the elbow and kept it aloft, as if awaiting the same gesture of enthusiasm from his interlocutor, initiating a triumphant high five. In his bewilderment, Muo took it for another secret sign, some code that the lawyer had forgotten to tell him about.

What a ghastly hand it was, with some of the fingers barely discernible and others in sharp focus, especially the crooked index finger with its dirty nail—the elite marksman's neglected trigger finger.

Evidently bemused by his visitor's lack of response,

Judge Di lowered his arm and resumed pacing the room. The television screen was filled by the red flag with five yellow stars (the largest symbolising the almighty Communist Party and the four small ones representing the workers, peasants, soldiers, and revolutionary traders) flying over the grandstand in readiness for the medal ceremony. The national anthem blared rousingly on trumpets, setting the miniature fighter plane on the television atremble.

Heaving a deep sigh, Muo took off his spectacles and wiped them with a slip of his jacket. This gesture did not escape the judge's notice.

"You are moved, too, by the success of our fatherland," he said. "I had taken you for the cold, reserved type."

Once more Judge Di raised his arm toward Muo, seeking the triumphant slap of hands.

Deciding to risk it, Muo raised one leg and stood balancing on the other in the manner of a war amputee.

"No, your hand, your hand," the judge said, winking with his right eye in an expression of exceptional indulgence.

Unprepared for any charade but the planned one, Muo pretended not to understand. He grabbed his ankle, and in an excruciating, painful effort, raised his foot bit by bit, all the way up to his shoulder, like a dancer warming up. The judge's left eye closed. The right eye stared coldly. Abruptly, he switched off his mobile phone.

"What sort of a circus act is this, then? Do you realise where you are?"

"It's all the lawyer's fault," Muo murmured, lowering his foot to the ground. "Forgive me . . . The lawyer acting for my friend, Volcano of the Old Moon . . ."

Choking guffaws from the judge drowned out his halting speech, a dark, hoarse laughter that chilled Muo to the bone. He took the laugh to be the prelude to some cruel pronouncement. The television relayed images of the Chinese judo champion lifting her face to sing the national anthem, then switched to the hockey finals between Russia and Canada.

"Volcano of the Old Moon?" asked the judge, sprawled on his Grand Inquisitor's throne.

"She is my friend."

"How unfortunate! The girl who sold photographs to the foreign press . . ."

"She didn't sell them. They didn't earn her a single yuan."

Tapping the keys of his phone, the judge said, "Just a moment, I must get in touch with the Party branch secretary."

Now Muo felt a terror he had not felt before. What had his stunt cost him? What further sanction would be visited on Volcano of the Old Moon, now that her case and her intercessor were coming to the attention of the Party boss? Drenched in sweat from his clumsy, foolish acrobatics, his shirt now clung icily to his skin.

The judge's ensuing conversation seemed endless. First Muo heard Judge Di propose a temporary lifting of the ban on firecrackers so that the people might have a fitting celebration of this latest gold medal. Then, changing the subject, he turned briefly to matters of general security, before continuing to enthuse about sports and grumble over budget cuts in the law courts and the laggardly construction of the new Palace of Justice. He ended by suggesting that they meet for a game of mah-jongg. It was at that moment that Muo heard the unforgettable phrase: "As exquisite as the ivory hand of a young virgin."

At the least shift in tone, the slightest clearing of the throat or harsh sound, Muo's heart pounded like a snared rabbit's, as new vistas of horror opened before his eyes. The terror was exhausting, and for that reason, as well as from a misplaced respect for the relevant social conventions, he refrained from doing what he was supposed to do: placing his lavish gift inside the third drawer.

The Chinese sports commentator shrieked when the Russian centre forward shot the winning goal in the final minutes of the match. The fans went wild, and the Russian flag was raised over the grandstand.

Sensing that Judge Di was registering his every move, Muo had another sudden realisation: it was not he who was waiting for the judge, but rather the judge who was waiting for him. He no longer felt like a secret agent on a mission, but rather a puppet on an invisible string, and the feeling made him sick. The shiny sequins on the fighter plane had ceased to dance. The brass of the shells had darkened.

As he looked more carefully, he realised that each shell's engraving consisted of a name and a date. And here and there, on several shells grouped together, the date was the same. A truth flashed across his mind: the name engraved on each cartridge was that of a prisoner personally shot by the former elite marksman, who on more than a few occasions had apparently executed sev-

eral men on the same day. Each cartridge was the relic
of a killer bullet fired into the small wedge of flesh
between the index finger and the thumb, into the heart
of a condemned man.

Even knowing of Judge Di's past, Muo was unprepared for the devotion with which this artefact had been
so lovingly fashioned. Suddenly it was not a man before
him, but a devil thirsty for blood, an incarnation of
pure terror, of gratuitous cruelty and evil. Where were
the phantom avengers? Apparently nowhere. Though
sceptical about the existence of God, Muo had believed
in ghosts since childhood, spirits in the inky dead of
night, the phantom freedom. Phantom justice. "But
right now I must pay tribute to a tyrant, whom even the
phantoms do not dare disturb, not even with a rash of
goose pimples. Not a single ghost haunts him." At this
Muo felt all his desire to take action on behalf of his
beloved melting away, dissipating, receding from him.
He replaced the envelope in his briefcase and turned to
leave the office.

He stole across the room and broke into a clattering
trot down the corridor, leaving Judge Di quite per-
plexed. Putting his head around the door Di saw Muo
passing the assistant and slipping something into his
hand—a twenty-yuan note. Here, for you. Mute thanks.
Good-bye.

5. BACKSCRATCHING

A revenant. For a minute or two at least, Muo had the feeling of seeing a revenant ghost. He could not recognise him at first, on account of his bruised eyes. Rather, it was merely a sense of having seen him before, the figure poised at the top of the long escalator in a glassed-in tunnel on the exterior of an ultramodern construction, rather like the Centre Pompidou in Paris. The rumpled suit said nothing, but the salt-and-pepper crew cut, the bony face, and especially the deep creases running down either side of the nose to the corners of the mouth—it was all uncannily familiar, and yet unrecognisable in the muted sunlight filtering through the milky glass of the tunnel. The escalators swished in parallel, one going up, the other down. The spectre came striding down toward Muo, who was on the rising belt. Muo's feeling of déjà vu was unbearable until he heard himself addressed by his childhood name. "Little Muo," called the man he now recognised as his old friend White Hair, the mayor's son-in-law, the one condemned to death by firing squad. Remembering that White Hair had been shot several years ago deprived the imminent reunion of any tenderness.

As the escalator continued upward, Muo felt his arm hooked inextricably by the wrist that still bore the fateful number 3519. He stepped backward, helpless to resist, as in a dream, pushing his way past the shopping carts of customers going up.

"What are you doing here?" he asked, so undone that his own voice seemed distant to him, more breath than sound. And as if to explain his own puzzlement to the spectre of White Hair, he felt compelled to add, "I have just escaped from the madhouse. What about you?"

"I'm on a tour of inspection."

"Inspection of what?"

"Restaurants."

"Restaurants?" asked Muo, the reality of his inter-locutor having become clear to him, though no less puzzling.

"My prison has opened two restaurants, and I am the manager. It was part of the deal my father-in-law wan-gled so my death sentence could be commuted to life imprisonment. I was able to persuade the warden to open a restaurant and make me the manager, with the promise that it would bring in a lot of money, which it did. In fact, he was so satisfied that he decided to open a second one, here in the shopping mall."

"So you've struck it rich?"

"No. All the profits go to the prison. But that's a rea-sonable price to pay for my daytime freedom. At dusk I go back to spend the night in a cell for lifers. It's right next to death row. Every time there's an execution I see a guard going past the door with a plate of meat for the man who's going to be shot the next day. That's when I say to myself, Shit, I've done pretty well for myself, avoiding that last supper."

They went to the prison-owned restaurant—The Mongolian Saucepan, a self-service establishment—to celebrate their reunion. Plate in hand, amid the pushing and shoving, each diner took his pick from scores of platters set out on counters down the centre line of a large hall: eels, pigs' brains, goats' blood, shrimp, squid, shellfish, snails, frogs' legs, ducks' feet, anything you could want, and all you can eat for just twenty-eight yuan (local beer included). The hall was filled with a hundred tables, flushed faces over saucepans set on gas rings, chunks of meat or vegetable being dipped into a thick, spicy broth covered with a red, oily froth of tiny bubbles, rising and swirling. The steam, the aromas, the voices of the diners bustling—it all made Muo dizzy. He found himself free-associating about the execution ground, the psychiatric clinic, Volcano of the Old Moon's lawyer, Judge Di . . . Underfoot, the floor was slippery with grease and filth, especially for a near-sighted klutz like Muo, who watched apprehensively as the diners cautiously crossed the floor, as if it were a frozen pond. A drunk in the washroom had lost his balance and tried to get up, but he kept slipping on the slimy floor and ended up asleep, with a urinal for his pillow. Such were the wages of unlimited abundance, The Mongolian Saucepan's innovative all-you-can-eat offer: "It's like a duel between the restaurant and the customer," White Hair explained to Muo. "The first to give up is the loser."

IT WAS RAINING. The son-in-law's car, a splendid, bright-red Fiat convertible with a driver built like a boxer, chugged valiantly up the hill to the judge's residence. Back in The Mongolian Saucepan, White Hair had told Muo he might be able to help with Volcano of the Old Moon's case, which offer had moved Muo almost to tears, now that he was fast losing hope in his mission and its promise of humanitarian and amorous relief.

At the top of the hill, the car stopped, and the son-in-law lit a small Dutch cigar and reflected. The furrows running from either side of his nose seemed deeper than ever. Muo did not dare look at him, let alone talk to him. Had he thought better of his offer? The chauffeur cut the engine and for a time all three sat motionless in the car. Muo peered through the rain at a stand of poplar trees and a peasant in a straw cape toiling in a distant paddy field. Then his friend motioned to the driver to continue. The Fiat spluttered to life and set off slowly, turning onto a back street before pulling up to a metal gate, set in a boundary wall that was two metres high. The driver got out first and opened the door for the mayor's son-in-law, who headed through the rain toward the intercom.

The rain did not lift for another hour, during which time Muo stayed in the car. Even through the clouds, stars were appearing in the sky; soon it would be time for his friend, manager by day, prisoner by night, to return to his cell. Just as Muo was beginning to feel sure things had gone badly, the gate opened and out stepped White Hair, grinning from ear to ear.

"Done," he said, sliding into the passenger seat. "But he doesn't want any cash. He's got plenty already. All he asks of you in payment is a virgin for him to sleep with, a girl whose red melon has not yet been slashed . . ."

THIS STRANGE IMAGE always reminds Muo of the sultry night, baskets of freshly caught crabs, lukewarm hard-boiled eggs, a sweaty rock wall in a cave in the side of a mountain in Fujian, his father's native province. It was there that he had first heard this expression for a girl's loss of virginity. He was ten years old at the time, and spending the holidays with his grandparents. One of his uncles was there, a former math teacher now made to work as a butcher for political reasons. He was only thirty but so bent that anyone would have taken him for an old man. He took Muo for a swim in a mountain river. They were caught in a summer storm and took shelter in a cave, which was already crowded with people of all ages—peasants, passersby, and men carrying baskets of dark, stirring crabs fished from a lake at high altitude and destined for export to Japan. One of the older crab fishers, whose face was cratered like the moon, settled down against a rock. In a low voice interrupted by much spitting and coughing he launched into a shaggy-dog yarn, while Muo shelled a still-warm hard-boiled egg given to him by a peasant woman. Under the Tang Dynasty, the crab fisher said, the Japanese, who had just rallied around their first king, were at pains to create a national flag, so they decided to follow the example of the Chinese. A spy was promptly sent to China, which, being more developed and civilised, was in the golden age of empire. After many adventures at sea, the spy set foot on the Chinese coast. Night had fallen, and the weather was mild. In the first village he came to he found a boisterous crowd. They were singing, drinking, and dancing around a white sheet with a large round stain on it, red in the middle and darkening along the edges. Observing the festive mood, the spy said, "It must be their national feast day, and that must be the Chinese flag." He waited in the bushes until everyone had gone home before reaping the fruit of his great endeavour, for which he had braved months of gruelling travel, beset by mortal perils and hunger. He snatched the venerated object and vanished into the night, not knowing that all he had pinched was a sheet stained with the juice of a virgin's melon, slashed on her wedding night.

The cave seemed to vibrate with laughter, but little Muo, without comprehending, just cupped his cold hands around the shelled egg to warm them. Then, without knowing why, he stood and marched right up to the storyteller, with his bare torso hunched by the fire. With all his might, he rammed the egg into the man's open mouth. The man swallowed abruptly, almost choking on the egg, and then leaned back motionless against the rock in the firelight, his face glistening and his small eyes rolling in their sockets. Muo still recalls the touch of the skin, which resembled waxed wrapping paper, and the smallpox scars he could touch with his fingers. That was how the expression came to be etched in his memory: a panoply of colour dissolved in a shadowy, rustling tide that coursed through his veins and took possession of his body; the smell of the sea in the cave; the jagged, rocky bluff.

On the way home his uncle proved to be exceptionally good-humoured about the whole affair. The heavy downpour had lacquered the mountain foliage. The air was deliciously fresh. The light was lyrical. Muo remembered them both sitting on a slope, wreathed in the fragrance of wet bracken and gazing at an iridescent, snow-capped mountain in the distance. In a low voice, his uncle taught him a poem from the Yuan Dynasty, eight centuries old and forbidden by the communists. He made Muo recite after him, word for word:

> *A magnificent wedding took place tonight;*
> *But when I set out to explore the perfumed flower*
> *I found that spring had already passed her by.*
> *Much red, little red, why ask for so much?*
> *No matter, it is of no matter!*
> *I am returning to you the length of white silk.*

Muo had never since imagined, even in his wildest dreams, that he would one day be tormented by such a desire on the part of an old judge in this lewdest state of corruption: to slash, with his bare elite marksman's hands, a red melon in the first flush of ripeness.

Could the case of Judge Di, or indeed of the whole Chinese people, have simply escaped the notice of his great master Freud, notwithstanding his demonstrable knowledge of every human perversion? No sooner does the thought enter his head than Muo remembers that in "The Taboo of Virginity," Freud argues that the man, suffering from a castration complex, regards the woman at the moment of defloration as a source of danger: "The first sexual act with her represents a particularly intense danger." In the man's view, the bleeding caused by the ruptured hymen evokes injury and death: "The man fears being drained by the woman, being contaminated by her femininity and thus becoming impotent." In fact, Freud entrusted the thankless task of deflowering his partner to a third party.

Ever since setting foot in China, Muo, the most doctrinaire of disciples, has faced looming doubts about his psychoanalytic vocation. He has allowed himself to wonder, *Could it be that the loves of Volcano of the Old Moon, past or present or future, including myself, are really nothing but substitutes for her father?* And now, *Why would Judge Di want to savour a slashed red melon, if he truly feared it might cost him his penis?* Muo has come to feel that he is being mocked from on high by a capricious tyrant, and the thought has kept him awake at night. He looks for orthodox answers in his psychoanalytic texts, but when he finds the answers, they seem only more outlandish here, in his true home. Nothing disconcerts him more than the prospect of renouncing his calling.

BY WAY OF THANKS, Muo presented the mayor's son-in-law with a very pretty fan from the twenties, decorated by an artist-monk with waxwing sparrows on rocky perches, preening with their feathers and ruby beaks. The son-in-law in return invited Muo to dine with him once more—not in one of the prison's restaurants this time, but in a place at the other end of the city. After dinner he took Muo to a tea pavilion on a bank of the river, decorated in the Shanghai style of the thirties with lacquered screens, low carved tables, and embroidered satin cushions. The soft music, barely audible, was wafting toward them from the far end of the pavilion. The son-in-law asked, "What do you think of the girl sitting on the bamboo chair in the hall?"

Muo turned to look at her. She was young, perhaps eighteen. Her shoulder-length hair dyed red was dull and lifeless. She wore a white blouse that reached down to her thighs. He got up and headed to the men's room for a better look. In the low, diffuse light he noted her plucked eyebrows, her sharp features, and, through her unbuttoned blouse and the black semitransparent bra underneath, her flat breasts and bony body.

"A young virgin for the judge?" he said upon returning to their table.

"No, a whore I have reserved for you."

Muo remained speechless for several seconds. In spite of himself, his eyes were drawn to the girl again.

"Reserved? For me? What do you mean?" he stammered, feeling the blood rush to his cheeks.

"Have fun. It's all paid for. You go ahead and relax."

"No, no . . . No, thank you, I'd rather not."

"Go on, be a sport, old friend. You've impressed me with your passion for your photographer friend, and for psychoanalysis. But I also feel sorry for you. You're tired. You don't look in the best of health. You're obviously tense. Why not follow Judge Di's example and take a girl's essence of yin to boost your vitality?"

Muo felt he was on the verge of an important discovery. His breathing became fast and shallow, and the heat of his eyes misted up the lenses of his spectacles. Perhaps it was finally at hand, the worldly wisdom whose lack he had so long suffered.

"Do you mean to say that when some jerk of a judge wants to take a girl's virginity, it's to boost his vitality?"

"Certainly. To boost his vitality, his power, his health . . . Forgive me for saying so, but you could learn a thing or two about sex from an old jailbird like me. When we Chinese men make love, it is for one of two reasons, which have nothing to do with each other. The first, of course, is to have children. That's work, purely mechanical. Ridiculous to contemplate, but that's the way it is. But the second reason is the more exalted: to nourish the self through congress with the woman's energy, with her female essence. And the female essence of a virgin—you realise what that means, don't you? Her saliva is more fragrant than a married woman's; her vaginal secretions bestow an exquisite grace on the sexual act. That is the most precious source of vitality on Earth."

Muo listened with fascination, taking care to veil his complete ignorance.

6. A MOVABLE COUCH

Two vertical strokes crossed by two horizontal ones, shorter and very faint, symbolising a bed. Beside it, three strokes, slanting and threadlike, represent the lowered lashes against the background of a closed eye, while a thumb points down as if to say, Even sleeping, the eye sees. The character for *dream* is in an ancient hieroglyphic script dating from thirty-six hundred years ago. There is a primitive enchantment about the character, a mysterious grace that hints at the divine, which deeply impressed Muo when he first set eyes on it as a twenty-year-old student at the Imperial Museum: an inscription on dark tortoiseshell so cracked and transparent in places, so ancient, he half-expected it to turn to dust if the air so much as stirred.

The scribe of old had no way of imagining that, several dozen centuries later, his character would become the logo of a travelling psychoanalyst. Muo set about tracing the outline on a piece of black silk, taking great pains to adjust the proportions according to the rules of enlargement. He then cut it out and instructed a tailor to sew it to a length of white cotton smelling faintly of detergent mixed with camphor, purloined from his mother's mahogany chest of drawers when her back was turned. Above the silk appliqué logo he printed three lines in red ink: INTERPRETER OF DREAMS (large script), followed by PSYCHOANALYST RETURNED FROM FRANCE and SCHOOLED IN FREUD AND LACAN (smaller scipt).

The final stage in the manufacture of his banner consisted of finding a suitable mast. Muo searched the furniture market and compared bamboo canes, but none had the sturdiness and resilience to support a flag in a brisk wind. Back in his parents' flat he dithered over the rod upon which his mother dried the wash and his father's collapsible fishing pole, made up of several lengths of lacquered bamboo. After due reflection he opted for the latter, less sturdy no doubt, but aesthetically by far the more pleasing.

Toward the end of a mild summer's night he woke from a brief and restless sleep. Since reading Kafka's *Metamorphosis,* he found his mornings had become a recurrent nightmare. That day, however, he felt oddly refreshed and energetic. He got out of bed, crossed to the window, and looked outside. He spotted a solitary star, perhaps the polestar, still shining in the northern heavens. It was the first time since his return that he had seen a star in the sky over this polluted city. He gazed at it for a time and interpreted it as a good omen for the psychoanalytic expedition he was about to undertake. Before the star faded, he got on his father's old bicycle and rattled down the streets, still drained of colour owing to the hour. He pedalled toward the outskirts of the city and dismounted in front of a skyscraper with a glass curtain wall like a vast mirror in which was reflected the sunrise over the Yangtze River in its full glory. He took out his banner and hoisted it on the fishing rod, firmly secured to the back of his bike, and then jumped on the saddle and shot off like a rocket with his banner streaming in the wind. Destination: the southern suburbs.

At this point let us reveal a secret: his vocational debut had become but a pretext, the cover for his quest to find a girl whose virginity he might purchase for Judge Di. Setting off with a clear goal at last, he was certain of taking a decisive leap forward to secure the freedom of his imprisoned sweetheart.

"And like an old flag volleying in the gale / Your whole flesh shudders in the blasts of sin . . ." The lines from Baudelaire went around and around in Muo's head as he pedalled.

Little by little he left the city behind. After an hour he arrived at the Red Gate commune. The first village, known as Jade Bamboo, had been selected for modernisation and presented a ghostly spectacle: parcels of land had been sold off, the old houses razed and replaced by high-rise office blocks rearing their unfinished skeletons, without roofs, floors, or partitions, the effort abandoned no doubt owing to economic vicissitudes. The empty frames of doors and windows were fringed with yellow wildflowers springing from cracks in the concrete and brickwork. Muo ventured into one of the buildings to take a rest and found the ground floor invaded by a lush weed, smelling strongly and wet with morning dew. A flock of sheep grazing within took no notice of him. Now and then a drawn-out bleat of contentment would drown out the faint rush of urine hitting a wall.

It was in this ruin, amid gaping holes giving onto the sky like so many windows, that he ventured his first professional interpretation. Here it must be remembered that whatever the faults in Muo's conduct of his own life, however crushing his ignorance, in matters of psychoanalysis, particularly as applied to the domain of dreams, his knowledge was vast and unimpeachable.

His first client was the owner of the sheep, a crippled man of fifty-four who hobbled to him on wooden crutches. Although he tried not to stare, Muo noted that one of the man's legs was shorter than the other, and surely thinner, too, for on that side the trouser leg flapped wildly as well as entirely concealing the foot. The man bargained the price down from twenty yuan to ten, which Muo accepted without further ado.

Smoking a cigarette, the shepherd related a dream in which he was walking, or rather wading, in a shallow stretch of water, probably along the Yangtze River, in the company of a fifty-year-old woman, a sexual partner of several years ago. In the dream, he was roused from a sound sleep by this former mistress, who in great excitement had come to show him a photograph of them taken by a neighbour who worked at a nearby tourist site. The Yangtze was so clear he could see the water plants and pebbles on the bottom. Farther along, midstream, he could see a barge with a line of clothes hanging out to dry. The woman was holding the man by his elbow, and he smiled, awkwardly supported by his crutches. His trousers, though rolled up and wet, were loosely flapping, and from his gaping fly protruded a very long, very straight rod reaching down to the surface of the water. The rod looked like crystal and shimmered with colour.

Asked to decipher this dream, Muo felt like a grand-master of chess called to play against the greenest beginner. Without hesitating or probing further, our psychoanalyst warned his client that it was plain from his oneiric report that another handicap—a sexual one—was stalking him, and that the temptations of Evil, known collectively as Satan among the religious and as the pleasures of the flesh among those of a more literary bent, would soon elude the poor cripple. Muo encour-aged him to seek a pharmaceutical remedy, modern or ancient.

Hardly had he uttered these words when he realized that this candor was pointless; the session should some-how have been applied to the furtherance of his supreme mission, but just as he was about to steer the conversation toward the subject of virgins among the local population, he observed that his patient was shak-ing with rage. Narrowing his mean eyes, the man show-ered abuse on Muo, excoriating him for mocking a man's disability. He flung his cigarette butt in his ana-lyst's face and, leaning on his left crutch, he swung the right one to strike Muo across the jaw. Muo fled, with the man in wrathful pursuit, hopping on one leg, lean-ing on one crutch, and swinging the other one overhead as in a kung-fu film, scattering the panicked sheep in all directions. In his blind dash, Muo was lucky to get away with his banner. He vanished as a feeble sun was still clearing the morning mist, without receiving payment for his services.

So Muo's tour of the suburbs as interpreter of dreams, his solo long march, started not so auspiciously. It would prove to be a test of patience. Every day for three weeks he set out in the early morning on his father's old bike. By midday the heat was so intense that the tarred surface of the road seemed to melt, and he felt as if he were pedalling through a bog. One time his front tire became flat, and by the time he managed to push the bike to the next village, where he could mend the tire, the seat was too hot to sit on.

At each new settlement, with his banner streaming from the fishing rod, he would hawk for clients. Without ever officially deviating from his rate of twenty yuan per session, he often lowered it to one yuan and sometimes even waived it altogether for the sake of referral business. At night, he would return to his parents' flat totally wrung out.

Some days he worked his legs so hard that it would seem he was no longer pedalling, that the old bike was carrying him along as a passenger. Then the fragrances of the fields, the buffalo, even the cars—everything struck him as beautiful, and as he sped along the roads shaded by plane trees he sometimes spied pretty girls riding the same way. He always thought women looked particularly sexy while cycling, and he dreamed of organising a fashion show in Paris with models riding bicycles down the catwalk.

His search for a virgin was not helped by demographics; the majority of the generation among whom the virginal were mainly to be found had abandoned the countryside to earn a living in the city. And of the few remaining, how many had not sold their virtue already? That was the question. Dreamers, by contrast, were to be found everywhere, and he encountered several interesting cases, always returning home to his exercise books and hefty dictionary to write up his notes in the language of Molière.

One morning in June, for instance, having turned off Highway 351, his bike swerving to avoid the puddles on a dirt track along a brook in a calm and verdant valley, he came upon a lone house with a tiled roof and a wooden palisade. It had a raised threshold half a metre off the ground and heavily carved double doors several centuries old, on the other side of which was a rectangular courtyard. There sat two old women next to two spanking new wooden coffins, stacked atop one another under an overhang (the local custom being to prepare the coffin of an elderly parent well ahead of time and to put it on view until the final day, as a sort of guarantee of abode in the next life). After parking his bike, he crossed the high threshold and approached the gossiping old women. Over the coffins' scent of freshly cut timber, he caught a whiff of something strange and indefinably foul in the courtyard. No matter; like an itinerant hairdresser, knife grinder, or cock castrator he advertised his services, calling out the offer of dream interpretation: "Best quality, best price."

The two old women—sisters, to judge by their resemblance—cleared their throats and expressed not the slightest interest in his magical exposition following the method invented by his master Freud.

This was nothing new. He had doubted the old sisters would tell him their dreams, was not even sure they were still of dreaming age or frame of mind, given the two

coffins under the eaves. After circling the subject for
some time, he was on the point of asking if they happened to know of any virgins in the area when one of the
sisters declared in a sardonic, almost riling tone, "We
are sorceresses ourselves, and we are famous in these
parts. Our father was a medium who specialised in
dreams. He certainly knew a lot more than your foreign
master."

At this news Muo was taken with a coughing fit, suddenly having located the source of the strange smell lingering in the courtyard. He laughed, excused himself,
and laughed again. He started back to the door but
could not resist the temptation to turn for a parting
shot: "You weren't in love with your father, by any
chance?"

The question, asked in a tone of perfect innocence,
was like a bomb detonated in the courtyard. Even the
coffins seemed to shudder. He continued, "According
to the theory I am applying, every young girl at some
stage feels the desire to sleep with her father."

He was expecting another fiery wave, and it was not
long in coming, albeit from one of the sisters only. She
threatened to cast a spell on him, whereupon the other
frowned and put her in her place.

"It's not all nonsense, what he's saying, especially in
your case. As soon as Mother got up you always used to
slip into bed with Father. He had to keep chasing you
away; don't you remember?"

"That's insane! It was you, you sneaky cat, who he
had to kick out of the bed every time. You even hid in
the dark to spy on him when he peed."

"You're lying! Only a few weeks ago you told me how
you had dreamt of him peeing in the courtyard, and

that in the same dream you'd imitated him by standing up to pee like a man, and it had made him laugh. True or false?"

Muo was deliberately slow in retreating from this sororal fracas, not wishing to miss a word of their mutual recriminations. Back on his bike, rolling down the dirt track toward the other villages in the valley, he regretted not having stayed for the inevitable tearful breakdown. He felt a deep sympathy for those two sisters—more, in fact, than for most other patients. He loved it when the settling of old scores took the form of a river overflowing its banks and breaching the dykes during epic, full-moon floods. Revelations, confessions, emotional apocalypse! Ah, the power of psychoanalysis!

In the valley he found only old villagers with their coffins in their courtyards, and women with babies strapped to their backs working in the fields or feeding the pigs. For a moment he thought Fortune might have smiled upon him when he spotted a plump girl, barely eighteen, behind the counter of the only shop for miles around. As he approached, he eyed her intently as she made entries in a ledger and then stuck a postage stamp on an envelope addressed to the tax office. She looked brave, determined to keep her business afloat. But her almost childlike face was marred by the imprint of fashion—plucked eyebrows. A session of dream interpretation ensued, free of charge, but it, too, turned to tearful confession: her bitterness over a brief sojourn in the city where, having secured a position in a restaurant, she'd lost her virginity in a vain effort to keep her job. Muo asked for the washroom and, having escorted him to the first floor, the girl held open the door of a grimy cubicle and quietly slipped in behind him. They were met by a swarm of buzzing, whirring bluebottles.

"Shall I help you open your fly?" she asked with a breezy, practised air.

"No, thank you," he said, taken aback.

"My price is nothing for someone as rich as you, Mr. Teacher."

"Get out!" he cried. "You must be out of your mind. Besides, who said I was a teacher?"

At this she left meekly and returned to her seat behind the counter. Had she insisted, had she pled for the sake of her business or her family, had she played the damsel in distress, it might have ended quite differently for Muo the incorruptible, Muo the true, Muo the knight in shining armour! Invoking the name of his own Dulcinea, he pictured her in his mind as he pedalled along the bumpy road just ahead of his dream-logo banner.

The highway was not yet in sight, but he could already make out the impatient honking of truck horns. In the distance he spied two black dots in the middle of the road, near the old wooden house he had visited earlier. The bicycle clattered, the basket creaked, the handlebars shook, and the chain seemed about to snap with each thrust of the pedals. He was thirsty and fantasising about an ice cream. The two black dots grew, crossed, and changed positions. He was labouring uphill against a long slope. His front wheel ceased turning, time stopped, and then, in a spurt, everything started up again.

For a moment the two black shapes vanished from view, then reappeared, still blurred but ever larger as he approached, until they revealed themselves to be the two

sorceresses, barring his way. The sight alone was enough
to make him dismount, but the heat exhaustion didn't
help matters. At no time since the start of his psychoanalytic *Wanderschaft* had he sweated so profusely.

They greeted him most cordially, apologising for
having doubted his competence, and even professing an
interest in psychoanalysis. He could barely believe this
about-face and made to continue on his way, but they
would not hear of it, instead pressing him to park his
bicycle outside and to step into their house for a bite to
eat. He complied.

The walls of their low-ceilinged dining room were
papered with old newsprint; the floor was of earth.
Hanging between the two closed windows was a framed
photograph of an old man, no doubt their dead father.
The smell of Tibetan incense filled the air. Two impressive bows of reddish ochre, which appeared suitable for
shooting arrows at demons, were arranged in a hollow
over the hearth. A fire was burning. Water was on the
boil. Tea would soon be served.

Muo had to admit that their noodles, their spicy carp
broth, and their pork kidneys with chives were well
worth returning for. While he savoured this virtuosic
performance of the culinary arts of boiling, frying, and
stewing, the two sorceresses told him there was one
dream they had never succeeded in clarifying, as their
late father had failed to instruct them in this area of
sorcery. (Not a single female adept is mentioned in the
Chinese annals of this art, although they are as vast as
the ocean.)

The dream had been dreamt by the elder sister's son,
who had died two months ago at age thirty-five from
natural causes, probably collapsed lungs. There was no

sign of violence. He had been working in a marble quarry for some years in Chongqing, five hundred kilometres away. An X-ray had shown a shadow on his right lung, a common development in quarry workers, and so he had been given five days off to celebrate the first of May, which opportunity he took to visit his wife and family back home in the house he had built the year before. It was one of the prettiest houses in the village: two storeys, balconies, and an exterior decorated with thousands of white tiles, which his mother and his aunt had affixed one by one while standing on bamboo scaffolding. The poor man had not had time to admire his dwelling by daylight, each square centimetre of which he had paid for with his marble-cutter's blood and sweat. He arrived too late; it was already dark, and being tired from the journey, he had no desire to eat or even take a bath. His wife filled a wooden basin with hot water and washed his feet for him, took his clothes off, and helped him into a T-shirt and clean underpants, after which he went outside to pee, more or less in that order. When he returned, he told his wife he wanted to say a prayer before going to sleep. He was a follower of the forbidden sect of Falungong. His wife left the room and he began to pray. By the time she came to bed after finishing her work about the house, he was asleep. The next morning she woke at seven and found him dead beside her. Owing to his involvement with the Falungong, she did not have a postmortem done for fear of involving the police.

When word of his death spread, it was learnt that on his way home the elder sister's son had dropped in on his mother and his aunt. He had stayed for about a quarter of an hour, during which time he'd checked the state of their coffins and told them what he had dreamt the night before he left Chongqing: he was riding a powerful motorcycle along the Yangtze River, when, looking down, he noted that his wheels had parted the gravelly sand of the riverbank, dividing it down the middle into two parallel tracks, dry and white on the right, damp and dark on the left.

Listening to the two sisters' story, Muo had fixed his gaze on the dusty portrait of the father, the medium of dreams, whose features, it seemed, betrayed a certain truly Chinese sensibility, while remaining otherwise quite illegible. He asked the old sisters for a few days' time to consider the dream and returned to his parents' home. The following nights he was unable to sleep more than two or three hours, and he smoked more than his lungs could bear. He continued his daily expeditions, but his mind was elsewhere. He thought of the famous English detective who could tell when footprints had been made by walking backward. One day he came across a decrepit old man trying to hitch a ride by the side of a road with no bus service. Muo obliged, for he was touched by the old man, so thin he seemed like so much livid skin over bone. As soon as he was settled on the luggage carrier Muo pedalled away, and the old man fell asleep. Engrossed in his ongoing attempts to analyse the son's enigmatic dream, Muo rode on for about an hour without hearing a word from the hitchhiker. Indeed, he had forgotten all about him until he slowed to a halt in the shade of a tall gingko and looked over his shoulder. The old man was missing—had fallen off, it seemed, somewhere along the way. Muo decided his distraction called for a few days and nights of sleep, and that he might have better luck unravelling the mystery of the dream having had some dreams of his own. One morning, as the pale blue light of day was sliding across his window, he awoke having dreamt of Volcano of the Old Moon in striped prison garb, accusing him of having forsaken her. At that very moment everything seemed to fall into place. He returned to the sorceresses with his answer: the dead son's dream was a premonition, and showed an unconscious suspicion that his wife was having an affair with another man, possibly a neighbour by the name of Fong, forename Chang, who would later murder him. (The Fong character is composed of two parts—one on the left representing water, and one on the right denoting a horse, a symbol for the motorcycle. Two superimposed suns make up the name Chang, and could be understood to refer to the two men, opposed in their designs on the same woman.)

The elder sister—the young man's mother—broke down in sobs. Her sister gasped, for they did indeed have a neighbour by that name in the village. A few days later the two sorceresses persuaded the police to arrest him. A confession was extracted after only ten minutes of vigorous interrogation.

Muo paid dearly for having dreamt another man's dream. At night, and sometimes in the middle of a psychoanalytic session, the motorcycle would roar into his mind's eye, ridden by him along the bank of the Yangtze, his head mobbed by sea gulls, who were whipping his face with their white wings. The machine was black, the river bottle-green. The sand on the left was light and dry; on the right it was dark and moist. And lending some depth to the picture were a sailboat in the background and a child peeing from a pontoon.

DURING THE SAME MONTH of travels Muo heard the dream of a night watchman. Much later he would still remember the corrugated iron roof of the man's shack, the solitary black form of which was flooded intermittently with light from the headlights of passing trucks. The watchman and Muo had met in a teahouse late one afternoon. The watchman had invited Muo home. "We'll have some fun tonight, with some girls from work," boasted the watchman, a man of about thirty and as short as Muo, but more energetic and by that time very drunk. Arriving at the shack, they found the door securely padlocked. When the watchman was unable to find his key he staggered around in search of a rusty crowbar, eventually managing to force the door with a terrible noise. As Muo stepped in, it seemed that the corrugated iron roof was still reverberating from the shock.

Inside Muo found the squalor of a man living alone, although at least the refrigerator was not empty. The man gave Muo a beer and proposed that they order up two whores.

"We'll have a foursome."

"Two whores? No! All these whores, I'm sick of them," said Muo, after a moment's pause.

Although naturally preferring a more oblique line of questioning, he decided to abandon his accustomed approach and forced himself to be direct. With impressive nonchalance he enquired, "You don't by any chance know any virgins, do you?"

"Any what?"

The night watchman stepped up to slap him on the shoulder.

"Virgins. Girls who are innocent and pure, who've never been . . . you know . . . Virgins!" he repeated, lingering over the word as if it were some obsolete verbal relic, savouring the curiosity of a sound seldom spoken.

The watchman roared with laughter, leaving Muo feeling a little sordid. When the drunkard's unseemly mirth had subsided, he grabbed Muo by one arm and propelled him to the shattered door, sending him packing as if he were a raving lunatic.

Muo maintained his composure. Adjusting his banner, he headed off slowly on foot, trundling his bicycle along the gravelly track. At a construction site where the building was almost finished, he paused to take a long look at the bamboo scaffolding towering into the sky like a vast chessboard. "Life is a game of chess," he reflected, "and my quest for a virgin is no exception to this rule. At which point did I make a mistake? Have I already been checkmated?"

He noticed a ladder with metal rungs spiralling up through the scaffolding. Seized with longing for a cigarette, he thought, *Why not have a smoke at the very top of these unfinished premises?* He slipped and almost fell off the narrow ladder, but imagined himself somehow protected, and so felt no pang of fear and continued on his way. His only concern was for his bicycle, as it occurred to him how disastrous it would be if on his descent he were to find it missing, and himself doomed to several hours' walking to get home. So he climbed down, lifted the bike on his shoulder, and started to make his slippery way up again.

The roof was a vast expanse of tar, a more or less fin-ished terrace. When the night watchman appeared on the roof—late for work, as it happened, his present job being the protection of the almost-complete building—Muo stood up on his pedals to race along a section of the smooth surface that was fenced off with steel cables. After he had winded himself, he dropped back on his saddle and freewheeled for a time before returning to the centre where, resting one foot on a steamroller, he came to a halt. Still on the saddle, he lit a cigarette and with a long puff abandoned himself to the combined lull of tobacco and depression before pushing off sharply to speed away again.

Fearing an accident—or worse, a suicide—the night watchman ordered him to dismount at once. But Muo just carried on, adding to his theatrics now by shouting at the top of his voice a phrase from the most illustrious of English poets: "I have stolen the moon, the sea, the stars," to which he added, "and virgins."

Rising up from the rack of his bicycle, the banner with the dream logo fluttered in the wind, and Muo alternately imagined that it was bearing him aloft or chasing him like a predator over the edge by the metal fence. He was drenched in sweat. The wind suddenly rose, howling and gusting so hard he was afraid the mast would snap, but just as quickly it died down into a soft moan and the air became as limpid as water. The sky seemed lower than usual, and Muo felt like a giant, as though he needed only to reach out his hand to touch it.

The watchman's voice reached his ears, but rather than ordering him to dismount, Muo heard it speak to him of a dream: "It was neither myself nor my late wife who had this dream, but someone who lived in our building in the southern district of Chengdu. He was a retired doctor of traditional medicine who on occasion still supplied herbs or plants to the neighbours. He was also a superb acupuncturist. He told me of a dream he'd had very early one morning, of my wife in front of a shop. There was no one else in the street. She was on her knees to gather up her own severed head from the pavement. She replaced it on her neck, rose to her feet, and hurried down the deserted street, holding her head in place with both hands. She ran past without seeing him."

Muo, feeling inspired and in excellent form, interrupted him: "Do you want to know what this dream signified?"

"Yes, please."

"Your wife was going to die quite soon, probably of some disease of the throat. Cancer, maybe."

No sooner had he made this audacious pronouncement than the night watchman fell to his knees before him and confessed that his wife had indeed died one month after the retired doctor's dream.

Sobered by Muo's powers of divination, the night watchman was virtually speechless from a surge of esteem for the psychoanalyst. He apologised desperately for having treated Muo so roughly before, begging him to understand that in his line of work, too, "you run up against a lot of kooks." Alas, he was unable to furnish Muo the one thing he sought, for the simple reason that virginity had ceased to exist among both "the girls at work" and the females of his social acquaintance. The best he could offer was to take him to the domestic workers' market, where he thought Muo might have better luck.

7. MRS. THATCHER OF THE DOMESTIC WORKERS' MARKET

Muo had never imagined such a dreamscape existed—a realm of only girls. His entry into the domestic workers' market affected him deeply: he had pangs of conscience at the social injustice of it all, to be sure, but at the same time his entire body was set alight by the sheer number of girls and the feminine fragrance they exuded. Even the sound of their voices struck him as carnal. *My God*, he thought, *what I wouldn't give to stay right here and be of service to these girls, loving them, kissing their young breasts, caressing their firm buttocks in their jeans, and offering them something infinitely more valuable than work or money, namely love and affection.* His knees were shaking; never had he been so close to his goal.

Situated at the foot of a rocky mountain, the domestic workers' market occupied the full length of a gently sloping paved alley, still known by the name it had been given during the Revolution: Great Leap Forward Street. Bordering the Yangtze River, it was often shrouded in mist, and its clientele consisted of well-off women, mostly city dwellers. Leaving their cars parked on the far bank, they would cross the river, arriving in small boats with outboard motors, and, much as at a vegetable market, would squeeze the merchandise and haggle over prices. Half an hour later, with their new girls in tow, they would depart via the same clanking boat, back across the famous Yangtze, its churning brown waters bubbling with sewage and industrial waste.

The market was run very strictly by Madame Wang, a fifty-year-old policewoman. Resolute and efficient, she was, at least from a distance, lacking in neither charm nor a certain stylishness owing to her trim waist, short hair, and fine wire-framed glasses. It was easy to imagine her as an attractive young girl, but for the smallpox that had ravaged her as a teenager and left her face looking like a colander. Her mastery of microeconomics, bordering on avarice, and her strict discipline, thanks to which no one had ever stolen so much as a yuan from her, had earned her the nickname "Mrs. Thatcher." The sobriquet was not lost on her, as Muo discovered when he went to apply for a permit to analyse dreams in the market. In her office in the only two-storey building, which loomed over the alley like a fortress, Muo spotted on a shelf, beneath the portrait of China's premier, a biography of Margaret Thatcher, tucked in among the usual government-issue publications and voluminous collected writings of diverse communist leaders.

After three minutes of Muo's laboured explanations, she interrupted him with a wave of her hand.

"We communists are atheists, as you well know."

"I'm sorry, but what's that got to do with psycho-analysis?" he stammered in bafflement.

"What you call psychoanalysis is nothing but fortune-telling."

Looking her straight in the eye (just as he had been warned not to do), he retorted, "Well, if Freud could hear what you just said . . ."

Before he could finish the thought, he lost heart, flattened by the repellent sight that was Mrs. Thatcher's face. But after a moment of gathering his wits and steeling himself, he widened his eyes and started again, more gently now: "If Freud could hear you . . ."

"Who is this Freud?" she asked, her own voice softening, too.

"The founder of psychoanalysis. A Jew, like Marx."

"Stop looking at me like that," she said in a timid, unlikely girlish tone. "I'm old and ugly."

"You're too modest."

"It is you who are too kind," she said, touching the sleeve of Muo's jacket. "I will tell you a dream, and if your interpretation is correct, I will give you permission to ply your trade in Great Leap Forward Street."

SUNDAY 25 JUNE. *That bitch Mrs. Thatcher is driving me insane. This is the first time I have resorted to coarse language in my psychoanalytic notebook (my custom being to employ neutral, objective words), but only the bluntest, most brutish terms can aptly describe my nightmarish encounter with this crone. Throughout my brief career as a psychoanalyst, I've come to understand that when listening to my patients' dreams, I can better sense the presence of invisible, unconscious forces if I shut my eyes. The narrators fade, their voices become distant, but those certain words that are charged with extra meaning ring in my head like a thunderclap. That is my method. Unfortunately, it has proved impossible to apply to the local Mrs. Thatcher, who is unnerved and offended by anyone's shutting his eyes in her presence. So I have had to force myself to look at her as she narrated, but repulsed as I was by her pockmarked face, the only thing to enter my head was a vision of her brain riddled with smallpox. I had a vague awareness of her having mentioned the image of a stuffed dog, for instance, but I was powerless to speak, much less interpret it. Entries in psychoanalytic tomes swirled in my head, Freudian and Jungian precepts interspersed with Chinese words and the teachings of Confucius, as I desperately wracked my brain for ideas. Finally, I decided I had to answer her expectations somehow—tell her fortune and reveal the key to her life as a woman of power. But what keys could there be to the life of someone like her?*

"The stuffed dog is a premonition that you will be invited to a sumptuous banquet in the near future," I told her. (Will you ever forgive me this sacrilege, Master Freud? It was her pox upon me that made me do it.)

"When?" she asked.

"Tonight or tomorrow," I replied, shutting my eyes for a moment's relief.

Again pawing my sleeve, she laughed with delight, a theatrical and imperious laugh that contorted her features and made the hundreds of tiny pits on her face seem to crinkle and bubble, growing larger and larger like dried peas after soaking, until I feared they would burst all at once in my face. But I would have had no regret of this horror if only she had given me my damn permit thereafter. The truth is that I had become enchanted by the domestic workers' market and only more certain of its promise as a gold mine in my quest.

MONDAY 26 JUNE. It's done. Mrs. Thatcher has granted my permit, owing to a fortuitous last-minute invitation to an official dinner hosted by the regional marketing authority. Soon I shall be filling the pages of my exercise book once again. This afternoon I raised my banner in the middle of the market (the good fortune brought to me by psychoanalysis has never yet failed me). And with my official installation in Great Leap Forward Street I know beyond a doubt that the mission I must accomplish on behalf of Judge Di is entering a crucial phase. What's more, I am beginning to enjoy life as an interpreter of dreams.

TUESDAY 27 JUNE. *Today's efforts were a bust. The women who came to consult me were mostly of the disagreeable minority I would classify as halfway to old age.*

I perch myself uneasily on a wooden crate, which I acquired from the only food shop in the alley, but for the comfort of my patients, I have rented a proper chair from a pensioner. It's one of those low, reclining chairs made of bamboo, and it accommodates well enough the necessity of their being supine, though the resemblance to a Western psychiatrist's divan is slight.

Most of my first patients had been previously employed by company directors, doctors, lawyers, and professors, or by people working in film or the theatre. I'd set my fee at three yuan, which seemed to me nominal, but treating oneself to a dream interpretation turned out to represent a small bourgeois luxury by which the "half-old women" set themselves apart from the girls, who haven't yet made a little money. The bamboo chair would creak as they reclined. No one wished to remain in that position for very long, deeming it a mild torture and preferring to be upright. They tried hard to disclose themselves to me, but with little success, for although they were eager to tell me their dreams they could never quite remember them but for the odd detail: a vase shattering spontaneously; half a green apple; the grand master of the Falungong; a dried fish; a head of hair turning white overnight, or falling out by the handful; a flickering candle; a rat squeaking in the dark; their own skin shrinking or wrinkling like that of a snake. One recurrent element is the domestic iron—not surprisingly—a symbol of conflict and servitude. ("It means you wish to be in a different situation," is the diagnosis I give women who dream of ironing.) One dreamt of yawning while she ironed (as in the painting by Degas, which bears witness to his compassion for the poor). She had been yawning and stretching frantically, and it finally emerged that in the dream she was wearing the clothes of her boss's daughter, aged ten.

My first client, a woman of fifty with a perm and a fancy ring on her finger, had dreamt of catching a fish. I asked her if the fish was large or small, but she could not remember. To persuade her of the significance of this detail I attempted to translate what Freud has to say on the subject. The specific terminology and phrasing, it must be conceded, does not lend itself to translation, but using the melodious dialect of Sechuan, I managed well enough to convey the gist, which amounts to the following: small fish stand for human sperm, big fish for children. As for the fishing rod, it obviously stood for the phallus. An indescribable pandemonium ensued, with all the women shouting and cheering at the tops of their voices, though my patient blushed and hid her face in her hands, as if a dream could dishonour her. I could not say that all found relief in these revelations, but from one moment to the next the fear of unemployment at least seemed to vanish from their faces, and if nothing else I have the feeling that Great Leap Forward Street has accepted me as a public entertainer.

Tonight, before closing up shop, I received a visit from Mrs. Thatcher. Unlike the others, she lay back easily on the bamboo reclining chair, her head resting on a wooden pillow. Her face was drawn, her eyes firmly lowered, and I detected an odd aroma, which was neither perfume nor the local eau de cologne. She called to mind Freud's description of hysteria in women.

She said in a low, halting voice, "I dreamt of the stuffed dog again last night."

I probed her for more details. Was the dog in the same position? Was it the same size? The same breed? And what breed was that?

Had it looked at her? Had it barked? She was unable to reply. She had simply dreamt of the stuffed dog, that was all.

"Astonishing, isn't it?" she said.

"No. In fact, the return of the familiar is a typical manifestation of the psychical unconscious," I explained. "Freud, in the early years of his practice, made a special study of this. He said, 'The repetition of an action in time is habitually represented in dreams by the multiplication of an object, which appears any number of times.' "

She seemed dismayed. I could not be sure that she heard the end of my Sechuan rendering, for laughter from the crowd erupted at the mere mention of the Master's name, which a few bystanders repeated like an incantation, perhaps attempting to usurp my analytic power.

"So who is this Freud?"

"As I've told you, he revolutionised the interpretation of dreams."

"Yes, but nothing he says makes any sense."

"He is teaching us, quite simply, to trawl our childhood experiences for the origins of what we dream. Do you remember the first time you saw a stuffed dog?"

"No, I don't."

"Please try to remember. One of Freud's great discoveries is the nefarious role of recurrence. The point is not to decode a dream or solve an enigma per se, but to find some way of putting an end to the repetition to which one is painfully subjected, and by so doing clear a path to further possibilities."

The policewoman's brow furrowed, and the lines running on either side of her nose deepened.

"Now you've lost me. The last time, you revealed that the stuffed dog meant I was to expect a dinner invitation, and that was true enough, but do these 'repetitions' promise further meals? Is that what your Freud is saying?"

Abruptly she sat up. Her voice became sharp, almost hysterical, and she started clicking her tongue as if she'd remembered something else.

"Come to think of it, the dog had a strong smell; it stank of mildewed books!"

She thrust her face close to mine.

"Rather like you."

"The stuffed dog is an omen that you will soon be a cripple."

Of course, this was neither an orthodox Freudian view nor a legitimate personal opinion. I just had a sudden urge to insult her in return. No doubt my id got the better of me, or perhaps my subconscious, since the Chinese refer to the disabled as "pocked, lame, and lousy."

In the hush that followed, only the creaking of the bamboo chair, the clicking of her tongue, and the whispers of the bystanders could be heard. Then she laughed.

When I rolled my bicycle onto the ferry, the boatman told me that the market women were already placing bets on the failure of Mrs. Thatcher's legs.

At two a.m. I woke with a start and tried to recall the dream I'd just had. I got out of bed to jot down notes, but it was too late; the essence had slipped through my fingers. What I did remember was a sequence of horrible images: an open-air political meeting in Great Leap Forward Street, awash with black-haired girls. It was very hot, the loudspeakers were blaring, and I was on my knees in front of a grandstand. A heavy slab of concrete hung around my neck from a wire so deeply embedded it was lost in the folds of my skin. On the slab were inscribed my name and my offence: MUO, ROBBER OF VIRGINS. Mrs. Thatcher was talking into a microphone, clearly denouncing me, though I could not make out what she was saying. In the brutal heat of midday, the sweat from my forehead was pooling on the ground before me. Then, with the absurd suddenness of dreams, I found myself lashed with ropes to my father's bicycle, the muddied front wheel spinning away, my dream-interpreter banner streaming behind me. In a pandemonium of shouting and screaming, the girls threw me—bike, banner, and all—into the Yangtze River. The deep, dark water, black at first, became emerald green, then darkened again to take on an olive sheen, though I could see vegetation—grass or algae—swaying along the riverbed. The banner detached itself from the bicycle, eddied around me for a while, then drifted quietly downstream.

WEDNESDAY 28 JUNE. I was obsessed by my dream during the entire long and arduous journey to the domestic workers' market. If the first image, the political meeting, could be placed in the category of dreams about trials (here I recalled the most spine-chilling first lines in all of literature, from Kafka: "Someone must have been telling lies about Joseph K., he knew he had done nothing wrong but, one morning, he was arrested"), the second image, that of being cast in the river to drown, was surely by the logic of analogy and chronology the verdict. One needn't be a trained psychoanalyst to recognise the hovering shadow of an impending catastrophe, and I could already see the policewoman's gun levelled at my poor head. What could I do but shrug, a telling gesture of resignation?

Something, however, kept me from accepting the plain truth of this analysis, as logic, fear, and certain tenets of my venerated masters became entangled in my head. True self-analysis or wishful thinking? I could not say, but as I stood on the bank of the Yangtze, waiting for the ferry, something Jung once said with reference to water flashed into my mind, and with it, I was certain, the correct explanation of my strange dream had come to me: the trial signified that something I was hiding (my project? my plan? my love?) threatened to be exposed; as for my being cast in the river, according to Jung, it is the primitive symbol of often unpredictable yet powerfully fecund forces, an insight he propounds in a work whose title now escapes me, but which I would be able to locate in the library of *any university in France. Elated by this new perspective, I took a few sips of green tea from my thermos, relishing it like an exceptionally fine whisky. I took off my shoes, tied them together by the laces, and hung them over the handlebars. Then I rolled up my trousers and waded into the water, carrying my bicycle on my shoulders. With my shoes dangling and bobbing at the ends of their laces I waded with faltering steps toward the waiting boat. Once on board I looked around and breathed in with delight and a sense of relief. The clouds were vanishing quietly, melting into the blue. The prow of the boat danced on the river. The current sang, as if to infuse me with renewed strength.*

"Thanks to Judge Di," I said to myself, "I have touched upon something primal at the core of being alive."

And so my entirely unexpected hero's welcome in Great Leap Forward Street was but icing on the cake. Upon my arrival I was met with a whirlwind of excited women, emitting shrill cries like the chirping of so many crickets, and as my newfound devotees fluttered gaily about me, one whispered in my ear: "Mrs. Thatcher sprained her left ankle stepping off the boat last night."

THURSDAY 29 JUNE. *Poxy Mrs. Thatcher did not show up yesterday, nor today, in fact, which is most unlike her, I am told. The cause of her twisted ankle remains to be clarified. In all likelihood there is a connection here with the psychological concept I call "counter-suggestion," namely that the more one fears an imagined danger, the more cautious one is and, paradoxically, the more one invites the misfortune. This insight has nothing to do with any prowess of mine at the art of fortune-telling, at least in the popular sense.*

Be that as it may, for two whole days I have reaped the benefits of what is rapidly becoming a legendary reputation, and my clientele is expanding accordingly. Suddenly everybody has a dream to tell me, especially after a brief post-prandial snooze. And I am particularly pleased to note that my relations with the younger women at the market are intensifying. (The eye of the would-be virgin-snatcher is ever alert, and can never succumb to pity or complacency.)

I can now well imagine the purely physical joy of a botanist exploring a new continent. Without neglecting his plant-finding mission as such, he nevertheless immerses himself in the new bitter-sweet odours, the tangy, musky perfumes, savouring the strange and exquisite forms and hitherto unseen hues. For my part, I began to fear that, faced with the varied wonders of creation, my memory would fail to keep straight all the different objects of their dreams, each more palpably significant than the last: a mirror; an iron gate; a heavy wooden door; a rusty ring; a card stained with soy sauce; a mother-of-pearl scent bottle; a dull glass; a long, thin cake of soap in a black box; a department store's revolving lipstick display; a collapsed bridge; a flight of steps hewn out of rock, with treads widening and narrowing by turns; a handful of crushed charcoal; the fall of a bicycle with a brightly fringed saddle; an antique belt; red patent-leather sandals on a muddy footpath . . . Never do the dreams of these poor young girls, most of whom came from the mountains, feature such things as dolls, teddy bears, or cuddly elephants, let alone white or pale pink wedding gowns.

"My dream—" giggle—"I often have the same dream; it's like the movies—" giggle—"I'm acting in a film. Which one? Can't remember. A scene? Wait. For example, I dreamt I was playing a girl about to be kissed, or who was watching other people kissing . . . very embarrassing. But I know, even before waking up, that I'm having a dream. Do you see what I mean? I told myself, 'You're dreaming,' but it went on anyway . . ."

This girl was one of the youngest at the market: barely sixteen, no breasts yet, a shiny comb in her hair, bare feet. Reclining on the bamboo chair, she rubbed the arch of her left foot up and down the mud-encrusted calf of her right leg. I remembered seeing her two *days before on the embankment, arguing with some other girls. As I listened to her, I glimpsed the "diaphanous, feather-light down, evoking the bloom on a peach," this dusting so highly praised by the poets of the Tang Dynasty, which softened the outline of her delicate thighs. Taking this to be a sure sign of her virginity, I had to fight back tears of joy.*

"How old are you?"

"Seventeen."

"I don't believe you, but no matter. I just want to return to one point you made. You said you dreamt you saw people kissing. Have you had any personal experience of such physical contact?"

"You sound like some kind of professor."

"Indeed, my mother very nearly became one. But please answer me; it is important for the interpretation of your dream. Have you ever kissed a boy?"

"Certainly not, sir. Not in real life, anyway. But I did once dream that I was watching a film, on TV, at home. And it was me acting in the film. There was a boy, played by a famous actor, who wanted to kiss me. It was dark, and we were standing on a bridge. He came up close to me, but then, just as he was about to kiss me, I woke up."

"Congratulations, my dear girl, there is about to be a change in your situation. That is what your dreams foretell."

"Really? Will I get a job?"

"More than that, I assure you."

My pronouncement elicited astonishment and envy among the crowd of bystanders. I decided to suspend our session for the moment, and pick it up with her again in private later on. Some of her successors in the bamboo chair tried to extract a similarly heartening interpretation from me, but stubbornly I would not oblige. Unfortunately, this tussling distracted me, and when I had finished with them my little film-dreamer had gone.

FRIDAY 30 JUNE. *This morning I woke up fully dressed, including my shoes, feeling like a chess champion who has been up all night planning a tactical offensive. Unfortunately, my shirt and trousers were badly wrinkled, unseemly for a professional, so I needed to change. A frantic search in my wardrobe ensued, but not only could I not find anything decent to wear, but my right index finger got caught in the stealthily swinging doors. At my howls of pain, my mother put her head around the door to tell me that my three pairs of trousers were tumbling around in the washing machine—another bright idea of hers. Having no option but to wait for the end of the cycle, I paced the shabby living room in my under-pants, fuming. It was unbearably stuffy, and I kept glimpsing my ugly body and incipient paunch in the pitiless mirror.*

I ended up putting on a pair of trousers that were still damp, and in my haste to be on my way, I forgot to dump the trash bag my mother had asked me to take down. I didn't realise this until I was several streets away, when I was flagged down at an intersection by an old man wearing a road safety armband. His suspicions must have been aroused by my fishing-rod flagpole, and he sniffed the air inquisitively until his eyes came to rest on my handlebars and the trash bag swinging from them, which, given a few taps by him, began to trickle dark liquid. Luckily the light switched to green just then, so I stood up on my pedals and shot away.

Reaching the suburbs, I dismounted in order to drop my unwanted load. There was too much wind for flying my banner, but as I pedalled along I felt a sense of tranquillity and fulfilment, and gradually my confidence returned. I was tempted to slow down and feast my eyes, perhaps for the last time, on the pretty countryside of southern China—the misty slopes, the paddy fields on either side of the road, and the villages screened by thickets of bamboo all along the Yangtze River. I was optimistic about finding the film-dreamer again, the girl whose virginity was assured, and told myself that if

*she accepted my proposition it would mean that I had brought my
latest psychoanalytical endeavour to a successful end. I would
treasure forever my dream-logo banner as a memento of my profound and eternal love for Volcano of the Old Moon.*

*The boat was waiting for me, and as I got on with my bicycle, the
ferryman wordlessly slipped an envelope into my hand.*

"A letter for me?" I asked with evident surprise. "From whom?"

"The policewoman."

*He cast off and the craft chugged slowly toward the opposite
bank. I opened the envelope and my heart sank to discover yet
another vile twist of fate. I couldn't even read to the end; I tore up
the letter and threw the scraps in the river.*

*"Turn back now, please. I won't be going to the market after
all," I said.*

*The ferryman cut the engine and for a long while remained
motionless at the wheel, looking at me pointedly.*

"What are you waiting for?" I said.

"You'll pay me for a round-trip, then?"

*I nodded assent, slumped in thought. Slowly and deliberately, I
lowered the banner inscribed with the ideogram for* dream, *from
the most ancient of Chinese scripts. I almost had to laugh at my
foolishness before tossing it into the river. It made a fluttering arc
before touching down on the brown surface, where it drifted into an
eddy and spun around a few times before being sucked into the dark,
deep current.*

*I can still see that fastidious schoolgirl hand, those sickening lines
in leaky ballpoint ink: "I cannot believe I have fallen in love at my
age. But it is true! I might as well tell you now that I never had those
dreams about stuffed dogs. Not the first, and not the second one,
either. I simply concocted them so you could demonstrate your professional competence. Do you find that endearing? Please give me a
sign. If you wish to marry me, come quickly, my love—all of Great*

Leap Forward Street is ours. But if you do not wish it, be so kind as to go away and never come back. Just leave me in peace, I beg you."

The rest of the letter had consisted of a page devoted to news about Mrs. Thatcher's children and grandchildren, and another devoted to her parents.

Muo could not help but wonder what uncanny force could have visited this undeserved fate upon him: the first marriage proposal of his life coming from a pockmarked grandmother.

The measure of the gallant man, he knew, was his conduct not in triumph but under the cruelest of reversals. The day after receiving the missive that put an end to his promising daily sessions at the domestic workers' market, China's only psychoanalyst-at-large sat in his bedroom in a corner of his parents' house at six in the evening, planning a new journey. He would go to Hainan, a province declared a Special Economic Zone by the government and known locally as "the island of desire" because of the many young girls who flocked there from the four corners of China. This trip would take him one thousand kilometres from the happy hometown of his parents, from Judge Di, and from the prison where Volcano of the Old Moon was being held.

He filled his pale blue Delsey with a portable radio, a clear plastic raincoat, sunglasses (actually a pair of thin, gold-framed lenses that could be clipped to ordinary glasses—quite a masterpiece of French optical design), two sweaters, shorts, several shirts, a pair of summer sandals, and flip-flops with wafer-thin soles. These more practical necessities having been assembled, he looked to gathering from his bedside table his true travelling companions and most trusted friends—the source of all his spiritual nourishment, the lack of which for more than twenty-four hours would have made him ill. Among them were a hefty hardback Larousse dictionary with gilt lettering on the cover; the two-volume *Dictionary of Psychoanalysis* in its slipcase, it alone weighed five kilos; Freud's essay on psychoanalysis in the 1928 French translation of Marie Bonaparte, revised by Freud himself and published by Gallimard; a volume in the *Connaissance de l'inconscient* series, edited by J.-B. Pontalis; *Journal psychanalytique d'une petite fille*, translated by Malraux's wife (wherein Freud describes "how the secret of sexual life emerges, indistinctly at first, then takes full possession of the juvenile soul"); Lacan's *Subversion of the Subject and the Dialectics of Desire*, which Muo held to be the ultimate authority on female orgasm; and *The Secret of the Golden Flower*, an ancient Chinese alchemical treatise that Jung studied throughout his life. As Muo wavered between *A Case of Mental Neurosis with Premature Ejaculation and Other Psychoanalytical Texts*, by Andreas Embirikos, poet and father of Greek psychoanalysis, and Claude Lévi-Strauss's *Tristes Tropiques*, another book slipped from the pile and landed on the faded carpet at his feet: Robert van Gulik's *Sexual Life in Ancient China*. The book fell open at a five-hundred-year-old wood engraving by Lie-nu-chuan depicting four women in various stages of undress, two having already shed their clothing while a third, rising up on the tip of one bound and twisted foot, raises the other foot to slip off her trousers, which are embroidered with tiny flowers. Muo's eye was immediately drawn to the inclined nape of the fourth figure as she unhooked her brassiere. He promptly took a small card from a drawer and jotted down the references of the illustration. He intended upon his return from Hainan to check in the library whether this was indeed the earliest depiction of a Chinese bra.

Preparing his spiritual repasts for the journey flooded him with pure and innocent joy. Like a greedy child, he could not resist dipping into the goodies he would have to leave behind, reading a passage or two before shutting the books again and running his fingertips soothingly over their covers. Now and then, coming across some concept he recognised from somewhere else, he would set about leafing through thousands of pages of print, as well as his exercise books. When he could not find what he was looking for he wracked his brain for any mention of the subject by some university professor, perhaps during a lecture. And then he riffled through cardboard boxes filled with notes he had taken as a student in more careless times, at university with Volcano of the Old Moon.

Sitting on his bed, he made a final check of his suitcase, now almost full. The blinds were drawn, and six or seven lamps were lit. He added the last-minute items on his list to his suitcase: the thermos for his daily cup of tea; a jar of extremely hot red peppers to season cooked dishes, especially tasteless ones, as he might find; a jar of pickled green peppers for breakfast; some canned foods; several packets of instant noodles; a comb with two or three teeth missing; several blank exercise books, for taking notes; two or three metallic ballpoint pens; and some markers. At the back of a drawer he discovered a pencil sharpener sparkling like a gem in the dark. He tried it, and although it was a little rusty, it gave a satisfying crunch as the shavings curled into the air.

Leaning his head against the wall, he shut his eyes as if he were listening to music. In reality, he was breathing with difficulty and feeling stabs of pain in his stomach, possibly caused by the toxic lead in his pencil, the point of which he tended to lick nervously while thinking hard.

He recalled the policewoman's words: "I never had those dreams of stuffed dogs. Not the first one, nor the second . . ."

"Get out of my head, you buzzard," he answered to the intrusive memory.

He got up and went into the bathroom and, without switching on the light, stripped down to his glasses. The white bathtub glinted in the half-light. As the water gushed from the tap, choking and spluttering amid a cloud of hot steam, he lowered himself into the tub. As he did so, his glasses were dislodged by the water and, after lingering afloat for a moment, sank like a torpedoed vessel. He ruminated on the moony gaze of the policewoman, and her remarkably low voice. The painful truth, he told himself, was that psychoanalysis, for all its merits as the best conceptual framework for gaining insight into the human soul, was no match for a female communist, especially an uncouth, grass-roots communist who had the gall not only to violate the sanctity of the therapeutic relationship and fabricate dreams but also to turn the tables on a professional interpreter's own analysis. He lay back in the tub and let the water lap at his chin. A wave of nausea swept over him. "I can't let her get away with it," he told himself, and leapt out of the bath with a great splash.

Drying himself quickly, he returned to his room and sat down at his desk.

"Dear Madame Policewoman," he wrote in a hand more legible than usual, but also more guarded, "I have the honour to declare that no one can escape the truth of psychoanalysis, not even an official representative of law and order. Allow me to inform you that, from the perspective of psychoanalysis, the dream you purport to have had, and which you disclaim as a fabrication, is just as revealing as a proper dream occurring during a state of suspended consciousness. It has, as we say, the same psychological resonance. In other words, both are equally revelatory as to your fears, thwarted desires, and complexes, as well as to the state of your soul: tainted, sordid, puerile . . ."

As the words poured from his pen he was reminded once more of the film-dreamer, the living embodiment of all the physical and professional joys he had known as a dream interpreter. He remembered the expression on her face when she told him she had dreamt of acting the part of a girl waiting for a kiss. He pictured her bare feet and the way she had rubbed her left instep up and down the mud-bespattered calf of her right leg. *A true virgin, an oriental, on-screen Alice in Wonderland! How close I was!*

Having lost interest in the matter and having some thought that she might reply, Muo did not finish the letter to Mrs. Thatcher. He put it away among other papers in a folder he packed in his suitcase.

Some days later, on a night train heading south to Hainan Island on 6 July, the unsent letter would disappear along with the pale blue Delsey, so ineffectually secured with a metal chain sheathed in pink plastic.

What happened next has been recounted already:

Muo crisscrossed this vast island for several weeks without success, but at the beginning of September a chance telephone conversation with one of his former neighbours in Chengdu presented him with a prospect—a girl (if a middle-aged female embalmer can be so called) whose virginity was still intact.

PART TWO

UNDER COVER OF DARKNESS

1. THE VAN IN THE NIGHT

A week or so after his return from Hainan, the phone rings in his parents' flat, past midnight. The hyperventilating voice at the other end is that of his upstairs neighbour, the Embalmer.

"He's dead. I just got back from his villa."

"Who is dead?"

"Judge Di. It's all over."

AT THIS NEWS, all he feels is a prickling sensation sweeping over his body, a cold sweat breaking out from every pore. His mind races: *He must have died making love, his heart must have stopped during the tryst I arranged for him. Could I be arrested, not for bribing an official, but as an accessory to premeditated murder? No doubt. Wait, I remember reading about someone in a similar predicament, but where? A novel, perhaps . . .* Soon, though, his mind refocuses on the present: What on Earth to do? And how can he possibly secure Volcano of the Old Moon's release now? When no answer comes to him, he begins once again to hear

the Embalmer's voice, still prattling on the other end of
the phone, her words seeping into the minute inter-
stices of his brain like an invisible liquid, making every
nerve throb and fizz against his eardrums and cranium
in a whirlpool of conflicting emotion: relief at the pre-
emption of an impossible mission, and terror at the
prospect of imminent arrest.

"NOW LISTEN," the Embalmer continues, "you told
me someone would come for me at the mortuary at
about eight p.m., but instead this guy turned up at
seven. Judge Di's sixth secretary, or so he introduced
himself. A very nervous little man. He said the judge
was waiting. There was no time for me to change my
clothes or take a shower, but I figured, okay, after all the
old judge wouldn't be expecting a movie star, and the
sooner we get it over with, the better for Muo. So we left
right away, although I did snatch a moment to put on
some of that Chanel lipstick you gave me for my birthday. We went down to the main entrance, where the
judge's secretary tried calling a cab. After ten minutes
of shouting into his mobile phone, still no taxi, which
got him good and worried—scared of you-know-who, of
course. Seemed he was going to lose it. He started bab-
bling about this and that, how he had just come back
from the United States, where he was studying law, how
he'd picked up a lot of English, big man. Anyway, just
to get on with it I suggested we take one of the mortuary
vans. I was half-kidding because there happened to be
one parked right by the entrance. It was an old van with
headlamps like goggle eyes and a split windshield and,
as I pointed out, it was just like the armoured police

vans they use to transport prisoners to the execution ground. Anyway, this wannabe American devil didn't know what to do. He called the hotel where the judge was playing mah-jongg to get instructions, but they said he had already gone home. Then he called the judge's villa, but there was no answer there. By then it was seven-thirty. Finally the poor jerk took a five-yuan coin from his pocket and flipped it in the air. Tails, we take the van; heads, he figures out something else. Looking back, I should have prayed for heads. If I hadn't mentioned the van at all, or if I hadn't had the key, Judge Di might still be alive. So really, it's thanks to you that I'm in this mess."

AS THE EMBALMER DRONES ON, the screen in Muo's panicky mind switches channels. A film called *Lenin in October*, which was was shown in the Kremlin sometime during the fifties. During the screening the director was sitting a few rows behind Stalin. Halfway through, in the half-light, he noticed the People's Little Father turning to his neighbour and muttering. Actually, what Stalin said was probably something like: "You must send a telegram to X," but what the director heard was: "This film is shit." Suddenly everything went black; the director slid off his seat, and when he regained consciousness he was still on the floor. When the guards came to take him away, they noticed he had wet his pants. Muo congratulates himself that his own panic—in a predicament no less dire than this director's imaginary one—has not yet brought him to that point.

"Once we were in the van with me at the wheel," the Embalmer continues, "it was my turn to be anxious and depressed. Naturally, I couldn't help thinking about what was awaiting me at the judge's villa. I may be a virgin, but I wasn't born yesterday. I knew the deal, Muo, and let me tell you one thing . . ."

"Yes?"

"I hated you for it. During the whole trip I hated you so much you have no idea. Do you know that deep down you're callous and cruel, not to mention completely selfish?"

"Can't say I have an argument in my defence. You may well be right."

"Oh, you bastard! So where was I? Oh, right—while I was driving, the secretary pulled himself together long enough to give me road directions and brief me for my rendezvous. Do you know how long the judge had been playing mah-jongg?"

"Before returning home to his villa, you mean?"

"Yes."

"Twenty-four hours?"

"Try seventy-two! Three days and three nights. From Thursday evening on, he was holed up with his cronies in a room at the Holiday Inn. Do you know it? It's that five-star property in the middle of town with the fake marble columns. There's also a manicured lawn with a fountain. According to the secretary, the entrance hall and the upper floors are lined with black granite, and the elevators have doors of hammered bronze. But the most remarkable thing he said is that when you're looking for a particular room in the corridors, the numbers aren't marked on the doors—they're beamed from the ceiling onto the thick beige carpet at your feet! They don't even have this in the United States, he said. Anyway, when the hotel was inaugurated three or four years ago, Judge Di was a guest of honour. That was his first marathon: he stayed at one mah-jongg table for twenty-four hours straight, without eating or drinking. Apparently he was insanely compulsive, desperate for something that can give him the kind of thrill he used to get in the firing squad, pulling that trigger. And you, you knew what a pervert he was, and you let me go to him."

STILL LISTENING TO HER in the dark, Muo fumbles vainly for the switch on the bedside lamp. He pulls on his trousers and jacket. He must go to the police station, or at least be ready to go. He wonders whether he has time to change his clammy shirt, and suddenly hears something drop out of his coat pocket onto the floor. In a flash it comes to him Singer! It was Isaac Bashevis Singer who wrote that story about a man in a similar pickle. The setting is some Eastern Bloc country— Poland? Hungary? Whatever. A handsome young man, charming and fun-loving, an inveterate womaniser, is moved out of compassion to sleep with a fifty-five-year-old teacher, a scrawny matchstick of a woman, who worships him. She waits in his house until midnight, then takes a shower and joins him in bed. But in the middle of their exertions her body suddenly stiffens and, convulsing horribly, she dies. The seducer is petrified at the prospect of being arrested for murder. So much for the parallel—the rest of the story, Muo recalls, is devoted to the young man's efforts to get rid of the teacher's corpse in the middle of the night. *That's exactly what I should be doing,* Muo thinks, with a sharp gasp, *thinking up ways to get rid of Judge Di's body.*

"During the whole journey I kept asking myself, Have I gone nuts? Am I really, at the age of forty, going to have my 'first night' with a judge whose biggest kick is mah-jongg? I'm sure I started to hallucinate. The streetlamps cast an eerie yellow light, and the horns of the other cars sounded strangely distant, as if I were in a dream or, let's say, as if I were actually living something I had only dreamt of before. Even now I'm not sure I'm not dreaming. Anyway, a strange sort of calm came over me as I was driving, while the sixth secretary burbled on. I pictured white mah-jongg tiles sliding apart, uniting, colliding, sliding apart again."

How to get rid of Judge Di's remains? Muo, the accessory to murder, sees a succession of film stills flooding into his mind's eye. First, the image of a heavy body floating on the surface of a river before sinking slowly to the bottom, where the rope that's binding it comes undone. The judge's uniform billows out; his stomach balloons. His feet twitch their final twitches, then become rigid; he loses a shoe in the muddy current, choked with dark green aquatic plants, dead leaves, rubbish, rotting trash, a cloud of black debris. Borne along by the current, Judge Di poses, stiff as a wooden doll, with long arms outstretched to form a cross, heading toward a bridge over the river. Just as his body is about to collide with a concrete pier of the bridge, in the shape of a prow, it is swept into an eddy and rolls like a fallen leaf into the eye of a whirlpool. Of course, a murderer with so much blood on his hands does not deserve such an aquatic funeral, the likes of which Tibetans have practised for centuries, any more than he deserves the Yangtze River, from whose waters rise the world's most ancient prayers: "In accents intertwined two by two, waves coupled with verbs." *Joyce? Valéry? Do I have that right?*

"I was driving on a road I've taken every day for over twenty years, and yet I had the sense of crossing a foreign city. We went past the open-air market, where butchers were cutting up carcasses. I could feel a migraine coming on at the sight of them, in their halos of sickly yellow light. We went past the grounds of the music academy. From behind the wall someone was playing the piano. 'How wonderful!' exclaimed Judge Di's sixth secretary, 'Beethoven's *Sonata no. 29.*' For the first time I was impressed. He told me about America, and about all his sleepless nights spent listening to the radio. He had fallen in love with jazz, and then with the piano repertoire. I complimented his musical taste. He thanked me, and made a confession: he had converted to Christianity while he was over there. This guy, escorting me like a prisoner to the execution ground—a Christian! In the end I actually felt sorry for him. He told me he had suffered horribly from hemorrhoids while he was away, and that his condition is now incurable. They're invading his bowels and sometimes when they break there's so much blood you'd swear the man was having his period. And as if that wasn't bad enough, it's ruined his career. He can't take part in the mahjongg marathons held by his superiors, which often go on for days. So he has never penetrated Judge Di's inner circle; the judge picks his confidants from among his gaming friends, so the man will always be the sixth secretary.

"Past the factory we turned into the road that goes to the bridge at South Gate. It's not as bumpy as it used to be, back when my husband would fetch me from

work on his bike. And of course we went past the public toilet. It isn't a shed anymore, but a building with
a tiled roof and white tiles on the outside, although it
still stinks to heaven. I can't bear to pass it, except now
the latrines seem like part of him, of me, of my life.
I think of Jian, wherever he is, free to have his assig-
nations with boys now that he's dead. At one point I
asked the secretary—his name is Lu—'You're a Christian, Lu. I suppose you've studied the Bible, and all the
rest?' And he said, 'What do you mean, all the rest?' I
said, 'Well, what about paradise and such? What d'you
think it's like? Would you say they have toilets in paradise? Not filthy ones, of course.' He seemed annoyed,
so I dropped the subject and concentrated on the road,
keeping both hands on the wheel, until we went past the
People's Park, and he said: 'Listen, I'm a lawyer. I don't
deal in ambiguities. Pissing and shitting are what your
body is for. And after you die your body doesn't go anywhere. Only the soul ascends to paradise. Goes up to
heaven to join the angels. And souls don't shit or piss.
So there's no need for any shithouses up there.' It
naturally occurred to me to ask, 'Do they have them in
hell, then?' but he said he didn't know. We both shut
up after that. In the centre of Chengdu I stopped to
buy something to drink. When I got back into the van
he was evidently still pondering my question because he
burst out with: 'Up in Peking, in the Forbidden City,
they don't have bathrooms, either.' I said, 'Oh, really?'
'No, they don't,' he said. 'Have you been? If so, you
wouldn't have seen any in the sections of the palace
reserved for staff, nor in the inner courtyard used by
the emperor, the empress, and the concubines, and not
in the eunuchs' quarters, either. No bathrooms any-

where, just as in heaven.' I said, 'So where do they do their business? In a bucket?' He got angry again, saying, 'Shit, use your head! A bucket's a bucket, not a bathroom!' "

HOLDING THE RECEIVER in his right hand, Muo feels around with his left on his back for the exact spot at which the elite marksman will aim before putting a bullet through his heart. He imagines being sentenced to death for the double crime of bribing a judge and instigating murder. Fortunately, they can kill him only once. One fine morning the execution squad will take him to the wasteland at the foot of Mill Hill, a place he has seen with his own eyes, perhaps not by chance. A hole will have been dug by two grunts. He will be bound with thick ropes, his arms stretched high behind him, and made to kneel with his back to the marksman, who will train his sight on the tiny square between his forefinger and thumb. The only question is whether he will wet himself, like the Russian film director. He runs his fingertips over his back, pausing at the sharp, jutting triangle of his left shoulder blade, tapping his vertebrae, exploring his frame to locate the fatal spot. Will his thorax explode the moment the bullet, popularly called a "killer peanut," hits him? With a jolt, he remembers the talk about "pay bullets" when he was a boy, about the executioner's bullet being billed to a condemned man's family. If they didn't pay up, they could not recover the body. Fortunate were those whose loved ones succumbed at the first shot; the parents would pay the price of just one bullet, which back then was sixty-five fens in Chengdu, one yuan in Peking, and one yuan twenty-five in Shanghai. Nowadays, they're at least ten or twenty yuan each. Muo imagines his poor parents paying at the rate dictated by progress.

"Have you been to Judge Di's house? It's pretty far away. Ten kilometres west of Chengdu, in the direction of Wenjiang. You follow the Yangtze until Sword Lake—you know, the one they built in the shape of the Olympic rings that's used as a water reservoir. The road is quite narrow, but in excellent condition. You go up a wooded slope and across a new-money neighbourhood—Western-style houses, terraces with electric lights, wide verandas, long arcades, lawns with statues, fountains, pitched roofs, and rounded belfries like Russian onion domes. Each one gaudier than the last. My migraine was getting worse, clamping down from my neck to my temples. It wasn't full-blown yet, but it was getting there.

"Judge Di's villa is halfway up the slope, behind a wall two metres high. I pulled up at the gate and the secretary got out to announce our arrival on the intercom. A blinding spotlight flipped on, and the heavy iron gate swung open, almost theatrically.

"The house was in the Western style, a stand-alone two-storey construction, but honestly I could barely see it at first. I steered the van into a dark drive that abutted a thicket of bamboo. Suddenly something jutted into the beam of my headlights—a strange, phantasmal figure a bit like a dragon or a tropical snake, with a flat head swaying to and fro about a metre above the ground. I thought it was about to open its saw-toothed jaws, and I let out a shriek. My escort cracked up. 'It's just a rare chrysanthemum,' he said, that someone had given Judge Di. The plant is so precious that it takes four gardeners working full-time to care for it, pruning it and watering it with a special solution to ensure that it keeps its shape. The bloom is priceless. I got out of the car to take a closer look. Sure enough, it was a true chrysanthemum, but with unusually large leaves and petals curling in on themselves in a scalloped spiral. I rubbed one of the flowers between my thumb and forefinger and the fragrance was so strong it seemed it would never leave my hand. There were more flowers of the same species in a variety of shapes, some of which I couldn't identify, although I did make out one shaped like a horse.

"I got back in the car and we took a turn, and he said we were approaching the peony garden. Our headlights beamed over low bamboo hedges, but as it isn't yet the season there was nothing much to see. The bonsai garden, on the other hand, was truly shocking. You can't imagine how many there were—a huge slope with plants serried on various levels, contorted, stunted growths like deformed creatures, bristling, with scales standing on end. They reminded me of those monstrous foetuses kept in glass laboratory jars. Some were clipped into perfectly symmetrical shapes. There's nothing more unsettling than nature made into something unnatural. I didn't bother to stop this time; in fact, I speeded up. But there seemed to be no end to the expanse of midgets, no escaping them: yews twisted into vases and lyres; aconites covered in poisonous spurs; miniature Indian fig trees with branches dropping shoots to the ground, taking root there and sprouting more trees; elms with black boughs. I even saw a dwarf papaw with a trunk like an elongated stump, fringed at the top with tiny green fruit under a tuft of leaves like an umbrella. Also acacias, limes, magnolias, and clove trees, all absurdly shrunken. The easiest to recognise were the cypresses because they always retain their campanile shape. But there were many more species I couldn't distinguish, some just altered beyond recognition. And so when I say I saw a magnolia, a jujube, an ilex, or a green oak, really it's just a guess.

"Finally the judge's villa came into view, guarded by yet another dwarf army—conifers this time—ranged on the slope like a host of savages in verdant headgear. I rolled down the window and inhaled the smell of resin and incense. Then something odd happened. A policeman in uniform stopped us, directing us to a parking space and ordering us to wait there. Judge Di's secretary, who was at first astonished and then outraged, produced his work permit and started making grandiose declarations. He was eventually allowed to approach the villa on foot, but without me.

"I, of course, was in no rush, and so I was perfectly happy with this unexpected turn of events. I stayed behind at the wheel, like someone who's early for a date. I checked out the house where my virginity was supposed to be taken. Rising on the far side of a lily pond was a brick building blending Western and Chinese styles, with creepers forming a little arch over one of the doors and climbing up to invade an arcaded balcony on the first floor. Through the greenery I could see large open windows, lit with red, drum-shaped lanterns, as if a party were going on. From time to time figures appeared at the windows, then flitted away, only to reappear elsewhere.

"The judge's secretary was taking forever, so I crept out of the van very slowly and carefully. The policeman was watching me but said nothing. I strolled around for a bit near the van, stepping on pine cones and broom-pods everywhere. I went over to a stand of eucalyptus; the fragrance was delicious, especially combined with the almondy smell of broom.

"Up in the windows with the red lanterns people seemed to be hurrying from room to room. There was a lot of talk and gesturing, but the voices were muted by the festoons of creeper. Somehow, though, it seemed like one of those moments in life when you know instinctively that an impending doom has lifted. My migraine was gone. A vehicle pulled into the drive, where it was met by the uniformed policeman. It was an ambulance, the revolving light streaking the tree trunks with garish shadows. This was when the sixth secretary came running to announce that Judge Di was dead. Having played mah-jongg for three days and three nights, he had to play some more when he got home. He summoned his staff and they played five games in succession. A sixth was about to begin when the judge was struck dumb and keeled over."

Muo groans a fatalistic groan.

"Aren't you relieved?" the Embalmer continues. "I'm at the mortuary right now—I'm on embalming duty for the night shift. Everything has to be done by morning, before the bigwigs and the relatives arrive . . . Of course, I'll wait for you here—where would I go? . . . Okay, see you . . . Wait—bring me something to eat, will you? I'm starving!"

2. TWO A.M.

An acrid smell stings Muo's nostrils the moment the door swings open. Rotting citronella? Camphor, perhaps? No, it is more searing, as hot peppers are to the palate. At last Muo realizes it must be myrrh. She must have burnt some sticks of it to mask the smell of formaldehyde, which can turn the stomach and tighten the throat of the uninitiated.

"Are you all alone here?" he asks. "Don't you get scared?"

"Only when it's very late," replies the Embalmer, continuing her preparations without pause, in her work clothes and high rubber gloves.

"Excuse me. I forgot to say good evening."

"Is it still evening?"

"Actually, it's almost daybreak."

The room is not as Muo had imagined it: not stark, nor empty, nor white. Indeed, it seems far less sinister than his room in the psychiatric hospital. There is a softness to the atmosphere, owing to the five or six small lamps that cause the shiny, chrome-plated instruments and brass locks to glint against the draperies covering the walls. Muo imagines an underwater world, like the hold of a sunken ship, an effect heightened by the rush of water filling the gleaming tub in the dark far corner. It is rather like a dream he once had: he was underwater, entering a submerged house, the roof of which was heavily encrusted with white shells, and with rafts of tiny red crabs settling on the woodwork of the door and the windows, their iridescent armour setting the dwelling alight.

Stepping across the giant chessboard formed by the black-and-white floor tiles, he almost expects to hear the crunch of crab shells underfoot. Everything seems steeped in the colours of deep water. He approaches the Embalmer.

"Where shall I put the food?" he asks. "The shop at South Bridge was the only place still open at this hour. I brought you a peppered-ham sandwich and two tea-boiled eggs."

"I love tea-boiled eggs. Shell them for me, will you? I'm starving."

Tea boiled eggs are cracked during immersion so the tea can do its work. When Muo picks the shell off, the egg emerges with a brownish scallop pattern, like a pinecone.

"I'll take out the yolk. They say it's bad for your cholesterol," he says.

She does not answer but throws her head back, mouth wide open to receive a piece of egg.

"More, please," she says like a child.

She devours the two eggs. Muo becomes keenly aware of the woman's greedy, burning tongue. With a pitiless gaze, he studies her familiar face, the curved forehead already lined, the fine crows' feet, the chin showing the first signs of slackness.

"Come on," she says, "why don't you go and say good-bye to your friend Judge Di, then wait for me outside."

On a table in the middle of the adjoining room, a bulging, translucent plastic body bag is laid out. She begins to unzip it, the metallic crackle of the resistant zipper ripping the silence of the room. Judge Di's head emerges from the stiff folds of plastic, followed by his black-shirted torso.

"Damn, it's stuck," says the Embalmer. "Can you give me a hand?"

"Are you sure?"

"Sure about what? Come on, pull."

For all their concerted and disconcerted efforts, the zipper won't budge past the point where its teeth are clenched. Muo can hear his breathing becoming labored. Now and then his hand glances off the judge's shirt, a silk woven more finely than anything Muo has felt. At this close range, the sharp smell of myrrh competes with the rank odour of yesterday's wine and stale tobacco, a mixture reminiscent of the clochards in Paris. It occurs to him that the mah-jongg addict probably hadn't bathed for more than three days prior to his heart attack—maybe a whole week.

"Wait," she says. "I'll get some scissors to cut the damn thing open."

While her back is turned Muo battles with the zipper once more, pulling the little metal clip back to the top, and then down again, inch by inch, until returning to the place where it jammed before; then he gives it a mighty tug. No use. Just as he is about to attempt another assault, he makes a most disturbing discovery: the judge's eyes are no longer shut. Muo makes to shut them but then notices that the glassy globes are rolling in their grotesquely wrinkled, red-rimmed

sockets, fixing him with the dull, glazed look of someone just returned from wandering in a blizzard. Could
the doctor who signed the death certificate have been
mistaken? Is this another communist miracle? A resurrection? Muo remains poised over the judge's face, only
half believing what he sees, but feels his tormented soul
yearning for refuge outside his body. A gleam comes
into the judge's eye as he catches sight of the Embalmer
returning with the scissors. Pushing the screen aside,
she freezes in midstep. The scissors slip from her fingers and crash to the tiled floor. The judge stirs and
throws his arms around her. She shrieks, but he hangs
on to her shoulders, pulling himself upright and then
drawing his body close to hers. She struggles hys-
terically, now unable to speak. He says, "You're the
Embalmer, aren't you?" She nods yes, still squirming
like a creature caught in a hopeless trap. He smothers
her with his cheek: "Don't be afraid," he coos, "every
virgin goes through this to become a woman."

As he tries to separate them, Muo's arms feel limp as
cotton wool, and he is thrown backward. Then, summoning more strength than he thought he had, he grabs
the judge by the collar so fiercely that he rips his shirt.
"Go on, run for it!" he yells at the Embalmer, who flees
just before a thousand stars explode in front of his eyes
as a blow from the judge's steely elbow knocks him to
the ground. Muo struggles to his feet, but his nose is
bleeding so profusely he is too light-headed to stand.

Finally sitting up, the judge surveys his surroundings. "Damn! I'm in the morgue!" he says, with
remarkable matter-of-factness.

Sprawled on the black-and-white tiles, Muo watches

the little judge looming above like a giant, bolting for the door, and vanishing into the night, at which point Muo feels free at last to pass out.

Coming to his senses after he knows not how long, he assesses the damage: a bloodied face like the hero in a Western or a film about a boxer, and sopping trousers like the Soviet director in the Kremlin's screening room.

"Not bad, Muo," he says to himself. "Here you are, the two global superpowers united within you."

3. THE CITY OF LIGHT

With his trousers and underwear soaked through, Muo has no choice but to leave the mortuary in the Embalmer's clothes, which he finds in a cupboard—a pair of pale blue overalls made of thick, sturdy canvas, something between a boilersuit and the robe of an ancient scholar, at once solemn-looking and ridiculous, especially given the words printed back and front: COSMOS FUNERAL SER-VICES (in white), with a picture of an astronaut astride a rocket fuselage (in yellow), phone and fax numbers and the address (in red). At least it has plenty of pockets, into which he transfers everything he was carrying: cigarettes, lighter, wallet, key ring, and his recently acquired mobile phone, still glowing and blinking, heedless of the preceding drama.

It is still dark. He dreads the thought of his parents waking to greet him in this macabre outfit. Rather than take a taxi, he decides to walk, and sets off across the slumbering city without any particular plan. He finds himself taking the Embalmer's route, past the gate of the deserted music academy, after which he turns right and follows the long wall until he comes upon an unlit block of workers' housing with no one in sight. He would like to catch his reflection in a shop window, just to see how odd he really looks, but there are no shops in this neighbourhood. Now and then a dog crosses his path, pausing briefly to observe him and then following him along the opposite pavement. He can hear rats in the trash cans along the curb.

Reaching an intersection, he is seized with strange doubt. *What is happening to me? I was born in this town, I grew up here, I know this area like the back of my hand, and yet here I am, lost.* Fighting down a rising panic, he distracts himself by inspecting the changes wrought by feverish capitalism. He strolls around the intersection, exploring one new street after another, all the same, row upon row of concrete apartment blocks, all virtually identical. After a quarter of an hour of wandering he decides he'd best head north. But looking up to scan the sky, he can't tell where north is. It's about to start raining, so he decides he'll just continue in the direction he's been going, down a street lined, like all the others, with young eucalyptus trees.

What would Volcano of the Old Moon say if I paid her a surprise visit in this outfit? he thinks. He smiles, imagining it. Her laughter is an abrupt roar, which some find alarming and others embarrassing. "See this astronaut on a spaceship? I'm in training for a new career." No, he can do better than that: "I've gone to work for the angels who escort human beings on the last leg of their journey to paradise. Embalmers: we are the beauticians of the dead." She'd laugh, pointing out that he never knew a thing about beauty. Then he'd lean forward, pressing himself against the Plexiglas window, and she, with her long, fine fingers, would trace the little man in the space suit on his chest, from the other side. Or would she, he wonders, dissolve into tears, having understood all without his having to explain a thing— their last chance blown, the finality of it all. Would she bury her head in her arms, laying it so leadenly on the table that all the screws together couldn't carry her away? *I'd better not visit her now, and not in the next few days, either,* he thinks. *She doesn't need that.*

Muo had first seen Volcano of the Old Moon in tears when they were both at Sechuan University. It was bitterly cold and it had snowed for several days, exceptional for the southwest. One afternoon toward the end of November he went to see Professor Li, who taught Shakespeare and was rather fond of him. The professor's office was spacious but freezing cold, except for an adjoining study, five square metres, lined floor to ceiling with bound volumes and heated by a coal-burning stove. They went into the little room to chat. Muo showed him a speech from *King Lear* he had just translated, and Professor Li put on his spectacles—the missing left support of which had been replaced by a piece of string—to compare Muo's text with the original. There was a knock at the door. Professor Li stepped into the main room to answer it, and Muo glimpsed Volcano of the Old Moon as she came in. He was puzzled to see her; she had never taken an interest in English, let alone in Shakespeare. She was unrecognisable, very pale, her eyes heavy and swollen; she was clearly in great distress, though physical or mental he could not tell. She did not speak. Indeed, she did not even return the professor's greeting, and it seemed it was all she could do to reach the table in the middle of the room and collapse in the cane chair before dissolving into tears, her head flat on the table. From his vantage point Muo could discern only her long hair shivering between her shoulders, tossing and rippling with each spasm of grief. He felt trapped in the little study, uncertain whether he should stay or go. He could hear the professor's voice, but without the venerable authority and wonderful resonance that kept his classes spellbound. He was apologising for the misdeeds of his son (a student of philosophy, whose inordinate good looks were known all over campus, and whose name often crossed the lips of female students, in whose dreams he was known to be a regular visitor). She remained silent as Professor Li blasted the boy as a rogue and a reprobate, someone not to be trusted. Muo leaned toward the little window in the little room and, peering through the dusty pane, he was startled to find tears beginning to well in his own distraught eyes. The stove, which had been purring like a homely old cat all the while, had gone out. He tried adding coal and blowing through the small vent, but the irritable stove answered with only a stifling puff of soot in his face. Smoke billowed out into the other room, and by the time the professor noticed it Muo had quit the study, coughing and wheezing, with Volcano of the Old Moon astounded to see him emerge from the billowing cloud. In fact, it was hard to say which of them was the more acutely embarrassed to see the other in this state. Wiping his face with the back of his sleeve left streaks of soot on his cheeks, which gave him the look of a clown in a Chinese opera. Perhaps it was the sight of him in this stage makeup, but whatever the cause, she was no longer crying. He took a chair and made to sit down, but instead found himself on his knees beside her. He had a look of such perfect comprehension and tenderness; anyone would have taken it to say, "Forget him." Shaking her head, she reached out to touch Muo's shoulder, to urge him to his feet. Her despair was palpable. He wanted to say: "Volcano of the Old Moon, I am nearsighted, unattractive, puny, uninteresting, and poor, but I am proud and I would do anything for you," but he was struck dumb, never one for enormous declarations. Instead, lifting his face up close to her anguished heart, he managed only to stammer her nickname as she leaned over to help him to his feet. "Go on, get up, he'll see us," she said, the effort interrupting her tears, at least for a moment. Muo wanted to wipe them away, as any hero in a movie would have done, but his hand was too sooty, and so, in one swift pass, he stole an awkward kiss on the mouth instead. It was not a proper kiss—their lips just met, and he got a fleeting taste of her salty misery. They both drew back from it at once. Sitting quite still, she kept her swollen eyes fixed on him, though without seeing him, he thought. She had the dull, suffering look of a patient in a hospital waiting room. But in a moment she had collected herself with all her usual grace, and she bade good-bye to Professor Li, who was still waving his arms to clear the air in his study.

Twenty-odd years later, trudging across town in the Embalmer's work clothes, Muo thinks back to that kiss—

his first, a kiss of love and desire, a complicated kiss, salted and unearned. In his mind's eye he sees Volcano of the Old Moon, her lovely pallor set against her black quilted cord jacket, and under it a turtleneck sweater in snow white. That day in November has remained ever since a secret anniversary for him, faithfully celebrated each year in solitude, always in the same ragged blue coat and greasy cap he wore then. (At this point it would hardly seem indelicate to reveal the other secret of our psychoanalyst friend: to put it plainly, he is still a virgin, but hardly one eager for experience, as becomes awkwardly apparent whenever he is in female company.) Laden with sentiment as they are, the clochard coat and cap infuse him with the happy glow of romance on these occasions of remembered grace in the month of November, whether in China or in Paris.

The rain is hardly noticeable, except when the drops slide down from the leaves of trees, soaking Muo's clothes and hair. A cab coming from behind draws up beside him, gliding along the pavement, hoping to be hailed, but he ignores it, thinking he has found his way. Indeed, beyond a stand of spectral plane trees rising almost ethereally in the rainy mist looms an unmistakable landmark: the public toilet, the homosexuals' happy hunting ground of old, the letters W.C. in neon on the roof. Upon reaching the building, Muo is moved by historical curiosity to step inside. Supervising the facility is a melancholy, hollow-eyed patriarch in overalls not unlike the mortuary uniform Muo wears, hunched like a pale ghost in the weak lamplight of his glass-fronted cubicle. "Two yuan," he announces, like a museum attendant. Inside, the tiled splendour seems unreal: not less filthy than the shack that stood there before, but now at least a squalor befitting a great modern country.

As he leaves the toilet and approaches the candy factory, Muo takes out his mobile phone; he stares distractedly at the small blinking object, for he can't remember whom he wanted to call. The only person in the world he feels like talking to is Volcano of the Old Moon. But a more realistic alternative occurs to him: Michel, his French psychoanalyst, who, given the time difference, should be awake at this hour. Sheltering from the rain under a tall bush with leaves as nervously aquiver as himself, Muo presses the long string of digits. He hears a click, then the very distant voice of his former mentor uttering a cool, tight-lipped sort of *"Oui."* (Because he is all too often harassed by patients suffering nervous breakdowns, Michel has adopted the habit of answering the phone with a most studied curtness and neutrality.) Muo's desire to talk evaporates, and he hangs up without a word. A few seconds later, his phone starts ringing in the pocket of his overalls.

"Do forgive me, Michel," he mumbles before the caller speaks. "I'm so sorry to have disturbed you, but I'm up to my neck in shit."

The voice at the other end is female, and Chinese. Muo is startled, and in his muddled state takes it to be his mother.

"Where are you, Muo? Are you mad? Why are you talking to me in a foreign language?"

It is the Embalmer. He can't imagine how she, or the recent macabre events, could have slipped his mind so completely. Apologising profusely, he promises that he is on his way home and will see her as soon as possible.

The Embalmer. Muo can't remember when his

upstairs neighbour's metier became her indelible nickname. Everyone calls her the Embalmer nowadays— even her own parents, Mr. and Mrs. Liu, both professors of anatomy, and both retired for ten years or so. They left her their flat: two modest rooms under the eaves of a six-storey walk-up with a whitewashed exterior decorated with thick bands of concrete and windows protected by security grilles like cages at a zoo. Over the main entrance is a relief in white and pink stucco portraying a worker, a farmer, and a soldier holding aloft a cogwheel as if it were a garland. It was here that the husband made the virgin a widow by jumping from the sixth floor on the night of their wedding.

After their phone conversation it occurs to Muo that he will need all the stealth of a burglar to reach her flat without alerting his parents on the second floor.

He is still mulling over the details of his covert night raid when, home at last, he finds himself entering the vast domain of the medical university: Little India Street, planted with mighty plane trees that form a kilometre-long tunnel of greenery that cuts the grounds in two; the southern half is given over to faculty premises and administration, the northern half to residential halls for teachers and other staff—several thousand dwellings for Chengdu medical faculty, just like his parents' and the Embalmer's.

The residential halls are arranged in five distinct walled cantons by the names of Peace, Light, Bamboo, the Garden of the West, and Peach Orchard, each of them a little city comprising several dozen buildings, five- to seven-storey walk-ups disposed in blocks. It is a long way from one end of this sleeping kingdom to the other. Muo walks his accustomed way, down Little India Street, for at least fifteen minutes before reaching Peace, after which he has the whole of Peach Orchard to cross before arriving at the one called Light.

The city of Light is plunged in darkness behind its locked gate. Muo rattles the door and shouts for the janitor, his voice echoing in the night until he is too hoarse to continue. Finally, a light flips on overhead, revealing the portal in all its grandeur. Surmounted by a pitched roof of varnished tiles and carved cornices with mythological figures, it consists of huge double doors of red-painted wood overlaid with layer upon layer of brightly coloured handbills: opening and closing times; lists of rules and regulations; pictures of wanted criminals; announcements of political meetings; American film posters; slogans; appeals for AIDS donations; personal ads; letters of public denunciation, dating from a different era but still perfectly legible; newspaper clippings spanning continents and decades. The small rectangular door in the gate opens with an earsplitting creak and from it emerges the janitor, a young man Muo has not seen before, with a People's Militia coat thrown over his shoulders.

"Thank you kindly for your trouble," Muo says, discreetly slipping the fellow a two-yuan note.

After admitting Muo the janitor locks the door behind him before turning around to size up the nocturnal stranger.

"Has someone died?" he asks, mesmerised by Muo's overalls.

"Yes, indeed. It's Liao, the cripple from building number eleven, in the third precinct," Muo replies, pleasantly surprised once again at his own knack for improvisation.

Liao the cripple, the Muo family's former next-door neighbour, has been dead for ten years, but the janitor shakes his head sympathetically and heaves a long sigh of respect before standing aside.

"Where's your hearse? Do you need some help with the body?" he calls after Muo.

"Not necessary. I have come for his soul."

Uncertain what to make of the metaphysical reply, the janitor follows with his eyes as Muo moves away, a ghostly silhouette in the rain. At the first block he walks past the entrance without glancing up at the six concrete buildings of exemplary uniformity, and at the fork by the entrance to the second block Muo turns left and disappears from the janitor's view.

He comes upon two further entrances piercing the brick walls, those of the third and fourth blocks, face-to-face in perfect symmetry. Both are fortified with chromed metal grilles lashed by the rain, iron chains painted green like climbing plants, and brass padlocks dripping water. One would think the buildings were treasure houses.

Again Muo rehearses a variety of scenes, adding dialogue this time in case he encounters his parents, and more particularly his mother. He knocks methodically on the left entrance. No answer. He knocks again and calls out, albeit in subdued, disguised tones for fear of being recognised by the maternal ear. He doesn't dare lift his eyes to the looming mass of cloned concrete whose sombre heights vanish in the rainy mist. Ever since he was a boy, waiting by these grilles for admittance—then they were rusty and shut at 8:30 p.m., instead of 11:30 as they are now—always filled him with the same dread of his mother.

The janitor lets him in—another young man, another People's Militia overcoat, but he is shorter and thinner than the fellow at the main gate. This one takes the proffered two-yuan note without expressing the least curiosity about either the giver or his advertised profession.

With all the residents sound asleep, the worker, the farmer, and the soldier in white and pink stucco over the entrance are the only witnesses to his arrival. He slips quietly into the empty hallway, which, as usual, smells foul, as if someone's vomit has just been mopped up. Shivering with cold, he cocks his ear. Not a sound. He starts up the stairs on tiptoe.

By the second floor, our night raider faces his greatest obstacle. With each step that brings him closer to his front door the smell of home becomes stronger, an indefinable yet unmistakable smell that he would know anywhere.

As on every other floor in every other building, there are two flats on the landing, on the left that of the Muo family and on the right the long-deceased cripple's. Approaching on tiptoe, he doesn't dare glance at either door—not that he can see them, as he is unwilling to risk switching on the light. He advances catlike, feeling around with the tip of his shoe before each step. Fortunately, ever since his eardrum was punctured his father watches television with the volume up high. Unfortunately, however, his mother's hearing is supernaturally acute; from the time her eyesight began to fail due to diabetes, she could hear a cat sneeze in the building opposite, or the scuttle of cockroaches on the fridge. Finally, steeling himself and holding his breath, he slides past what he takes to be his parents' door, for a moment very nearly losing his balance. Then, just as he imagines he has made it, the minefield traversed, all is suddenly lost with one cocksure step on an errant plastic trash bag: rubbish spills out everywhere, cascading down the stairs in an echoing thunderclap, a tumult without end until a last empty Coke can clatters to a halt against the neighbours' door.

Motionless in the dark, he waits for what seems like an age for the pandemonium to cease. Once it has, to his amazement and relief, no one has stirred—not even his mother. Perhaps such noise is routine given the marauding rats in Light, "the biggest in the world," as he once confided to Michel, not to be outdone by any westerner's report of childhood trauma.

He hurries up the next flight, and the next, quickening his pace as he approaches the top, a triumphant spiral of physical lightness akin to that of a bird taking flight. And like a lover speeding to an assignation, he runs his fingers through his hair, patting it down as best he can, blows into his cupped hand to check his breath, and wipes his spectacles.

The Embalmer's flat is on the right, at the end of the passage. The light from a nearby window bathes her door in a pale glow. It is a faintly yellow glow, suggesting the pearly sheen of glass, a strange effect that stays Muo's hand just as he is about to knock. Inspecting the door with his fingertips, he finds something stranger still: it is, in fact, glazed! Just the previous evening, when he visited the Embalmer to arrange her rendezvous with Judge Di, this door was made of metal like all the others, reinforced and outfitted with high-security hinges, latches, several locks, and a peep-hole. Some metamorphosis, he supposes, has occurred, either in his psyche or in the door, since the resurrec-tion of Judge Di.

A disposable lighter splutters to life and in the flicker fuelled by its last drops of butane Muo makes a further unearthly discovery as he holds the torch to the glazed door, in the mullion of which is pinned a small card reading MR. AND MRS. WANG—not the Embalmer's family name.

There is indeed some sorcery at work since the spec-tacle at the mortuary, he decides, or else he is totally mad. To investigate the latter hypothesis, he immedi-ately starts to test the workings of his brain. The sim-plest, most efficient way he knows is a memory test, so he prompts himself to recall as many words in French as he can. Surely his knowledge of the French language, so difficult to learn and requiring so many years of inces-sant hard work, could not have survived a total loss of reason. But not to depend on logic alone, he prays for divine protection.

The first French word that springs to mind is *merde*. He recalls *Les Misérables* and recites by heart a passage in which an expletive is delicately indicated by the initial followed by three dots, "to spare the sensitivities of the French reader."

Savouring this little triumph, he thinks of another exclamation he likes very much, one which means mar-vellously different things, depending on the circum-stances. It is his pet word, *hélas*. He calls to mind the famous exchange between Paul Valéry (his favourite French poet) and André Gide, wherein the former's claim that the greatest of all French poets was Victor Hugo is met with the latter's stunning retort, *"Hélas."* Then there is *l'amour,* a word whose resonance, whose silken mellifluousness, is more pleasing by far than its counterparts in Chinese or in English. During one of his weekly visits to Volcano of the Old Moon in prison, from his side of the glass partition he had told her about this little linguistic fetish of his, and had thrilled to hear her repeat the word several times. Being unable to distinguish between the sounds of the *n* and the *l,* however, she left out the definite article, saying only *"Amour,"* first in a whisper, then more and more loudly, until the grace and magic of the word resonated like a note from an oboe in the visiting area teeming with prisoners and their relatives, all of whom, young and old alike, were enchanted by the sound. Such are the mesmerising, voluptuous overtones of this foreign word! It would have been taken up in chorus had the screws not intervened.

Having verified the state of his memory, and knowing not how to prove or disprove the alternative theory of enchantment, Muo thinks to call upon the Wangs whose name is on the card tacked next to the door. But imagining the distress any couple would feel at the sight of him in his mortuary outfit, he thinks better of it, preferring to try calling the Embalmer on his mobile phone. A panicked voice answers at the other end.

"Where are you? . . . The Wangs'? Of course I know them, they teach physical culture . . . You're where? . . . Muo! They live in the fourth precinct; you and I live in the third! Can't you even find your own building?"

Too relieved to feel even the least embarrassment,

Muo flies down the stairs four steps at a time, running past the flat he had taken for his parents', pausing there to deliver a vicious kick to the half-empty trash bag, spilling into the stairwell what was left in it to spill. Outside it is still raining, and when Muo finally reaches his building he is soaked all over again, dripping water from his nostrils, like an otter that emerged from its hole to swim across a lake only to pop into another hole.

IMAGINING HIMSELF UNDERWATER, Muo can scarcely breathe; he feels as though he were wading through marshland, soggy, fertile, and pestilential, as in a dream he once had in which he was crossing an expanse of marble veined with grey and black, which softened under his long strides and finally metamorphosed into a huge slice of ripened cheese.

It is the Embalmer who has put our suggestible and sensitive psychoanalyst in this state, for she is at his side, holding his hand as he mounts the stairs.

When he entered the building moments ago, having groped in vain for the light switch, he had no choice but to make his way upstairs like a thief in the dark. But as he neared the first floor, the light on the landing above went on. He heard the sound of plastic flip-flops coming down the stairs, and a shiver of apprehension ran down his spine, as he imagined who might be flip-flopping at this hour.

Holding his breath, he'd strained to identify the prowler. However, since leaving China he has lost the ability to make distinctions as he once could, just by the sounds on the stairs: what the slippers are

made of (plastic? leather? rubber?), the nature of the
wearer (man, woman, timid, violent, tender, stern),
and sometimes even the person's mood. (When someone was accepted as a Communist Party member, for
instance, that person's footwear always changed its
tune, seeming for a long time afterward to mimic the
strains of the Chinese national anthem.)

The flip-flops descending the stairs suggested to
Muo a strange mix of high spirits and heedlessness. The
light went out again, but the darkness did not alter the
rhythm of the footsteps. They reached the second floor
without slowing down. Muo resumed his ascent with
trepidation, the *pad-pad* of his own shoes gradually
falling into a regular counterpoint with the crisp patter
of the flip-flops until the syncopated sounds combined
in a percussive serenade.

The stairs rose up, made a turn after about twenty
treads, and rose up again. Muo heard the Embalmer's
voice: "Is that you?"

"Shush," he said very softly. "You'll wake my
mother."

Just ahead of him on the second-floor landing, he
discerned a shadow that seemed slightly pale in the
darkness. The pace of the slippers neither quickened
nor slowed as the slight figure descending the stairs
continued its rhythmical tread. Without knowing why,
he heard himself say in a low, muted tone. "Careful, my
mother's hearing is—"

He did not reach the end of his sentence before the
slipper serenade fell silent. In the hush, the Embalmer
clasped his hand. He could feel her sweaty palm and
nervously clinging fingers, and something hard, which

he realised was her wedding ring. Her face, so close to his, emanated a faintly chemical smell. He put his cheek against hers.

"What scent are you wearing?" he whispered.

"None. It must be formaldehyde."

"No."

"Are you sure?"

"Yes."

"I'm glad. I hate smelling of formaldehyde after-hours."

"What, then?"

"Must be my aromatic moisturising lotion. Your Judge Di gave me such a fright that I couldn't stop shaking when I got home, so I rubbed it on, head to toe. You have no idea how soothing it is. Look—I've stopped shaking. I've almost put the whole ghastly business out of my mind."

"I almost died of fright, myself."

Hand-in-hand they advanced in the dark, groping and staggering like a pair of drunkards. When they passed Muo's parents' flat, the front door was blessedly shut and the lights out, but he thought he could hear his mother cough.

"How cold your hand is, you poor thing. I can't get it warm."

"I'm soaked to the skin. And these overalls are too small for me. Maybe they're yours?"

"Hmmm. Anyway, you can change at my place. I've kept my husband's clothes as mementos. The fit should be about right."

4. STEAMED DUMPLINGS

A few minutes later, Muo's bare feet are shod in dark blue suede slippers embroidered in different shades of mauve with three small flowers: a eupatorium, a sea lavender, and a scabious. The slippers are worn, and their smoothed soles slap the floor.

Like all Asians, the Embalmer keeps her shoes on a rack by the front door. Perching on a plastic stool in the narrow hallway, Muo has taken off his shapeless, sodden, mud-spattered shoes and lined them up alongside pairs of red and black sneakers, espadrilles, flip-flops, and high white lace-up boots—all the same size, but quite a bit smaller than the suede slippers that belonged to the Embalmer's late husband, which are too big for Muo, so that when his legs are crossed one dangles uncomfortably from his big toe.

"Not bad, those slippers," the Embalmer says to him. "We bought them a few weeks before the wedding, in the people's shopping centre. Five yuan five fen, if I remember. They've remained there on the shoe rack, where they were when he went out the window."

There are faint reminders of the embalming hall in her apartment, which is lit with five or six weak lamps dispersed around the room. Their pale, blurry halos create an atmosphere of almost subterranean confinement. She trips about with the lightness of a bird and the joy of regained youth, her face covered in a creamy mask, her short peignoir of pink silk embroidered with white birds and flowers in a golden landscape.

"What would you like to eat? I've got some frozen dumplings in the fridge. With celery and lamb stuffing—how does that sound?"

Without waiting for a reply, she disappears into the kitchen.

"A man in the house at last," she sighs.

The flat is pervaded by the cold melancholy of a childless spinster, which floats in the air like dust in a lamp beam or the scent of incense. On the floor is a mat of finely woven bamboo, here and there—by the sofa, the television, and the two leather armchairs—overlaid with bits of carpet in different colours. There is no dining table. Does she eat in the kitchen? The sofa and the armchairs still wear their protective plastic from the factory. The television, enthroned on its pedestal, has a purple velvet cover; the remote control is cased in cellophane, which crackles at Muo's touch. Even the telephone is draped in pale pink towelling. A family portrait in colour, enlarged and framed, hangs on the wall. Muo sees no individual photos of her or her husband, but there are several paper cutouts of his silhouette. There is just one picture of them together: Jian pedalling his bike against the wind, hunched over the handlebars, raincoat flapping, and she on the rack behind him, knitting a sweater that streams like a scarf behind her.

Her one treasure is a collection of puppets. Muo is enchanted as he peers at the small figures in their costumes of brightly coloured satin and silk, emperors in robes embroidered with dragons, empresses laden with jewels, scholars holding fans, generals bristling with sabres and lances, even beggars, all looking back at him through the dingy glass of a display case resting atop a chest of drawers. Her husband had inherited the collection, about twenty ravishing specimens, from a great-uncle. Muo could spend hours admiring them. Tiny lights had been installed in the display by the Embalmer's late husband, with individual switches hidden in the folds of the crumpled velvet lining the base and sides. On his knees, Muo opens the case and flips one switch after another, spotlighting each puppet in turn. He is soon joined by the Embalmer, who holds her purring blow-dryer to his head. The puppets' clothing ripples in the breeze; the scholars' fans fluttering, the empresses' jewels tinkling. In his rapture, Muo cannot resist touching the Embalmer's flip-flops, then her shapely left foot, its finely boned instep trembling under his fingertips.

The sound of dumplings boiling over abruptly ends this idyllic overture. She draws back and rushes off into the kitchen. Muo remains on his knees, gazing as the puppets come to life in his hands, quivering, swaying, nodding their heads topped with crowns or tall hats, saluting their solitary spectator. Through his steamy glasses a blurred panoply of colours dances, melting, transforming into a thousand stars, leaping flames, myriad glowworms, a twinkling drama of the night.

At the insistence of his hostess (who, being a perfectionist in such matters, deems this delicacy to have been ruined by overcooking and puts a fresh batch on to boil), Muo changes out of his wet uniform. Opening the wardrobe, he loses himself in the forest of hangers with all the Embalmer's clothes on one side: satin slips with scalloped hems, a fake-fur coat, shirtwaists, blouses, dresses, and skirts. And on the other side, her husband's things, smelling strongly of camphor: a blue Mao jacket, a slate-grey suit with matching waistcoat, a white shirt with starched collar and attached bow tie of black silk, several pairs of trousers, a worn leather jacket, belts, army caps—but nothing for the summer. The sight of these carefully hung clothes, so evocative of their dead owner, unsettles Muo. In another cupboard, among the piles of clean laundry, whites and pinks and blues fresh with the scent of detergent, Muo spots a likely garment and pulls it out. He unfolds the tracksuit with care, as if cradling a living thing, and shutting the door, he steps into the bathroom to change.

The fluorescent tube on the ceiling spreads a trembling shimmer of seeming twilight, an icy pallor on the white bathtub, toilet bowl, and washbasin. Above the basin is a little glass shelf bearing a toothbrush, a makeup bag, tubes of cream, and bottles of lotion. Above that an oval mirror reflects Muo's transformation from imposter mortician to a student in the eighties: the sky-blue top with open underarm seams bears the red torch and yellow insignia of the Communist Youth League. Muo remembers it as the uniform of the university basketball team. Gazing at himself with nostalgic fascination, Muo recalls the mannerisms of the departed point guard and imitates them to impressive effect—especially his boyish pout.

He remembers with a start the fear smouldering inside him since the incident at the mortuary. *The time has come to take action, Muo!* he tells himself. *You can't very well end your protracted celibacy out of duty and gratitude, to honour a moral debt. You must find some way out of this. Even at the*

*chance to furnish sensational proof of your virility, you must be true
to your principles! You don't owe anyone anything. Not a thing.*

He shuts the door behind him with feigned nonchalance. The latch drops with a dull, metallic click. He
listens and catches the sound of his hostess, busy in the
kitchen. If he is going to make his escape, this is unde-
niably the perfect moment, but he is distracted by an
effort to recall some words of Freud's—or of another
master; his mind is so muddled that the source eludes
him—". . . Many a murderer seeks refuge behind the
mask of a war hero, just as impotence is frequently
passed off as asceticism."

"I am not impotent, thank God. Nor am I disguised
as an ascetic, but as a varsity basketball player," he
chuckles to himself, regretting the absence of anyone else to appreciate his wit. "But can I be sure of my
virility?"

Looking down at the indiscreet bulge in the dead
husband's tracksuit bottoms, he reconsiders. "Just a
minute—think! It could be now or never, a prime
opportunity to acquire a skill that will come in handy
one day," he muses. The truth is that, for all the
abstract knowledge stuffed in his head on subjects ranging from psychoanalysis and ethics to the history of the
breast or of sex since antiquity, he is sorely lacking in
practical experience.

In the living room, he is astonished to find his legs
not taking him left, in the direction of the front door,
but striding purposefully, like those of a famished husband returning from work, to the right—that is to say,
to the kitchen.

"Are the dumplings ready?" the make-believe husband wants to know. "They certainly smell good."

Turning from the stove, she feels her heart pierced to see her husband's clothes on someone else. Her little gasp mixes shock with a certain joy. Feeling faint and shivery, she opens her eyes wide, taking in the tracksuit of long ago, torn and patched in places (she recognises her own hand in the mends), with its little standing collar and the V neck above a button dangling from a thread. As Muo moves closer, the button swells until it fills her field of vision.

"I must sew that back on," she says, touching him with one hand and stirring the dumplings with the other.

Muo lunges and grabs her roughly by the waist. He kisses her awkwardly, but with such passion that she very nearly falls backward against the stove. He can feel the Embalmer's toned muscles rippling under his hands. She twists around and their tongues meet, with courteous surprise at first, and a hint of embarrassment, which rapidly gives way to wild intoxication as they mingle, caress, and explore, rolling about like a pair of dolphins. Innocent Muo loses himself in the aroma of celery and lamb dumplings, the pharmaceutical odour of her facial mask, the perfume of her mouth, the hardness of her teeth like rocks in a grotto, the murmur of the fridge, the creaking of the sink, the groans escaping from their throats, the vapour from the saucepan rising and swathing their entwined bodies like a mosquito net of milky tulle, a floating veil, a sublime mist. Closing her eyes, she moans voluptuously as he caresses her thighs. He is startled to see her like this, barely recognisable, absent and dreamy, her face newly radiant, consumed with a lust akin to beatitude. They burn like two sticks of dry wood in a fire. They have no time to move to the bedroom. The Embalmer's hand grips the tracksuit pants and pulls them down around Muo's bony ankles. She in turn strips off her trousers and pink panties, which she sends flying with her foot. They make love on their feet, propped against a sideboard, the small doors of which give way under the seismic upheaval, spilling fistfuls of bamboo chopsticks and plastic forks and spoons with each thrust. Then the wave travels along the wall, making the wooden shelf above their heads rattle and dance, so that a bag of flour set among the pyramid of jars and pots falls onto the draining board with a dull thud. Puffs of white powder billow forth with each rhythmic thrust, dissipating in clouds carrying bits of paper—notes? unpaid bills?— which settle all around them, even on the steaming dumplings. Some snippets stick to the Embalmer's moisturising mask. Muo whispers, "It's snowing!" but she does not respond. Again he is amazed to see her in such ecstasy. He knows that she has not heard him. At that very moment he believes he has grasped the quintessence of modern art. Here she is, his dear old friend, incarnating all those portraits in museums, women with both eyes on one side or heads of disparate, flat, rectangular planes, especially the Picasso that he realises now he will admire unconditionally for the rest of his life: *Woman with a Mandolin.* Suddenly it all falls into place—the melting breast, the dislocated shoulders—for now he knows the cause of that exalted frenzy. He recalls the rudimentary head, a small square filled by a huge eye, emerging from a pear-shaped mandolin of a sombre shade. Muo's first copulation, which proceeds in textbook fashion, is in danger of turning into a doctoral thesis. He dreams of becoming the great artist himself, not for his genius or celebrity, but for his penetrating, cynical, unblinkered way of seeing. A hedonist in full, Muo casts a Picassoesque eye as well over the dumplings dancing in the bosomy foam like a surging tide with white horses rearing, neighing, and galloping. Just as the soup threatens to boil over, the Embalmer seizes a spoon. Watching her hand stirring the pan and the dumplings obediently sinking to the bottom, Muo is struck by the automatism of her gesture, which proves that she is still in this world. His thoughts shift to the dead bodies she has handled with this same hand, now slick with cream and sweat, glistening, almost fluorescent, this virginal, flour-dusted hand, to which he has surrendered his sex. He can hear her hot, shallow breathing and her whisper of "my man." The effect is heady and seductive. He feels slightly in love with her. He wants to tell her, but the words get stuck in his throat. Then, from one moment to the next, her body becomes rigid and her eyes pop as she moans, "My husband." A complete hush descends, in which Muo hears neither the murmur of the fridge nor the water bubbling in the pan—only that phrase resonates in the air.

He cannot decide whether the appellation vests him with the responsibility of a future head of the family or reduces him to the status of a mere stand-in, even a victim.

She removes his spectacles and puts them down on the sink, then takes his face between her hands and covers it with kisses.

"Hold me tight, my husband," she pleads with an earsplitting shriek. "Don't ever leave me."

Still thrusting, now in blindness, he rolls his eyes to

the ceiling several times, takes a deep breath, and says, "Your husband sends you his regards."

She is so taken aback by this that she looks at him blankly for a moment, then throws her head back and, quaking with laughter, shakes them both. This delectable convulsion is Muo's undoing—his untimely release.

"What, already?" she exclaims. "The dumplings aren't done yet."

"Forgive me," he mumbles, pulling up his pants and searching for his spectacles.

Having regained his sight, he is bowled over by the sheer incongruity of what is revealed to him. The first thing his refocused eyes behold is a dumpling, a slit dumpling struggling like a wounded butterfly, swirling around before sinking slowly to the bottom of the pan, leaving a trail of celery and cooked meat in its wake.

He sits on the floor with his back against the purring fridge. She takes a scrap of paper and wipes the rivulet of blood from the inside of her thigh. Then, with another scrap, she cleans Muo of his own effluent.

I'm no longer a virgin, she thinks. The tears trickle down her face, carving channels in the bluish crust of her floury moisturising mask.

"Come on," he says, kissing her on the cheek. "Let's eat. I'm incredibly hungry."

"Wait, I want to take a shower first."

The dumplings have an ashen taste, but the sauce she has prepared is deliciously spicy, with sweet vinegar, chopped chives, crushed garlic, and several drops of sesame oil. Face-to-face across the low table laid with a sheet of newspaper, they eat wordlessly. In the slightly lugubrious silence, Muo forces himself to eat all she serves him, for fear of offending her. Fortunately, she sets out a bottle of a pricey liquor called Phantom of Intoxication, famed for its potency, its exquisite aroma, and its trendy stoneware container in the shape of a crumpled bag. A few gulps are sufficient to raise his spirits, thereby reducing the sting of his preempted demonstration of virility. Muo is good-natured; he cannot help braving perils to which he has already succumbed. And so, having struggled his whole life to overcome setbacks, he has ended each time in deeper trouble. That's just the way it goes. Now he can only await the next occasion to take up the challenge and redeem his honour and self-respect.

He knows instinctively that he has another two or three hours in which to regain his manhood before leaving the flat and facing the world.

Eager to conserve the energy unleashed by the Phantom of Intoxication, he declines to share the watermelon she has taken from the fridge. She slices the fruit with a kitchen knife, causing the juice to run along the blade and drip on the newspaper covering the table. With every bite she takes, the red juice spills down her chin. She spits the seeds into a porcelain bowl. Muo is overcome by drowsiness. He has never known such a leaden somnolence, with his mind seeking voluptuous refuge while his body feels as if it is dropping down a chute. Making a manful effort to stay awake, he slides his drooping spectacles up the bridge of his nose, stifles a yawn, stands up, and heads for the bathroom, the bottle of Phantom of Intoxication in his hand.

"I'm going to take a bath, then I'll be back."

"Wait for me," she says. "I don't want to be left all alone."

In the tub he dunks his head several times to focus his thoughts. There is quite a battle ahead. He still feels languid, and notes with alarm that his member is shrinking to the point of retreating like a turtle's head into a tuft of floating hair, while the Embalmer, sitting on a chair with her feet on the edge of the tub, paints her toenails with pearly varnish.

She says, "In all the years I've worked there it has never happened before—a dead man coming to life, I mean."

She talks and talks like water gushing from a tap, wallowing in the blissful aftermath of love, so conducive to casual confidences. She little realises how much of her outpouring concerns her dead husband, with scarcely a mention of poor Muo. He is dismayed by the unmistakable signs of transference, which he perceives not as a therapeutic phenomenon but as harsh retribution for his earlier misfire. *How cruel women are! And how splendid!* the hapless stand-in thinks to himself as he lies back in the tub, immersed up to his ears in an effort to drown out her voice.

"Of all the embalming jobs I have done, the one I'll never forget is my husband's. In our line of work we don't normally handle anyone close to us, be it a member of the family, a friend, or even a neighbour. It's a golden rule. So my four colleagues were given the assignment and I stayed downstairs, waiting. They started by washing the body prior to the massage. As he had fallen from the sixth floor, naturally some of his veins had burst. It took a lot of concentration and care-

ful manipulation to get the congcalcd blood to flow
again. Suddenly I decided to go upstairs. I asked them
to leave, and despite great reluctance, they let me take
over. The hardest job was still to be done: the restora-
tion of the skull, a complicated, thankless task that they
were probably glad to be spared, especially since even
the most heroic effort would inevitably produce a disappointment: his head had split virtually down the
middle, like a melon hacked in two. The blackened
blood, the crusted brain matter, and especially the
cracks zigzagging over the skull made it so that with the
slightest false move the whole cranium would fall to
pieces. It was the worst of nightmares, impossible for
anyone to repair. I fought down my tears and barely
dared to breathe at all, holding as still as possible to do
the work. I selected the finest needle. The thread,
imported from Japan, the kind used by surgeons, was of
such quality that I couldn't break it with my teeth. The
crack in the skull was about twenty centimetres long and
at least five centimetres wide across the middle. I started
sewing from the narrowest end. Meanwhile, on the
ground floor, my colleagues were dancing to a tape of
piano music; it was a slow, sad waltz. (You know there
was a waltz craze at the time, a billion Chinese dancing
the waltz—before the mah-jongg fever, of course.) It
was the saddest tune I had ever heard, even sadder than
those requiems they sing in the West on television, with
flickering candles and women wearing little veils . . ."

His senses dulled by exhaustion and alcohol, Muo
listens to these confidences, pouring forth in an other-
worldly voice made of tones more of some sonorous,
ambient presence than of a human being. *Could this be
what a ghost sounds like?* He can no longer tell whether the

scene is real or imaginary, whether she is talking to him in real life or in a dream. Opening his eyes, he glimpses a little snake wriggling in the water between his thighs and reaches out a cautious hand to catch it. It slips away; all he catches is a handful of dark hair. He grabs the bottle of Phantom of Intoxication and pours it down his throat as his other hand resumes the game of hide-and-seek with the elusive little snake.

"The cranial sutures took ages to do—a veritable marathon. Stitch by stitch, millimetre by millimetre, I sewed up his skull. The bone was hard, the hair was tangled, and I had to change needles twice. Next I applied a coat of wax to his face. By that time the slow, sad waltz had given way to a lively tango. But still there was a hint of melancholy in the music, and even in the footfalls of my dancing colleagues, and it brought me to tears, which, in fact, interfered with the setting of the wax—supposedly weather- and climate-proof, but two millimetres thick, and it was still soft. Just awful. I had to coat his face all over again. Then the makeup. Some colour on his eyelids to make them lifelike. I did his hair. I was on the verge of wrapping it up when I got the strangest feeling that I had forgotten something. I retraced my steps, and soon realised what was missing: the smile. With my fingertips, I gently massaged the corners of his mouth, and just as the faintest smile began to appear I heard from within his skull a loud, long-drawn-out crunch like the creak of an old wooden door. It made me jump. I saw the wound opening up again, gaping and black, as the sutures snapped one after another. Taking his head in my hands, I screamed like a madwoman, trying to hold the pieces together, but no one could hear me over the rollicking music.

The tango was entering a romantic passage, with soaring, dreamy arpeggios. I had to make a tremendous effort to calm down. God knows it was difficult. Then I summoned my last bit of courage and started again from scratch, first stitching up the wound, which stubbornly refused to close, and I had to . . . What's the matter, Muo? Are you crying? Wait, give me your glasses. Calm down, will you . . . Tell me why you're crying. Is it because of me? Oh, look at you—you've got a hard-on! Look! A hard-on in the water! Wait, what are you doing? Are you crazy?"

She makes quite a splash entering the tub. "We must be crazy, the two of us! Yes, put your hands there . . . D'you like that? Unhook my bra. Ouch! You're hurting me. Don't bite! Gently. I'm a she-wolf. Your she-wolf. That's it." And as she takes him in her arms, muscled from lifting cadavers, her weight bearing down upon him, from under her engulfing body he can hear her lingering refrain: "My man, my man, my man . . ."

THE LIVING-ROOM WINDOW, fitted with mosquito netting in a wooden frame, is both wide and low enough for Muo, hapless on dry land but triumphant underwater, to sit on without difficulty despite the persistent effects of the Phantom. He even has the impression that he could leap over it quite easily.

Feeling giddy, he straddles the frame, one leg inside and the other swinging insouciantly over the mysterious void, the almost shimmering gloom of the abyss to which he feels himself inexplicably drawn. The rain has lifted. An invisible chaffinch twitters gaily, and a canary responds with a crystalline song. In the distance the milky white beam from a television relay sweeps its horizontal cone across the night. Muo is certain that he has seen this before, without knowing where.

Such potent stuff, this Phantom of Intoxication! His throat is scorched, his chest convulsed with boozy hiccups.

This is it, he thinks to himself. *I've gone out of my mind.*

He regrets not having brought his exercise book. The night is almost over and he has made no entries on this eventful, momentous day. And he knows that by morning the Phantom will have blotted it all out, leaving him not the slightest recollection. He dismounts the window frame, steps into the husband's slippers again, and hunts around for a pen and something to write on. The Embalmer is still in the bathroom, humming a tune as she washes her underwear in the basin.

Without removing the slippers he gets back into his saddle on the sill. Balancing precariously, he scribbles on one of the large matchboxes he found in the kitchen: "I am no Fan Jing, but I have truly lost my mind. In this world where success is a cardinal virtue, my insanity has nothing to do with my sexual exploits—quite the opposite."

(Fan Jing is the name of a famous personage in *The Secret History of Chinese Men of Letters,* a withered, white-haired student who entered the annual mandarin competition year after year in vain. The day he received news of his belated success, at the age of sixty-one, he was overcome with such joy and excitation that he went clear out of his mind.)

Muo looks up. There is still a smell of rain in the air,

but the sky has cleared, and the stars, whose names he does not know, seem close enough to touch. The white paint on the window frame is flaking, possibly gnawed by rats, and the wood is crumbling in places. He studies his face, mirrored in the windowpane: his hair is standing on end like a tussock of weeds. Two pinpoints of light, the concentrated reflection of lamps in the living room, dance on the lenses of his spectacles like twin fireflies shimmying up toward his forehead and down to his cheeks by turns, and vanish when he bows his head to reread the note on the box of matches. His satisfaction at what he has written soothes his overheated head and refreshes his swelling heart. On a second matchbox he writes: "S.O.S. I'm going mad. S.O.S. The revelation of my true nature is dire: every woman I want to make love to becomes the woman I love. Volcano of the Old Moon's absolute power is no more. The love of my life is in ruins. Another me resides within my body, younger and more vigorous, a species of underwater monster, in whose existence I have just witnessed a supreme moment. Which of us is the real Muo?"

A mosquito no bigger than a gnat circles him, whining like a violin, until it tumbles down on to the thickly veined wrist of his left hand.

"What did you have in mind, my little friend?" he asks the mosquito.

Gently, very gently, with the fingertips of his right hand, he stretches the skin where the poor insect is about to draw blood. Then, abruptly, he lets go, imprisoning the mosquito's proboscis in the creases. He watches the insect retract its wings and fold itself up until it has shrunk almost to the size of a pinhead, after which, with a sudden flurry of wings, it takes off, passing Muo's nose and then swooping down into the void outside.

Muo tells himself that he too should make himself scarce, just like the dapper mosquito.

His instinct and habitual cynicism concur that the Embalmer, aged forty like himself, is seeking not only adventure but a second husband. It makes sense in ordinary human terms: she did him that enormous favour with Judge Di; it is only fitting that he should return the courtesy. She wants a family. And why not be the wife of the first Chinese psychoanalyst? He can't fault her admirable choice.

"How to get out of this predicament?" muses Muo, shivering with cold astride the windowsill. "How am I to explain all this to Volcano of the Old Moon?"

He imagines strapping the matchboxes to his person and lighting them, like a fuse, after which he would tumble down to earth like a burning aeroplane in free-fall, somersaulting in the void, traversing clouds and mist and trailing a ribbon of black smoke.

But through this imaginary smoke he catches sight of his other self, the underwater monster, butting its head against a porthole, clamouring to get out.

It occurs to him to pray.

He has never done so before. How does one pray? He is of two minds—should he opt for Buddhism or Taoism? Both entail roughly the same manner of prayer, on the knees and with the hands joined at chest level. As for Christianity, he is not too sure. When he was a boy religion was so strictly forbidden that his parents never took him anywhere near a temple or a church. The first time he saw anyone pray was when he was seven years old, at the height of the Cultural Revolution. One day his mother was taken away by Red Guards for interrogation. At midnight she still had not returned to the flat, which was being shared by his grandparents at the time. That night Muo did not sleep a wink. He got out of bed, and as he crept past the old people's bedroom his attention was caught by a strange glow. Glancing inside, he saw the pair of them kneeling at the foot of the bed, facing a candle. (Had they not dared to light a lamp?) No one had ever explained to the child what prayer was, but he understood instantly, even without any notion of what divinity they were supplicating. Their precise gestures escape him now, but he clearly remembers the pale, vibrant aura of sacrament surrounding them, and how their lined, careworn faces beamed with rapturous veneration and dignity. They looked beautiful.

"What can I ask the heavens to do for me?" he muses. "Take an interest in me? Help me escape? Deliver me from this woman? Isn't it too presumptuous to expect Heaven or God to take notice of us at all? If I committed suicide right now, would he care? Would he notice the stench of my decaying corpse filling the courtyard and permeating the clothes of every resident of the building? Or would he sit back and take the credit for my deliverance from all further troubles by this total, radical act of destruction?

"It's probably the window that is having a strange effect on me," he thinks. "Is it so unusual, this temptation to jump? Or is this a window with maleficent properties? Ten years ago it held a fatal attraction for the Embalmer's homosexual husband. Perhaps he had no intention to commit suicide at all; perhaps he came under the spell of this window, which lured him into the depths of some profound shame. In any case, I belong to that race of men in whose minds something snaps whenever we look down from a great height. All my years of psychoanalysis and all that study of Freud's wise, insightful books have not altered this reaction, which like a woman's perfume is beyond my power to resist."

Turning these things over in his befuddled brain, he begins to imitate his pastor grandfather's gestures on that night long ago. He draws up his legs and assumes a crouching position on the windowsill, like a bird on a perch—a bird with spectacles and bony talons, on the edge of a six-storey cliff. He tries to rise up, barely managing to keep his balance, and seems on the verge of taking flight when suddenly he sinks to his knees, onto the ledge jutting beyond the sill, where the rain-soaked, pale pink brickwork dampens his borrowed trousers. He surveys the dark lake, into the waters of which he aims to dive.

A brisk wind is blowing, cold but bearable. The cloudy sky is reflected in the sombre glass behind him. He searches for fitting words to make a vow, reflecting ruefully that the most wonderful promise in the world would have been to keep his virginity until Volcano of the Old Moon's release from prison. But it is too late for that now. Thoughts of Judge Di and the Embalmer fill Muo with bitterness.

He feels like a torn, shrivelled mosquito, his wings scrolled tight and legs—surprisingly long—crumpled up, a tiny, trembling body cowering in the palm of an unknowable giant called Destiny. Abruptly he puts his hands together before his chest and prays as his grandfather did before him. But the words passing his lips are those of an old childhood ditty, which he has not sung for many years:

> *My father the canteen chef*
> *Stands accused of stealing tickets.*
> *Tickets for what?*
> *Rations of rice and oil.*
> *My father kneeling on a table*
> *Bound with thick ropes,*
> *Called to account by the mob,*
> *To account! To account!*

His voice, still somewhat slurred by the Phantom, is barely audible at first, no more than a murmur. But soon, gaining confidence, it resonates with joyous irony, growing louder and louder until it vies with the raucous cries of a bird, which answers him from its perch on the roof across the way. At the end of the first verse he hums the refrain through a trumpeter's pursed lips, delighted to discover in his own voice the intonations of his boyhood hero and neighbour, nicknamed The Spy. The Spy was the son of a professor of pathology who, during his reeducation, became the leader of a gang of robbers, and was sent to prison for twenty years for a bank holdup in the seventies. The song was much favoured by The Spy, who hummed it with savage glee as he walked with his cap cocked atop his springy hair or whistled it in the staircase to attract girls.

Muo concludes the second verse with a series of tremolos and launches into the refrain, at once sad and gay. It clears his head of his recent setbacks and betray-

als, of Judge Di's sordid addictions. He rocks his conscience to sleep with the bank robber's chorus until he
feels two strong arms grabbing him by the hips. With his
startled cry the starry sky reels, heaves, capsizes around
him, and his embroidered slippers drop into the void
like two shooting stars. His cry resonates among the
buildings, mingling with those of the two birds, a
thrush and a waxwing, and is quickly muffled by the
rain, which, in his brief lull, had resumed its patter
against the glass. Muo lies stunned on the living-room
floor.

Weeping profusely, the Embalmer bundles him into
a cupboard and fastens the metal doors with a large
padlock.

"I have no intention of stitching up your skull, too,"
she says in response to his kicks and desperate cries.
"It's for your own good, I promise you."

PART THREE

LITTLE ROAD

1. DON'T SWALLOW MY TOOTH!

Muo gazes at the rails gleaming silkily in the sunset as they stretch away from the station of Chengdu. He is standing by a window in the ticket office. A golden light filters through the broken, cobwebby panes. The rusty window bars are the colour of ancient copper, a splendid green. Thinking of the prison where Volcano of the Old Moon has now been joined by the Embalmer, he wonders whether this same light, so pure and soft, can be shining on those four watchtowers and on the armed guards poised there, motionless as statues.

For the past half-hour he has been waiting in line for a ticket, his face half-hidden by a grey hood. A loud argument erupts between two women next to him, turning into an intergenerational free-for-all when their relatives join the fray. A confusion of voices and loudspeaker announcements, the smells of human sweat, stale tobacco, and instant noodles . . . the long queue shuffles forward in disheartening torpor before coming to another halt.

Outside the broken window, the night begins to enfold the world in its mysterious, inescapable embrace. Red and green signals flash along the track, flickering in the haze like fireflies in a fairy tale and reminding Muo of police cars with revolving lights, which may even now be patrolling the city streets in search of a bespectacled psychoanalyst who has become the sworn enemy of Judge Di.

You must pull yourself together, Muo, he tells himself. *The police are too busy dining in restaurants at this hour.*

Still, the moment he spots a uniform on the threshold his legs begin to give. The official pushes through the crowd in his direction, and as he draws near the tremors turn into a violent twitching just below the knee and remain unrelieved until Muo realises that the uniform is merely headed to the toilets all the way at the back.

The closer he gets to the ticket window, the denser the crowd gets and the safer he feels in the heaving, shoving, stifling bustle. A woman has lost a high-heeled shoe with a broken strap. But no matter: it is Muo's turn at last before the chrome-plated grille over the window.

"One way to Kunming," he shouts. "For the nine o'clock tonight."

"Speak up, I can't hear you," the clerk bellows into a microphone. "Where did you say?"

"To Kunming."

A scramble ensues, during which his hand misses the grille as he is shouldered out of the way. He lunges forward again, but by the time he can make his destination known, he discovers that the sleeper tickets are sold out. It will be a hard-seat carriage for him, like the one he

rode that night several months ago when his Delsey
suitcase was stolen.

A few minutes later, his head ensconced in the grey
hood (which, being totally unseasonal, gives him a
suspicious, clownish aspect), he dines incognito at a
fluorescent-lit fast-food restaurant, one of the innu-
merable booths lining the shadowy, grim, Soviet-style
high colonnade, which has been given over to small
eateries, souvenir stalls, checked-luggage counters, and
newsstands with magazine covers of sexy film stars both
Western and Chinese.

A buzzing fly circles overhead.

No plate, no bowl, just a rectangular polystyrene box
for his pieces of fried chicken, the sliced squid with
pureed red peppers, and a serving of fried noodles
swimming in oil, all of it cold. Cheap, anyway—five
yuan, and a glass of soy milk is included—less than a
metro ticket in Paris for this man on the run. The
chicken tastes of nothing at all. The fried squid is even
worse, and though he chews furiously, he can't get
through the hard, leathery flesh. Hearing the crackle of
the loudspeaker, he pricks up his ears. It is a page for
one Mr. Mao, a name that sounds alarmingly like his
own. The squid surrenders to his teeth at last, but
though he chews it furiously, it's never ready to be swallowed. "What on Earth?" he exclaims under his breath.
Suddenly he feels as if the inside of his mouth is no
longer his. Minutely, his tongue explores each tooth in
turn; one of his incisors is gone.

The fly buzzes.

With the tip of his tongue he probes the hole, aston-
ishingly wide and deep. Curiously, there is not a trace
of blood.

Still with his tongue, he searches his mouth for the stray tooth, and not finding it, he fears he may have mistakenly swallowed it like a fishbone. As his anxiety intensifies he can't swallow even what little saliva his mouth can produce. Imagining the tooth stuck in his throat, and then his gut, he is jubilant at finding it at last, buried among the fried noodles in the polystyrene box. It is still intact, the colour of tea smudged with brown, almost black at the tip. It is the first time he has beheld a tooth of his own face-to-face rather than in a mirror. He is impressed by its ugliness and by its length—at least three centimetres. Its pointed root is shaped like a stiletto heel and makes him think of the fangs of vampires. As for the other end, with which he has chewed his food for forty years, the tooth resembles a sliver of flint, fissured and darkened by time.

With the care of an archaeologist, he wraps the tooth in a scrap torn from a paper napkin. He lights a cigarette, but the smoke, percolating through the gaping hole, does not taste the same.

Disgruntled, he leaves the fast-food counter and crosses to the far side of the square, opposite the station. The girl he met a few months ago on the night train flashes into his mind. He decides to buy a bamboo mat and spread out under the hard seat later on, the way she did.

He is startled by a whiff of sickly perfume and a female voice hissing in his ear: "Looking for a hotel, boss?"

"Sorry, my train's leaving in two hours."

"In that case," the woman, all rouge and mascara, persists, barring his way, "we've got a karaoke bar, pretty girls. Come on, boss, a little relaxation would do you good. Life's too short."

"Thanks, but no thanks. And I'm nobody's boss, by the way."

"What would you prefer to be called? Something naughtier, perhaps?"

"Mind your own business!" he barks, up close to the woman's face.

The effect is instantaneous: the gaping hole in his mouth, more ghastly in the dim lamplight, comes as such a shock that she flees.

The only shop still open does not stock bamboo mats, so he will make do with one of those paper-thin plastic slickers for cyclists, in pale pink.

The train to Kunming departs after a mere ten-minute delay. The Chengdu cityscape so reminiscent of Judge Di is receding at last, and Muo tastes a moment of release. He takes out his exercise book and writes, "When Ezra Pound was arrested, he picked up a eucalyptus pod as a keepsake. For my part I will have my tooth to preserve the memory of my escape."

The Embalmer is about to pass her first night in prison. Her arrest took place the morning after Judge Di's resurrection. The sky was a serene blue. The venetian blinds in the embalming room rustled in the air-conditioned breeze. A telephone rang. It was the mortuary director, summoning her to discuss a dossier of medical reimbursements. She stripped off her gloves and, still in her white smock, presented herself at the director's office, where two plainclothes policemen were waiting to take her. Somebody reported having seen her in handcuffs as she was bundled into one of the tribunal's black vans in front of the administration wing.

"Looked like a hearse to me," a mortuary attendant had told Muo when he'd arrived in a taxi to take her out to lunch.

The two hundred metres separating him from his waiting taxi had seemed like an ocean. With uncontrollable spasms, his calves quivered, and when he finally made it to the car he had to press down on his muscles with both hands to still them.

Should he give himself up to the police like a penitent or make his getaway like a bandit on the run? After much deliberation, the first course seemed the more sensible, and he decided with remarkable sangfroid to do some shopping in anticipation of serving a long sentence. In a zombielike voice he told the cab driver to take him to The City of Books, a bookshop in the centre of town. He purchased all seven volumes of Freud in Chinese translation (how he had changed during his sojourn in France, how careless he had become—he had not even thought to find out whether books were permitted in Chinese prisons). In addition, he bought a two-volume French dictionary of psychoanalysis in a blue slipcase—that cost a fortune!—and a book of commentaries on Zhuangzi, his favourite Chinese author. The bookseller gave the prospective convict two plastic bags in which to carry his spiritual provisions. Finally, wishing to avoid returning home and having to say good-bye to his parents, he bought sheets, towels, a toothbrush, and a pair of heavy-duty black tennis shoes, which would serve him as work shoes. Of one thing at least he was certain; everyone talked about it: prisons in China are places of work.

Another taxi dropped him off at the intersection where the horse-and-mule market was, not far from the tribunal. Fearing the demented Judge Di might view his arrival by taxi as a further insolence, and therefore go harder on him, Muo went on foot the rest of the way. With each step the bags seemed on the verge of bursting, the plastic handles stretched almost to the breaking point. Then there would be a great spectacle, and everyone would turn to look as the books tumbled onto the pavement strewn with dead leaves, gobs of spit, and dog shit. Catching sight of the Palace of Justice on the hillside, he was seized with renewed muscle spasms, which almost paralysed him. He halted, resting the bags on the ground, sitting on them and waiting for the ache to pass.

Forty-eight words, he had read somewhere, no more and no less, just forty-eight, were all a person needed to survive in a prison anywhere in the world. How many would he need to survive in a Chinese penitentiary? A hundred? A thousand? Whatever the case, these ten books in French and Chinese would undoubtedly place him in the prisoner aristocracy.

The spasms in his legs subsided as little by little he staggered along the pavement, lugging the plastic bags full of books. "If I ever become a millionaire," he vowed, "I'll just buy books, books, and more books, and store them in different places, according to subject. I'll keep all the works of Chinese and Western literature in Paris, at an apartment I'll buy somewhere in the fifth arrondissement near the Jardin des Plantes, the rue Buffon for instance, or else in the heart of the Latin Quarter. All my psychoanalytical volumes will go to Peking, where I'll spend most of my time on the university campus by the side of the Nameless Lake"—yes, indeed, that is how the beautiful lake is known—"all the other books, on subjects from history to painting to philosophy and so on, I'll leave in a small studio-cum-office in Chengdu, near the home of my parents."

Suddenly remembering his current state, he reflected that he had never had anything to call his own and now probably never would have, not even an attic room or cubbyhole. *Maybe these ten volumes represent my only fortune, the only riches I will ever possess,* he told himself morosely, and he began to cry. He limped on and would have hidden his teary face in his hands had they not been encumbered with his heavy burdens. His sobs attracted attention from passing cars and buses.

"Unbelievable! Imagine crying over money!" Muo muttered under his breath. "Here I am, about to be slung behind bars, and yet I'm so preoccupied with money that I make a spectacle of myself in the street."

It occurred to him that if he were filming the story of his life, this would be the crucial scene. He pictured himself penetrating the Palace of Justice, his footsteps echoing down the long hall of marble columns. The lenses of his spectacles would turn golden in the sunlight, but soon he would descend to the murky depths, where the judges lurked in their subterranean offices. He would pass through twilight zones of deepening horror before he reached the door of Judge Di. As he pushed it open, the judge, believing the plastic shopping bags to contain explosives, would scream blue murder and beg to be spared. But Muo (wide shot followed by pan and close-up) would wearily take off his glasses, polish them on his sleeve, and beseech him nobly, like the captain of the *Titanic,* who ordered women and children into the lifeboats first: "Go ahead, handcuff me, but release the Embalmer!" (It is extraordinary what associations a film can trigger, even when one is on the point of turning oneself in at the Palace of Justice.) He could already see himself among snoring convicts in the obscurity of an overcrowded cell, making his first entries in his secret prison diary. He would write in French: "Wherein lies the difference between Western civilisation and my own? What have the people of France contributed to world history? The first thing that springs to mind is not the French Revolution—it is the spirit of chivalry. And that is the spirit that has guided me today."

The Palace of Justice was an ultramodern structure designed by an Australian architect, a dazzling fortress of glass set on a slope that, according to legend, harboured the legendary tomb of General Zhang Fei of the Three Kingdom Period. The midday sun beating down set this vast diamond ablaze, silvering the lawn sprinklers and glinting on the tower, which dominated the palace, its dazzling marble clock-face indicating three o'clock against the clear blue sky. (The architect, it could not be denied, had a sense of humour, if he knew of the old Chinese saying attributed to the powerful king of the underworld: "When it is time, it is time.")

One, two, three . . . with bowed head, Muo huffed and puffed as he counted the steps to the entrance of the glass fortress, where several soldiers, some of them armed, stood watch, indifferent to his laborious ascent. Halfway up Muo paused again to rest, looking up at the sentries, dark silhouettes against the glass façade. One of them, who was unarmed, descended a few steps, and with his hands on his hips called out imperiously: "What have you got in those plastic bags?"

"Books," replied Muo, relieved to hear that his voice was sounding calm and neutral. "I've come for Judge Di. I assume you know him."

"You're out of luck. He's just left."

"I'll wait in his office," said Muo, adding solemnly, "I have an appointment."

He continued his climb and had only another dozen steps to go when, following a reflexive gesture, he pushed up his glasses, which were sliding down his sweaty nose, and Freud's great works tumbled out of one plastic bag, followed by the Zhuangzi commentaries from the other. He watched in dumb horror as the other volumes followed, cascading down the steps in all directions.

The soldiers roared with laugher, shaking like marionettes. One of them cocked his rifle, aimed at a book, and pretended to pull the trigger. He simulated the kick of the gun against his jaw before training his sights on another book. He mouthed a make-believe blast and then affected triumph at hitting the mark.

The toiletries Muo had purchased earlier were the next to escape his grasp. The Gillette shaving cream made the most spectacular clattering descent until it finally came to rest at the bottom of the steps. Muo finally conceded the climb and returned to the base to gather his belongings and start again. There a tall, gaunt figure with a bulging leather briefcase under his arm was bending over to inspect one of the fallen books. He was about fifty, with a small, pointed head and a long neck. He resembled a stork.

"Are you familiar with these books?" he asked.

Muo gave a nod of assent.

"In point of fact, my boy, I want a straight answer. Just say yes or no," the Stork said in a somewhat hoarse, reedy voice. "I shall repeat my question."

"Yes, I am familiar with them," said Muo.

"Don't reply until I have repeated my question. Now, are you familiar with these books?"

"Yes, I am."

"Do they belong to you?"

"Yes."

"Follow me. I have left my reading glasses in my office, and I shall need them to check some details," he said, producing his identification card. "In point of fact, I am Judge Huan, president of the Clandestine Anti-publications Commission. It is my sober duty to inform you that Freud's books are strictly forbidden."

"But I just bought them in a downtown bookshop."

"Precisely. In point of fact, I need to establish by whom and under which false licence number they have been published."

Unlike his colleague Judge Di, who preferred a sub-terranean lair, the Stork had opted for a perch on the top floor of the five-storey glass fortress.

In the lift going up, a misunderstanding arose. At Muo's mention of Judge Di the Stork took him for an acquaintance, possibly the judge's advisor in matters of psychology. Wishing, perhaps, to make up for his authoritarian manners earlier, he adopted a friendly tone and became quite talkative, complaining of understaffing in his department and of having to work so hard in monkish solitude, often very late. It was a somewhat wearisome conversation, not least because he was unable to utter more than three sentences without saying "in point of fact" (a phrase undoubtedly adopted from televised interviews of the general secretary of the Party). He spoke of his modest origins as a communist schoolteacher and his good fortune to have been singled out for a career in the judiciary in the late nineties. He had resigned himself to his disadvantage vis-à-vis certain colleagues, who were drawn from the ranks of the army.

"In point of fact," he confided in a fawning voice edged with bitterness, "the omnipotent Judge Di, with whom you have your appointment, frequently makes me uneasy."

The entrance to his department was secured with three locks: one on the sturdy, shiny protective grille and two others at different levels on the glass-panelled double doors. The Stork deactivated the alarm system by pressing a practised sequence on the keypad on the wall. And soon the clicks of the locks being turned, the squeak of the grillework, the whoosh of the glazed double doors, all these sounds were subsumed into the hum of the air conditioning. But the ventilation did nothing to dispel the stinging secret odour of doctrinaire virtue, power, parallel existences, desiccated lives.

In the Department of Clandestine Anti-publications, Muo found himself in a vast anteroom, which was quite dark, owing to the lowered blinds. He followed closely behind the Stork, feeling as though he were in some grotto in which his myopic eyes could discern only vague shapes and occasional blurs of light, but after a moment or two it dawned on him that he was surrounded by forbidden books, some worth a fortune, jumbled together on shelves from floor to ceiling. The smell of damp paper wafted about the room. There was a small opening in the middle of the ceiling, a traditional feature of Chinese architecture, through which a cone-shaped beam of greyish light was projected onto the middle of the floor, leaving the walls in shadow. Among the unmarked shelves of cheap plywood sagging under the weight of the books, likewise without rubric or number, Muo felt as though he had stumbled upon an ancient treasure house.

In the centre of the space, where the light was strongest, Muo took advantage of the Stork's momentary inattention to put down his bags and pluck a book from the shelf nearest him. It was the memoirs of Mao's personal physician, on its cover a black-and-white photograph of the author in shorts, smiling ecstatically beside Mao, who wore a floppy shirt and wide trousers and squinted in the glare of the sun. Furtively, Muo opened the book and happened upon a page devoted to a condition that Mao attributed to phimosis, which, while no trouble to him personally, had infected all his sexual partners. The physician had advised him (with the same ecstatic smile?) to wash his member, to which the president of the People's Republic had replied that he cleansed it regularly in the sex organs of women. Muo shut the book and replaced it where he'd found it. He walked on, passing shelves crammed with political books, mostly reports and analyses of the events of Tiananmen Square in 1989, but also documents pertaining to power struggles in the bosom of the Party, the suspicious death of Lin Biao, the true personality of Zhou Enlai, the famines of the sixties, the massacres of intellectuals, the reeducation camps, even cases of revolutionary cannibalism . . . His head reeling, Muo had nearly lost himself in this forest of compilations, archives, and records of bloodcurdling cruelty and connivance when he suddenly found himself afloat in a sea of erotic novels; licentious writings by libertine monks; the works of de Sade; old manuals, clandestinely reprinted; albums of pornographic woodcuts from the Ming Dynasty; various editions of the Chinese Kama Sutra; and several dozen versions of *Jing Ping Mei* (the novel that had so inspired Muo in France that he almost devoted a psychoanalytic dissertation to it, although the idea had never developed beyond occasional jottings in exercise books). There were even two stacks filled with antique volumes sewn with thread. Muo enquired what kind of subjects they dealt with and why they had been banned.

"They are esoteric Taoist treatises on ejaculation," replied the Stork.

"Do you mean masturbation?"

"No, ejaculation, or rather non-ejaculation. For centuries they studied ways of making human sperm circulate in the body during sexual congress, with a view to drawing the fluid to the brain so that it might be transformed into some supernatural energy."

Muo almost took out his exercise book to note down the titles of the ancient volumes. *A pity I can't have them with me in prison,* he mused to himself.

The second space, smaller than the first, was no less gloomy. Here Muo found not books nor shelves but metal boxes of film reels, bathed in a sepulchral glow. Spools of film in piles, stacks, layers, dozens huddling together, hundreds—thousands—of them, in the sinister penumbra of the luminous cone. Some columns had collapsed, the films escaping from their spools, uncurling like dead snakes, forming bows, circles, blossoming in enormous knots, calcinated in places or covered in greenish mould.

The Stork, presiding and sole member of the commission, held office in the third space. Having put on his reading glasses, he pored over the volumes of Freud, craning his neck to examine each and noting down the suspect references in a large ledger bound in fake black leather, leaving Muo to make a discovery even more bone-chilling than those of the two preceding rooms: the desk was strewn with letters of denunciation. "My personal collection," the Stork declared proudly.

Those already read had been minutely labelled, classified, and locked away like museum fossils in seven cabinets of richly carved ebony fronted with glass panels. Each cabinet had its own theme. The first contained denunciations between fathers and sons, the second between husbands and wives, the third between neighbours, the fourth between colleagues. The fifth and sixth cabinets were reserved for anonymous denunciations. Within each cabinet the letters were arranged according to subject in a rainbow of coloured folders. Red was for political subjects, yellow for matters of money, blue for extramarital fornication, violet for homosexuality, indigo for sexual abuse, orange for illicit betting, green for thievery and housebreaking.

The seventh cabinet contained letters of self-denunciation. Seeing the key in the lock, Muo ventured to ask permission to look inside. The majority, dating from the Cultural Revolution, were long, some running to over a hundred pages and resembling those relentlessly confessional novels in which the author reveals the darkest recesses of his being, complete with lascivious fancies, hidden desires, secret ambitions.

Cardboard boxes with red labels were stacked in the corner, waiting for their contents to be read and classified. The Stork was clearly kowtowing to a personal whimsy.

"Perhaps," said Muo, "I might add a letter to your collection."

"Whom do you wish to denounce?"

"Judge Di."

The Stork could not help laughing out loud. Returning to his work, he said: "In point of fact, I know why Judge Di called you here with those books of Freud's."

"Tell me."

"In point of fact, he is hunting a criminal, some sort of psychoanalyst who organises assassinations in the local mortuaries. He probably thought some clues might be found in your books."

Muo's laughter died in his throat. Once again, a searing pain shot through him from his calves down to his ankles and up again, toward his kidneys.

"Do you think Judge Di will have the psychoanalyst shot?"

"He will, undoubtedly."

"Would you mind telling me where the toilets are?" Muo asked, with mightily forced composure.

"At the end of the corridor, on the left."

Upon leaving the Department of Clandestine Antipublications Muo made straight for the stairs for fear of crossing Judge Di in the lift. Despite his cramped legs, he flew down four steps at a time, all the way to the ground floor of the glass palace. *I bet the judge has alerted the airport,* he thought to himself. *I'd best take a train.*

Ignoring his aching limbs, he sketched an escape route in his mind: by train from Chengdu to Kunming, and by bus from Kunming to the Sino-Burmese border, where he would have to find a smuggler to lead him into Burma on foot. Then from Rangoon to Paris by plane.

A LOCOMOTIVE EMERGES from the shadows, looming larger and larger with a deafening roar and filling the entire window before disappearing. Next a succession of gigantic, teetering freight cars cast their shadows on the glass. This crossing with another train concludes with a momentary glimpse of the last carriage, in which the armed guards are crowding around the feeble light of a green lampshade.

The dark reflection of an old man appears in the window, blurry and vague at first, then coming into focus as the train enters a tunnel, much as a photographic print reacts to developing fluid. Clearly mirrored in the glass is the tip of a tongue running the length of the dingy teeth in the upper jaw and probing a black hole near the middle. The gap, which looks enormous, grossly distorts the face.

Muo stares at the reflection with narcissistic fascination, tears welling in his eyes. "A foretaste of what will become of me, twenty years hence—Grandpa Muo, or else Muo the aged convict, slaving in a mine shaft. But at least for now, all is well. To be on the run is to be alive."

Suddenly, in the glass, he catches sight of a girlish

figure pausing by his compartment on her way down the corridor. He has a feeling he has seen this girl, who can't be more than eighteen, somewhere before, and though he can't think where, she, too, seems to recognise him. He whips off his glasses, pulls his head into his hood like a turtle, and feigns the deepest of slumbers. Not daring to move a muscle, he remains thus until the train rumbles out of the tunnel, by which time she has vanished. He can breathe freely again. Filling his lungs, he indulges in a bit of idle eavesdropping on the animated couple next to him.

Their topic is the ethnic minority known as the Lolo—or Yi, in Mandarin—who inhabit the mountainous region that is now filing past the window. Muo knows little about these folk other than that the men are seldom seen without their voluminous cloaks made of hemp, even wrapping themselves in these robes at night to sleep by the fireplace they hollow out in the earthen floor in the middle of a room. A Lolo's true home, Muo has heard it said, is his cloak. Another passenger, a workman familiar with this stretch of railway, recounts the adventure that befell him a month earlier in broad daylight, between the stations of Emei and Ebin. With a detached, impersonal smile, he describes a raid on his train carriage—"common currency in these parts." They were beset by a gang of about fifteen knife-wielding Lolo, three blocking the door at one end, two or three more posted at the other, the rest fleecing the passengers. There was no shouting. Everyone kept quite still, even the children. With the efficiency of ticket inspectors, the Lolo split up into two parties to work their way to the centre of the carriage from opposite ends. The Lolo snatched it all—handbags, briefcases, peasant hods, and various other personal effects—with their iron-hard fingers. Suitcases too large or over-stuffed for their convenience were emptied onto the floor. The booty was all the more considerable, as bank cheques are not used in the countryside and everyone travels with cash, sometimes a life's savings or money worth the price of a house. When the Lolo were done they didn't even wait for the train to slow down going up a slope, but leapt off to the ground, the engine's full speed as nothing to their dazzling acrobatics.

Muo fears for the dollars hidden in a secret pocket of his underpants. In the lush, slumbering landscape slid-ing past the window, which had filled him with nostalgia a moment ago, he now sees only menace: in the lofty mountain ranges, mountains as far as the eye can see, he sees the cloaks of the Lolo in shades of grey, black, and tan. The forests, marshes, and gorges flitting past seem filled with phantom shadows casting glares of racial hatred, that most implacable of passions. Even the few lights twinkling feebly in a hamlet clinging to the mountainside or in the depths of a distant valley seem resentful.

If only the train would speed up, if only he were out of here.

The conversation beside him heats up. He rises from his hard seat and moves to the smokers' corner.

His cigarettes taste decidedly different since his tooth fell out. The first puff has an unpleasant, unfamiliar aftertaste, and there is a general absence of aroma and subtlety. Instead of sliding in between his teeth and rolling about in his mouth, caressing tongue and palate, the smoke is funnelled in through the dental gap and passes directly to the back of his throat. His mouth has been reduced to a conduit, a vent, a chimney flue.

Shielded from prying eyes, he removes his tooth from its paper napkin and awkwardly pushes it into place, pressing the root up into his gums. By some miracle it stays put, wedged between the teeth on either side. The hole is gone.

For a time at least he rediscovers the taste of Marlboro, which he savours like a delicacy, with dainty little puffs. At his side, the door of the toilet swings in the draught (a sleepy occupant has neglected to shut it), wafting the foetid air. But nothing can spoil his enjoyment now. As the train enters yet another tunnel, the electricity fails and the carriage is plunged into total darkness. The glowing tip of his cigarette reminds him of his first smoke, a lifetime ago, when he was a boy. He was thirteen—no, fourteen. The brand was Jin Sha Jiang (River of Golden Sands), thirty fen a packet. He had composed the opening lines of a naïve and clumsy little poem called "Little Four Eyes" at the time, in praise of that first cigarette:

> Ah, my first kiss
> On the fine sensual thigh
> Of a River of Golden Sands
> Glowing in a February night

He rejoices in the vibrating echo of the train in the tunnel, exults in his restored tooth, relishes his boyhood reminiscences, and before he knows it the lights have come on again. Then he hears a female voice behind him: "Hello, Mr. Muo!"

Silence. Muo is transfixed with fear. Everything seems to stop: the air, the train, his body, his brain. "A female cop," he mutters under his breath, feeling faint.

The voice repeats its greeting, accompanied by a mysterious clicking sound. The sound of handcuffs? Expecting a Chinese Jodie Foster to hold a gun to his temple, *The Silence of the Lambs* à la Sechuan, he stammers, "Take me to . . ."

He is about to say "Judge Di," but he stops midsentence. It is the girl he saw reflected in the window a while ago.

His jaw drops as he takes her in. She is too tall. Indeed, everything about her seems oversized: the denim jacket, the red polka-dot trousers, the bright yellow backpack, even the Heineken six-pack under her arm. The cans vibrate to the rhythm of the train.

"Do you remember me, Mr. Muo?" she asks. "You interpreted my dream at the domestic workers' market."

"My name is not Muo," he responds gruffly. "You are mistaken."

As soon as the words are out of his mouth he quickly stubs out his cigarette in an ashtray affixed to the side of the carriage and ducks out. On no account must he be seen acting furtively, so he does his utmost to maintain a gentlemanly demeanour. But his consternation is so great that he takes the wrong door and steps into the filthy toilet. He slams the door behind him. "I'm going nuts," he rages, grabbing hold of the washbasin and doubling up as if vomit is rising to his gullet. "I must be stark raving mad. Of course it's her. How could I not have recognised that country bumpkin who dreamt of being in a movie? Damn her for disrupting my meditation, my last refuge!"

The vituperation dislodges his tooth, which falls into the washbasin, which—thank goodness—has been blocked since goodness knows when. Dredging the bottom of the blackish pool with his fingertips, he recovers his errant incisor. He cleans it and dries it several times over, but the penetrating smell of drains, trains, and latrines will not go away.

Suddenly there is a ruckus in the corridor. Putting his ear against the door he can hear the conductors shouting and the little film-dreamer whimpering. She is travelling without a ticket. They fulminate at her as at a thief caught red-handed. She has no defence. She has no money, she stammers; in all her eighteen years she has never done this before, and she swears she will never do it again. They say they'll take the Heineken as security. She pleads with them, explaining that it's a present for her father and cost her two months' earnings as a domestic worker. But the thirsty inspectors are implacable in their lack of mercy. She resists as one of them tries to wrest the pack from her, and then lets out a terrible, piercing cry like a wild beast in agony. Muo opens the door and steps out into the corridor with a thought to intervening but, as usual, unsure what to do.

"Mr. Muo, please, please explain to them what happened just now as I was fiddling about with my ticket," she says, frantically revising her story. "You are the only person who saw it snatched away by a gust of wind when I put it on the ledge by the window."

Muo confirms her account, adding as further corroboration three bills from his pocket for the three ticket inspectors.

"For you, my friends," he says. "Ten yuan each, and we won't mention it further."

THE VOICES OF THE TRAIN passengers seem to be travelling on some distant other vessel, like the boat Marlow navigated through the heart of darkness in search of Kurtz. Muffled, somnolent voices. Men reaping a harvest of anecdotes. Swags of talk floating, alternating, rising amid bursts of laughter, coughs, a spectacular sneeze, then dying away in a low sigh or a yawn. It is hard to tell who is speaking and who is listening.

Crouching under the wooden banquette, his ears pressed against the floor of the carriage, Muo listens to the wheels. When the train heads up a long mountain slope he can hear them skating on the rails, now with the dull rumble of thunder, now with earsplitting screeches, transforming his secret sleeping-berth into a crow's nest in the eye of a storm. He can almost see the sparks flying. But once the train rolls downgrade, devouring the night, the wheels produce a more muted sound, a smooth, barely perceptible cadence, echoed by the mountains, distant, ethereal, like a conch shell held to the ear: the murmur of a calm tide lapping a shore of polished shingle, blue-grey in the morning light. Best of all is when the train pulls into a station. He can hear a long sigh passing through the wheels, one after another, like someone gasping in their sleep—like some living creature in the undercarriage, so near that he can almost feel its tepid breath.

Snatches of the insomniacs' conversation reach Muo's ears. According to one, whose low voice evokes the storytellers of old, each mountain range and each mountainous district breeds its own folk, just as each

ocean breeds its own sailors. The Lolo in this region all
have a talent for jumping off trains. It is an inborn
knack, not the fruit of any rearing or training, an apti-
tude that, in some, approaches genius when they per-
form their death-defying leaps from cars hurtling at
top speed. By this talent, the Lolo distinguish themselves from other folk. And among themselves, the Lolo
are distinguished when they assault a freight train;
those cars carrying goods lack the proper doors and
footboards of passenger trains, as well as being secured
with iron bars and padlocks. You will see a band of Lolo
strolling nonchalantly along the track. A train goes
past. One of them breaks into a run. After a good start,
he takes a flying leap, a saltation of great beauty, perfectly calculated for him to grab hold of one of the iron
bars, whereupon he clings to the side of the carriage as
his voluminous black cloak flaps wildly in the wind.
With a hammer from his pocket, he smashes the padlock, lifts the iron bars, gives the heavy sliding door a
push, and slips inside. A second or two later he reap-
pears with a television set. He takes another leap, in
free-fall this time, or rather in lyrical suspension, with
his cloak floating in the air and his loot in his arms.
Like a ski jumper, he lands without losing his balance,
as far away from the takeoff ramp as possible. He hands
the television to his confreres, who have been keeping
pace. They tie it to his back with ropes, and off they all
go. Sometimes the odd railroad guard will go after
them, taking potshots, but when a Lolo takes to his heels
on a mountainside, even with a television on his back,
he is unassailable.

"Are you there, Mr. Muo?"

It is too dark for him to see anything. His mind is quite blank for a moment, then he focusses: it is the film-dreamer once again. The attentive trance in which he has been listening is instantly and totally dispelled. She has her charms for a country girl, but mindful of the last disaster that befell him on such a night train, he decides to keep silent, feigning slumber. A fugitive he may be, but he is a virtuous one, an ascetic.

She repeats Muo's name two or three more times, in a low voice, so as not to wake the other sleepers. But the softness of her tone confirms a good humour and affectionate nature. Muo, the ascetic fugitive, tries his best to snore convincingly, but the rhythm of his breathing is too erratic. Even with his eyes shut he knows that she is now insinuating herself into his secret sleeping-berth.

"Not bad, this little cubbyhole," she says, crawling toward him on her hands and knees. When she knocks into him in the dark, both of them cry out.

"Not so loud," he says.

"It's all right, everyone's asleep."

"What is it you want?"

His voice is as cold as ice.

"D'you like jujubes? I've brought you some."

"Not so loud," he repeats, girding himself to keep his ascetic vow. He doesn't want to smile, even if she can't see him. He adds: "Keep them for your father."

"I've got some more, don't worry. Go on, have one. A small token of thanks. They're clean. I washed them."

"Well, just one, then."

But in the gloom she misses his outstretched palm.

"Where's your hand?"

After a fair amount of fumbling, one jujube changes hands. Muo puts it into his mouth with caution, so as not to dislodge the loose tooth.

"D'you want another?"

"Wait."

He chews the fleshy, fresh-tasting, juicy fruit-gum carefully and with relish.

"I want to show you a book I bought," she says. "You can tell me what it's worth. Got a light?"

He strikes a match and the girl appears in the light of the flame, very close to him, her back hunched, her elbows propped on the floor. *How pretty she is,* he thinks.

Another match is needed to light up the book in her hand: a slender, worn volume with six Chinese characters on the cover, reading *Elementary Grammar of the French Language.* Some pages have folded-down corners and comments written in the margins.

Muo remains silent and keeps very still, scandalised by his arousal, however invisible to the girl. It is the first time this has happened since he lost his virginity. He can't tell whether it was triggered by the taste of the jujube or by the sight of the book.

As the match burns down to the last, a long, soft ember drops on the cover of the book, bounces up, and falls again on the plastic slicker he is using for a mat. The girl deftly extinguishes the spark.

"It must be worth five yuan, don't you think?" she asks, engulfed in darkness once more. "I bought it second-hand. To impress my father. He paid for my brother to go to secondary school, not for me."

"How were you going to impress him, not knowing any French?"

"I told him what you explained to us at the domestic

workers' market: that French is a language of words whose sole purpose is to please women. How did you put it? To woo them. I don't give a damn about not knowing the language. All I want is to stick it to my father. He has a husband in mind for me—the village headman's son. I don't like him at all."

"Maybe he is in love with you."

"I don't want him to love me."

She pauses. Although Muo cannot see her, he can feel her eyes on him.

"Muo, why are you hiding?"

"What?"

How crafty she is! Taken by surprise, he finds that anxiety gets the upper hand, and his erection subsides.

"Do you want to know the truth? Will you swear never to tell a soul? I am leaving the country. And as I loathe farewells, I have decided to give the land of China a final hug from under a bench on a night train. I am a patriot."

"You're lying."

"You know Burma? Well, that is where I'm going. It's a wonderful country where people spend their time chewing betel nuts and spitting out jets of bloodred juice. There are temples everywhere. I shall enter a temple. Become a monk. Buddhist monks are allowed to eat meat over there. I am very partial to meat."

"Don't make me laugh. No temple would accept an interpreter of dreams as a monk. You're running away. It's obvious. Just now, you even said your name wasn't Muo."

Then, fearing she might anger him, her tone softens again, mellifluous as before.

"May I lie down beside you? I'm exhausted."

"Be my guest. You can share my mat. The floor is filthy."

After that he holds his tongue. He listens to the sound of jujubes being chewed in the dark. She chews like a true peasant girl, making loud smacking noises that Muo is sure must be audible at the other end of the carriage. Little by little, the sound of chewing dwindles, giving way to the regular breathing of sleep, until there is only the burble of passengers and muffled snores, and the thunder of the train becomes a background silence. Suddenly he wakes her, saying, "I don't even know your name."

"Everyone calls me Little Sister Wang. Why d'you ask? Are you getting off at the next stop?"

"No. I want to ask you something, but if you prefer not to answer, I will understand."

"Go on, ask."

"Are you a virgin?"

"What?"

"A virgin. Someone who has never made love to a man."

"Yes, I'm a virgin."

In the dark he can hear her spluttering with laughter.

"Honestly?" he asks.

"Of course."

"If you save us, my friends and me, I'll take you to France."

"What d'you want me to do?"

"A magistrate in Chengdu by the name of Judge Di has sent two of my friends to prison. Now he is after me. He has been offered money. But he has declined it. He's got plenty already. All he wants is to meet a virgin girl."

Having made his statement, he awaits her reaction, imagining it even before his last word is out: a blood-curdling and earsplitting howl, almost feral, just as she had unleashed on the ticket inspectors. But she says nothing, and an ineffable sadness hangs silent in the air, and lingers awkwardly, to the point where he wonders how he can possibly retract the injury he has inflicted on this poor, simple girl. After an eternity she makes her halting reply: "Will you really take me to France afterward?"

"Yes."

"All right, then, you're on."

In the gloom, he feels utterly light-headed. Forgetting the ascetic fugitive, he takes her in his arms before she can speak another word.

"Thank you," he mumbles in a fatherly tone. "Thank you, thank you. And I'll teach you French."

A flood of verse from Hugo, Verlaine, and Baudelaire enters his head, passing through his lips and into the girl's ear as he covers her hair, her eyes, her nose with kisses. She keeps her head down, in the dark, but she does not resist him. And abruptly the lothario lately born in him shoves the ascetic aside: he kisses her hard on the mouth. Ah! The jujube all swollen with sap! But before he can gauge the fate of this bold overture he is interrupted.

"What's wrong?" he asks.

"There's something in my mouth," she murmurs. *"What is this?"*

"My tooth!" he exclaims, spraying saliva through the ruins of his smile. "Don't swallow it!"

2. THE HEAD OF THE DRAGON

CHENGDU, 5 OCTOBER

My dearest Old Moon, my splendid Volcano,
    Do you still have a taste for riddles? Or has
your imprisonment robbed you of that
pleasure, too? My dear little class champ of
1975, cleverest of all the female students,
riddle-solver to rival Oedipus. Remember
how you won first prize in the first-year
competition? A juicy red watermelon
weighing five kilos, which you shared with your
seven roommates in your ten-square-metre
room, without even a knife to help you.
Everyone rounded on the poor fruit, jostling
and laughing, battering it with spoons. The
following year you won the book you gave to
me, a dictionary of slang used in novels of the
Ming Dynasty, a rare book that I so love
leafing through, which I have read so many
times I could write a novel of my own in the
Ming style.
    Here is a riddle for you to ponder: my
motive for writing you a letter of as yet
indeterminate length in a foreign language,

that is, French, of which the dearly addressed understands scarcely a word.

It is a small enigma, resonant with the sweet sound of happiness, like the tinkle of coins. My surprise at finding that my swollen hand had begun writing in French soon grew into excitement at the ingeniousness of this spontaneous gesture. I was quite enchanted, really impressed, not to say filled with self-admiration. I am sorry I didn't think of it before. What a pleasure to envisage the screws charged with censoring your mail! I can already see their long faces confronted with pages upon pages by your tireless correspondent, your passionate and mysterious lover. Given budgetary strictures and the ever-growing numbers of prisoners, one could hardly expect them to bother having this cabalistic missive translated. (At Chengdu, the only three or four people who understand the language of Voltaire and Hugo are professors at the University of Sechuan. "Tell me, professor, how much to translate one page?" "About a hundred and twenty yuan." "No!" "That's the going rate.")

From now on, my dear Old Moon, my splendid Volcano, we can look to this foreign tongue to unite us, reunite us, bind us together in a magical knot that blossoms into the wings of an exotic butterfly—an alphabetic language from the other side of the world, whose orthography, complete with apostrophes and diacriticals, lends it the heady, impenetrable air of esotericism. Your fellow prisoners, I can well imagine, will envy you your passing the time poring over love letters, to extract even the slightest triumphant particle of meaning from them. Do you remember those wonderful times we sat together listening to records of our favourite poets: Eliot, Frost, Pound, Borges? Their voices, each with its own personality and sonorous beauty, enveloped us, uplifted us, and made us dream, even though neither of us understood much English, much less Spanish. Those accents, those incomprehensible phrases, remain for me, even today, the loveliest music in the world. Music for the elect few, filled with the spirit of romance and melancholy. Our music.

Do you know what I think, writing these words? It is not my ignorance of English and Spanish that I regret, but rather my not having learnt other, less common languages. Vietnamese, for instance. I have only a smattering of that six-tone tongue with its complicated, subtle grammar. Just think if I could write you in Vietnamese—even Judge Di could not find at any price someone competent in translating it, even if he were to scour the University of Sechuan. Or another language, even more recherché, such as Catalan. Could even one soul capable of translating a letter in Catalan be found in this province of one hundred and fifty million? If

I could, I would immerse myself in the study
of Catalan, and along with it Tibetan,
Mongolian, Latin, Greek, Hebrew, Sanskrit,
the Egyptian hieroglyphs. I would like to
penetrate those inner sanctums, kneel down
with three sticks of burning incense, and pray
for us in the languages of the holy of holies.

We made off together, Little Sister Wang
with the six-pack under her arm and I, the
fugitive, with my blissful smile of ruined
teeth, on the run from Judge Di and the
police; I who, after but a few hours on a train,
abandoned a flight to Burma and emerged
from my rock-hard hiding place having
enlisted a new recruit, a potential saviour, a
true and oh-so-precious virgin to return with
me whence I came.

It was three o'clock in the morning when we
got off the train at Meigou. The platform of
beaten earth was full of puddles from a
downpour moments earlier. It was a dismal
place, wedged between two high mountains.
When the Chengdu-Kunming train I was on
pulled out of the station and disappeared into
the night, the echo of the stationmaster's
whistle lingered in the air forever, it seemed,
among the rocks and the wind, the rustle of
leaves, the lapping waters of an invisible river.

The most urgent business was to contact the
son-in-law of the mayor of Chengdu—he's the
fellow I've often written of, the one with whom
the whole virgin nightmare began all those
months ago. He had directed the first

approach to Judge Di, and only he could direct another. But we had to wait until morning to telephone because, though he is a restaurateur by day, like you he sleeps in a prison cell, with his mobile switched off.

Meigou is the river at the foot of the mountains, which flows past the small town of the same name, not far from the station. The long, thick trunks of trees felled in the forests at high altitude float downstream, heaving and colliding to a strange, somewhat muted, phantasmal rhythm. Along the riverbank, our footsteps sounded alien. Our breathing, even our speech, took on a different rhythm. We felt apprehensive, as if we were entering a foreign land of menacing shadows and hostile sounds, where we ourselves were ghostly intruders. On the bridge at the entrance to the town there is an ancient stele, its inscriptions in Chinese and in the language of the Lolo still legible, proclaiming that the river rising at the summit of the mountain of the same name, to the north of the town, issues from a deep spring of divinely limpid waters. In times of drought, they say, it is enough to throw some stones in it for the rain to come down in sheets all across the region.

A karaoke bar in the main street was still open—incredible that such a backwater could boast a joint called Shanghai Blues, open past 3 a.m. I wish you could have seen the little film-dreamer sing. Her pretty face beamed with youth, coquetry, and love of music. It was

hot and dark inside, too dark to see the other
patrons. She took her jacket off and moved
close to the screen. For a country girl she is
not shy. Her build is slight, her chest flat, but
her arms are lively and her skinny body in that
floppy T-shirt was possessed of an adolescent
charm that even a nearsighted Muo could
appreciate. In point of fact, the more I looked
at her, the more she reminded me of you. Not
that she looks like you, but there is something
of you in her profile, notably in the curve of
the skull, the high forehead, and the elongated
eyes, and in her way of pausing now and then
to scratch the roots of her hair, which is
cropped along the ears, like yours. In her
voice, too, there is an echo of yours: low, a
little husky. Her imitation of a black blues
singer is priceless. She must have worked for
some people with quite a record collection.
One of her numbers—"I Take This Road But
Once in a Thousand Years"—was sublime. You
know I could never carry a tune but,
emboldened by her example, I actually joined
her at the microphone. She was radiant, a
natural star. In my elation I told her that, as
far as stage names go, "Little Road" sounded
much catchier than "Little Sister." She tried it
on for size, repeating "Little Road" several
times after me.

"All right," she said, finally convinced.
"From now on, you can call me 'Little
Road.' "

Superstitious as I am, each time I think

back to what happened the next day, I wonder
whether the name of the song was an omen. It
would indeed be the rarest of roads, one not
to travel more than once in a lifetime.

The proprietor of the karaoke bar, an
amicable thirty-year-old, seemed quite taken
with Little Road. When the crowd had gone
home, he asked her if she liked to dance. She
said she knew hip-hop, having learnt it while
employed in a house with a balcony
overlooking the quadrangle of a polytechnic,
where she observed the students doing it every
day during break. The owner of the bar
offered to DJ while she danced. He played a
track called "I Have Nothing," by Cui Jian,
the eighties rocker. The hoarse, despairing
intonations of Cui Jian were magically
modernised by the deft techno manipulations
of the accidental DJ, who, rather than fiddling
incessantly as some do, would let Cui Jian
work himself up to a pitch of agony before
going on the attack. Carried away by the
music, Little Road, all smiles, stepped and
twirled across the floor. After a moment her
shoulders were shaking, then her arms, legs,
hips—her entire body became disjointed, the
limbs seemingly dislocated and jerking
ecstatically. The next record was by a Chinese
rapper. He rapped the famous poem from *The
Dream of the Red Chamber,* which begins
"Everyone loves money." Little Road did a
backward somersault and, putting her hands
flat on the floor, holding her head down,

started spinning around on her arms and
head. Round and round she turned, bending
and stretching her legs in the air, faster and
faster until her whole body was pivoting on
her head alone. "Let Grandpa here show you a
revolutionary dance," I chimed in. And I did
an old-time jig for them—you know, that silly,
old-fashioned one we learnt at school about
the valet of the evil landowner who goes
around collecting the rent from starving
peasants. I played it for all it was worth:
sidestepping like a crab, pirouetting,
cavorting, cracking the whip—I used my belt—
but then, in the middle of a capriole, I lost my
footing and fell flat on my face. Taking pity on
me, the DJ switched to a more sedate selection
from the revolutionary ballet *The White-Haired
Girl,* but at his command was everything from
the Beatles to U2, Michael Jackson, and
Madonna, and even Red Sun of Our Heart,
Red Orient, and speeches by Chairman Mao,
sung by Hong Kong stars to electronic music.
What an evening!

I got through to the mayor's son-in-law
right after breakfast. He was in a taxi, this
prince of the condemned, and was perhaps a
little surprised to be hearing from me again.
He listened patiently as I explained matters
before asking whether he thought arranging
an encounter between Judge Di and a second
virgin might help the situation.

There was a moment's pause. I thought he
was pondering my question. Suddenly he

burst out: "How are *you* doing, sexually speaking?"

I was taken aback.

"I'm doing all right," I said modestly. "I have even made some progress in that field."

He laughed. It was not Homeric laughter, but I heard him nonetheless.

"Bravo! Listen here: according to old Sun, the shrewdest convict I have ever known, life boils down to three things: eating, shitting, and fucking. If you're doing all three, everything's fine."

"An amusing bit of wisdom."

"Come here as soon as possible, with the girl. What is she called? Little Road? I like it. Give me a ring as soon as you arrive. In the meantime I'll get things rolling with the judge."

Then, switching from our dialect to Mandarin, he added an afterthought: "Muo," he said, "this is a bombshell." And with that he hung up.

My heart pounded with joy. I knew my parents would already be at the hospital administering the morning rounds of injections, but with no one else to call, I dialled their number anyway. No one was there to reply, but it calmed me all the same. I had begun plotting how to make our way back to Chengdu when we stumbled upon a Blue Arrow.

It was parked at the entrance to the town, splattered with mud and with the paint all

chipped and flaking. The flatbed behind the
driver's cabin lacked a tarpaulin, and its door
panel was haplessly secured with a piece of
string. Little Road and I tracked down the
driver in the greasy spoon where we had
breakfast. He was bearded—or, rather,
unshaven—stooped, sallow-faced, and wracked
with fits of coughing. After each fit, he cleared
his throat of great gobs of phlegm, which he
ground with the sole of his shoe while he went
on talking.

As there was not a train to Chengdu
stopping in Meigou for another five or six
hours, I decided to make the journey in the
Blue Arrow rather than risk letting our
scheme falter on bad timing. We negotiated
twenty yuan for the driver, and off we went.

To the end of my days I will remember this
drive, bouncing along the potholed road
through the Mountains of the Great Cold.
The seat next to the driver had been
eviscerated and repaired with tape, but
practically speaking we were seated on bare
springs. The radio, missing almost all its
buttons, was affected worse than we were by
the bumps, cutting in and out of "Let Us
Crush Our American Enemies." I felt a bit
like the wounded soldier of the song, who,
gun in hand, makes straight for the American
front as bullets whistle past his ears and an
inferno of shells explodes at his feet.

The window on the driver's side wouldn't
crank all the way to the top, leaving a three-

finger gap through which the wind rushed in. Above the deafening gust, the trucker asked me to tell him some dirty jokes, for he had not slept the previous night and despite all the bumping around on "this shit road" he was afraid of falling asleep at the wheel.

"You know, raunchy stuff," he said.

I replied coolly that while my profession gave me access to people's dreams, and these often have a clear sexual component, they are never laughing matters.

With him looking at me quizzically, his eyelids in a drooping drowse, I felt an urgency to wrack my brain.

"With that kind of joke," I said, "it's a bit like psychoanalysis."

"Meaning what, exactly?" he asked, still plainly confused.

"I mean that to retrieve one, it is necessary to descend into the subconscious."

We were driving across a former pine forest recently devastated by fire, when suddenly flowering azaleas and rhododendrons came into view, splashing the mountain slope with colour.

"Shall I have a go?" Little Road suggested with a sigh.

"A kid like you, what joke would you have? Some kiddie tale?" said the trucker with a crooked, lecherous smile.

This is the story she told. Once upon a time, very long ago, a solitary monk lived on a remote mountain with an orphan who at the

age of three had been entrusted to his care.
Time passed. The child grew up having no
contact with the outside world. When he was
sixteen, his master took him to see what the
outside world was like. They went down the
mountain and, after walking for three days,
they reached a plain. As the young man knew
nothing, when they came across a horse the
monk told him, "Now that is what you call a
horse." In the same way he indicated a mule, a
buffalo, and a dog. Then a woman appeared,
heading in their direction. The youth asked
his master what this creature was called.

"Lower your eyes," Little Road said,
imitating the voice of an old man. "Don't
look. It's a tigress, the most dangerous beast in
the world. Keep away, or you'll he devoured."

That night, when they returned to their
mountain refuge, the old monk noticed that
the novice was wide awake, tossing and turning
in his bed as if lying on hot embers. It was the
first time the old man had seen him in such a
state. He asked what the matter was. The
novice responded, "Master, I can't stop
thinking of that man-eating tigress."

There was no reaction from our
confounded Blue Archer, who maintained his
impassive reserve, even as I began to guffaw
like a child and slap him on the shoulder.

"It's funny, but too vegetarian for my
taste," he said. "I prefer something meatier."

We were high up on the mountain. The
Meigou River, which we had been following

for some time, was now visible in the depths of a ravine, a thin ribbon of yellow with tiny sparkles. The driver announced that he would now tell us a joke.

"I bet you can't wait to hear one of mine," he said.

Just then, I spotted a heap of large stones, black as the rock of the mountain all around us, obstructing the pass we were heading for—a dark, dispiriting obstruction against the blue sky and the yellow earth of the road.

"Shit," cried the driver. "Shut your window, quick."

While Little Road did so, he tried cranking up his own window, but still couldn't close the gap of three fingers.

As we neared the pass, the black stones loomed ever larger, majestically imposing, until these petrified formations began eerily changing shape, a surreal metamorphic geometry, and soon we could make out the cloaks fluttering in the wind like the standards carried into battle by warriors of old.

"Are they bandits?" Little Road asked.

"They are true-blue Lolo," I said.

"True blue?" scoffed the driver. "We'll see which is truer—these savages or my Blue Arrow."

He floored the accelerator and honked furiously, hoping to scatter them. But the road was too steep for the rickety old vehicle to gain speed, and even the blasts from the horn,

resonating in the distance of these Mountains
of the Great Cold, made little more
impression than the drawn-out, plaintive
wailing of an exhausted camel in the
Taklamakan Desert, the endless Desert of
Death.

The shadowy figures stood stock-still,
sinister silhouettes against the yellow earth. As
the truck lurched forward, a strange optical
effect occurred: the shadows lay down under
the wheels. I yelled at the driver to brake.
Little Road did, too. But he barrelled on. The
Lolo remained motionless, a huddle of black
rocks. The moment of truth had arrived. The
Blue Arrow charged, jolting violently over the
bumpy road. In a final spurt, the truck lunged
at the Lolo. The springs of our seat sent us
flying to the ceiling of the cabin.

I shut my eyes. The driver slammed on the
brakes. Mass homicide had been avoided by
only a hair's breadth. But now there were
about thirty of them—long-boned and
muscular to a man, fearless train-jumpers—
wrathfully surrounding us. They beat the
window with their fists, cursing the driver in
their incomprehensible tongue, peppered
with a few words of Sechuanese—"Bastard . . .
You wait and see . . ."—a ring of swarthy,
glowering faces, so coarsely featured it was as if
they'd been hacked out of wood. Their
earrings glittered. After a time they drew back
and regrouped around a young man swigging

beer, who seemed to be their leader. He circulated the bottle among the others in the black scrum.

Discreetly, the driver took out his wallet and tucked it under his rump, among the shreds of padding and springs of the ragged seat. I wondered whether I should do something about the dollars stashed in my underpants, but it was too late.

The leader, who had a fearsome scar across his angular face, approached us. He hammered the windshield with his beer bottle, sending a white froth cascading down before our eyes.

"There's a tired horse for you!" he roared in Sechuanese, baring his blackened molars in an explosion of triumphant laughter.

"Who do you think you are, you bastard? Thought you'd just run us over, did you?" The humiliated driver said nothing, but a tremor passed through the seat as he tensed his muscles to rev the engine.

"Do you know where you are?" the scar-faced Lolo said. "This is Dragonhead Mountain. Open your eyes and look. In this place we slaughtered thousands of soldiers in the Qin Dynasty."

Testing the accelerator, the driver's foot began to jerk about, as though resisting the more audacious message coming from his brain.

"We are headed for our village," Scarface said. "Will you take us there?"

"All right, then, get in the back," the driver said as he tried to figure his next move, still not daring to look the Lolo in the eye.

The truck started up again. We were headed for who knows what calamity.

Beyond the fateful pass the mountain rose up in the shape of the strange mythical beast it was named for, a gigantic crouching monster stretching from east to west, which, in the light mist, seemed to be lying in ambush—a rocky skull, a scaly forehead, a chin bristling with foliage growing in its clefts, clinging to the cliff-faces, swaying in the wind.

"Do you know the expression 'to drop a bombshell'?" I asked the driver.

He eyed me as if I were mad.

"Turn the car around as soon as you can, and head back to Meigou. The Lolo can't stop us from going back to where we came from."

"Cowardly fool."

The brash master of the old jalopy rejected my sensible idea. Little Road was wide-eyed and openmouthed.

The Blue Arrow struggled up the slope of Dragonhead Mountain. It stopped several times to muster its strength before arriving at the summit. Beyond the crest were two more dragon heads, uncannily like the first, hanging breathtakingly from the edge of a precipice several hundred metres high. And to think, the Lolo spend their entire lives in these mountains, which for me would be vertigo without end.

"Hey, you two," said the truck driver. "I just remembered, I never finished telling you the joke I started when we were set upon by these savages."

Under the circumstances, I was beginning to think his fearlessness was nothing more than insanity, and he did nothing to make me think otherwise. Our terrified silence did not discourage him in the least.

"Well, I'm going to tell you."

The Lolo were now stirring in the back, Little Road observed. "They'll be wanting to get off when we reach the summit."

One of the cloaked terrors began pounding a fist on the roof of the cabin. The driver took no notice, however, having become engrossed in the telling of his tale. Two years ago, he said, he was working as a driver for the army (he was enlisted for eight years), at the headquarters of an infantry regiment. One day he was chauffeuring a communist commander on an inspection tour. The trip was to last four days. On the second evening they checked into a shabby hotel in a small town. The commander, a temperamental cuss of about fifty, spent the night with a fat, ugly whore, the only one the hotel had to offer. "He must have been pretty hard up to sample the likes of her," said the driver, who for his part passed the night unaccommodated, in "vegetarian" fashion.

The driver continued his tale through fits of coughing and the infernal pounding by the

Lolo until we reached the summit of the
second dragon's head, where I told him to stop
the truck so the unruly terrorist bandits could
disembark. The driver gave me a look of utter
contempt and condescension.

"Are you kidding?" he said. "This is the
place they mean to let us have it, to strip us of
everything but our underwear. They may take
me for an idiot, but they won't take my money
without a good fight."

He floored the accelerator, and once we'd
cleared the summit, he resumed his story, as
the Blue Arrow plunged down the steep
gradient.

"The next day, as we were driving along, the
commander told me that the whore had cost
him five hundred yuan and that some way had
to be found of justifying at least half of the
expense for the army accounts. I couldn't
think of any, but in a flash one occurred to
him: I was to file a report to the effect that in
the course of the inspection tour our vehicle
had struck an old sow crossing the road, and
that her owner had claimed two hundred and
fifty yuan as restitution."

With that he burst out laughing, first in a
high-pitched falsetto, then in a throttled
squeal. "Oh, man, I'm suffocating—an old
sow, you get it?" he spluttered between
guffaws.

Leaning back in his seat, he held his side
with one hand and steered with the other.

The interior of the cabin darkened, as if a

solar eclipse had caused a sudden, maleficent darkness to descend: it was the voluminous black cloak of a Lolo, drawn by an invisible, iron-fingered hand across the windshield. Little Road and I were speechless with terror, the silencing of the driver's vile laugh our only comfort.

"Stop the truck, please!" begged Little Road, clapping her hand to her mouth.

But the driver continued, as if possessed, poking his head out the window intermittently to judge the road. The car radio, which had been silent for the longest while, suddenly came on again, blaring Ravel's *Bolero* as we zigzagged up the third dragon's head. The Blue Arrow spluttered and slowed, which the Lolo took as a good opportunity to press their attack. Through the windshield, upside down, appeared the scarred face, swathed in black, as the other Lolo held him by the feet.

Malice, primordial hatred, racial animus, a lust for violence and blood: it was all carved in the rough-hewn features of the phantom that clung to the truck frame, resisting the driver's every attempt to hit any hump or stone that might loosen the black barnacle's iron-fingered grip. Indeed, the driver's mighty efforts only seemed to strengthen the Lolo's body and soul. And the *Bolero* was the bandit's trumpets of Jericho; his frenzied acrobatics mounted in synch with the radio's crescendo.

When a strong headwind spread the cloak over not just the windshield but also the

windows of the cab, it was as if a curtain had
fallen, a black curtain edged with sunlight.
The doughty driver, hanging on to the wheel
with both hands, leaned over almost
horizontally, resting his head on my knees to
peer out at the merest slip of visible road,
along the luminous selvedge of this black
curtain. And only when the wind died and the
cloak began to flap chaotically again did the
driver lift his stubborn head.

Now, having reached the limit of his
reason, the mad trucker poked his head out
the window, hissing a stream of
incomprehensible invective at the clinging
Lolo. In a wrathful reflex, he cleared his
throat and, with a precision to rival that of an
elite marksman, hurled a gob of phlegm at the
scar-faced bandit, hitting him square between
his fiery eyes. It seemed to me and Little
Road, now limp with terror, that the Blue
Arrow's apocalypse was upon us with this last
reckless deed. But as the road rose between
two rocky outcrops several dozen metres high,
the cloak miraculously peeled off the truck.
The Lolo chief dismounted as well,
somersaulting onto a nearby overhang before
disappearing into the peaks, followed by his
cloaked acrobatic troupe, until all of them had
disappeared, one after another, into the
mountains like so much black smoke.

As we breathed a puzzled sigh of relief,
here and there the rocky slopes gave way to
fields of yellow earth planted with maize or

spindly wheat, or to miraculous paddies just below the sheerest cliffs. Finally we approached the peak of the third dragon's head, another vertiginous drop of several hundred metres, bristling with leafy bushes, naked crags, and shadows. And as I pondered what totem or taboo the trucker's spit could have represented to the scattered Lolo people, I saw down below the River Meigou, like a yellow shoelace, its distant current the only sound after the *Bolero* had swollen to its thunderous conclusion.

As we zigzagged down the other side, Little Road and I stared in astonishment into the mists where they had last been seen. The way ahead wasn't clear, but the doughty driver, proud of routing his attackers, paid no heed. Until everything went black once again.

It all happened with such breathtaking speed and such heart-stopping violence that I cannot now recall whether any of us even had a chance to call out a warning. At a bend in the road a few metres beyond where the Lolo had unclenched his claws, scaly as an eagle's, stood a rocky promontory which would surely have crushed the bandit had he not disengaged. Unfortunately, the King of the Road was not so prescient, and just seconds after we'd breathed a sigh of relief, the reasons for our deliverance were made clear. The windscreen shattered first, with a deafening noise. On reflex I took Little Road in my arms and pushed her head down to protect it from the

impact. As the truck bounced back from the
point of collision, a blanket of broken glass
covered us. The worst of it I seemed to have
taken on the side of the head, though my chest
and knees were battered as well. At least I did
not lose consciousness. As the driver struggled
to regain control of the old truck, which still
had not come to a halt, we glanced off a tree
on the other side of the road and hit the rock
face again, before we skidded finally towards
the edge of the road where the ground fell
away. Thank goodness the truck did not
overturn. It came to a smoking standstill, on
the brink of the precipice.

My body was paralysed. Excruciating pain
in my skull. Had I suffered serious head
trauma? Would I be handicapped for life? I
couldn't rule out motor impairment, but at
least I would know whether my mind was
spared. Do a test, I said to myself. Right away.
A memory test: "When was Freud born?"
When the answer didn't come to me, I almost
wept, and then mercifully four digits appeared
in my mind's eye: "1856."

I went on quizzing myself with the rapid
fire of a sadistic teacher: "When did Freud
die?" The answer came faster this time:
"1939."

I interrupted my self-examination when I
heard moaning coming from close by in the
cab. It was Little Road, the sacrificial virgin.
She mumbled something unintelligible.

"What's your date of birth?" I said.

"Never mind that. My leg is broken."

Worse was to come. The Lolo, having observed the wreck, reappeared as eerily as they'd departed. They attacked the door on the driver's side so ferociously the handle snapped off in the grip of one black-cloaked assailant. As for the driver, the crash had drained the fight out of him, and he was leaning forward with his head in his arms over the steering wheel, as if transformed into a rag doll.

He was not wounded, apparently, but did not react when they meanaced him with their fists. He just gripped the wheel with all his might. Outside, atop the promontory, were gathered Scarface and his crew, each of them heaving a great menacing stone overhead. In his barely intelligible clipped Sechuanese, Scarface issued the death sentence: "With these stones we will smash your skulls like walnuts and feed your brains to the vultures, dogs, and worms."

Brushing off the broken glass and my transient paralysis, I clambered out through where the windshield had been and on to the hood, from which I delivered a pronouncement of my own. I raised my arms and shouted, "Help! My daughter has broken her leg!"

Although baseless, my claim to paternity brought tears to my eyes. But no one took any notice. I saw trickles of blood on the truck

bed—two or three Lolo were badly hurt. One
of them, bleeding profusely from the head,
was helped down by his comrades. And then
followed a shrill call as a horde of Lolo
peasants materialised out of the blue: a great
flapping of black, brown, and beige cloaks as
they charged down the slope, screaming and
brandishing picks and other farm
implements. In a moment the Blue Arrow was
surrounded by swarthy angry faces.

I stepped up to Scarface and grovelled
before him, a plea to defer his vengeance and
think first of the wounded, his own and my
precious daughter.

One enraged old Lolo pushed through the
crowd toward me. He was at least sixty and
wore the "Lolo horn," the unmistakable
headdress fashioned with black ribbon.
Despite my protestations that his son's injury
was not my fault, he landed an unexpected
blow to my right ear. His bony fist was so hard
that my head reeled and buzzed and I lost my
balance. As I lay stunned, the old-timer gave
me a sharp kick in the belly.

The shame of it! Hot tears of boyish
cowardice sprang from my eyes and trickled
down my cheeks. I drew myself up and heard
myself sob, "How dare you attack a
Frenchman?"

I was filled with self-loathing. But the
imperative of survival outweighed my pride.

"I am not some Chinese émigré, but a bona

fide Frenchman come to fetch his adopted
daughter. You have attacked a French citizen.
Do you realise where that will get you? In jail!
You know who Judge Di is, don't you? The
king of hell!"

The word "Frenchman" was picked up
by the Lolo, who started to mimic me,
some of them knowing what it meant,
others not.

"Can you prove it?" Scarface asked, with
only slightly chastened defiance.

"I don't believe it," growled the old man in
the turban, and then, after a pause, "Go on
then, say something in French."

I could have taken the opportunity to
deliver myself of a most satisfying string of
insults, incomprehensible to these marauding
savages. Instead, what I said—and my memory
is vivid—was this: "France is situated in
Western Europe. The earliest inhabitants were
the Gauls. Their name lives on in a popular
brand of cigarettes: Gauloise. The greatest
contribution of France to global civilisation is
the spirit of chivalry . . ." I carried on like a
professor in a lecture hall, not looking at my
class as I spoke. I was quite calm; I narrowed
my eyes and focused on the three peaks, the
three sombre, savage dragon heads. The Lolo
listened attentively. They put down their
stones and sat on them, the better to immerse
themselves in the sounds, accents,
intonations, rhythms of my French discourse,

by which they were evidently intrigued. I produced my French residence permit and presented it to Scarface. "Here is proof of my French identity," I said.

He got up from his stone to inspect it and like a customs official compared the face on the card with mine before passing it on to his cronies. While my *carte d'identité* passed from one dark, callused, mud-encrusted hand to the next, I showed Scarface the rest of my credentials: credit card, student ID, library card, and so on. But his attention was caught by something peeking out of a corner of my wallet.

"What's that?"

"It's called a 'Carte Orange'—it entitles you to take the metro in Paris."

I handed it to him. A gleam came into the eyes of the leader of the train-jumping fiends. "What is metro?" he said.

"The metro is a train. It runs underground through tunnels."

"Only in tunnels?"

"Only in tunnels."

He stared at me in slightly amused puzzlement.

"Never in the open air?" he said, with half a smile.

"The whole network consists of tunnels. Endless underground tunnels."

"Not a country for the likes of us, then," he chuckled.

His fellow train-jumpers and the peasants all roared with approving laughter.

"No, not a country for the Lolo," I replied amicably.

Are they really the savages the driver had claimed? I am not so sure. It is said they do not attack westerners, even unlikely ones who don't have blue eyes, fair hair, or big noses. The Lolo, it turns out, have a code. They are chivalrous in their own way, but also sensible. They take no unnecessary risks, knowing that the Chinese police take the safety of tourists seriously and that the slightest infraction can carry the death sentence.

Not to rely on intimidations alone, I presented the chief Lolo a two-hundred-yuan note, a gesture of gratitude if he could see his way to allowing the Frenchman, his adopted daughter, and their mad driver to be on their way, leaving the wreck of the Blue Arrow. Not to be outdone in courtesy, Scarface and his cronies stoned the first vehicle that happened by to make it stop. It was a minibus serving the employees of the local hydroelectric power company. "Take these folk to hospital double quick—the girl has a broken leg!" The minibus driver recognised that there was no discussing the Lolo's command, which seemed to ring out over the entire mountain.

Little Road lay on the back seat with me kneeling by her side to immobilise her broken leg with both hands; the least bump in the road made her howl with pain. Still, little by little the world recovered some semblance of normality. The memories of threats and violence melted in the monotonous calm of a purring engine, the rush of air conditioning, and another driver with a surfeit of phlegm. ("Ah! that was scary!" he confided in me. "I almost wet myself.") Down the yellow track the minibus glided like a silvery bird darting effortlessly among black rocks, dark trees, green grasses, and azaleas in flower. A bird in free flight, as light as a sunbeam.

The deposed King of the Road told the chauffeur his joke about the sow. When I looked out of the rear window I noticed that, from the vantage of the minibus, Dragonhead Mountain had ceased to seem the monstrous beast of legend sprawling from west to east. Instead, three crests rose up in north-south alignment above the green swathes of forest: the one in the middle was cone-shaped, while the other two, more rounded, resembled the splendid dark-veiled breasts of a goddess. A poem, whose author and title escape me, came to mind. We used to read it together, you and I:

> *And the sun high on the horizon*
> *Hiding in a bank of cloud*
> *Lines the clouds with saffron.*
> *Dove sta memora.*

3. THE FLYING SOCK

In the days and nights that follow, Little Road is plagued by nightmarish visions of a giant, spider-black cobra coiled at her feet, suddenly raising its head half a metre high to lunge at her, its fanged jaws stretched wide. In another dream, a quivering arrow cleaves the air on its way to pierce her with a point whose silvery sheen indicates that it is poisoned. In these dreams she hears the vibration of the invisible string, like the dying note of a cello. The arrow pierces her leg, always the left one. Sometimes, the images of the serpent and the arrow are conflated with that of a human bone, fleshless and phosphorescent—her fractured tibia, exactly as it looks in the X-ray.

The Hospital of China and the West, renowned for its department of osteopathic surgery, is the finest medical facility in all of Sechuan. It occupies a ten-storey building with thousands of beds and several operating theatres outfitted with all the latest American, German, and Japanese equipment.

Five hundred metres to the north stands the Palace of Justice. From the window of her ward, Little Road can see the glass palace, which is often wreathed in mist, especially in the mornings. Judge Di is not there. According to the mayor's son-in-law, the leading mag-

istrates of the country are all in Peking to attend a fortnight of conferences.

"When I return," he had told the mayor's son-in-law
on the phone, "I will be glad to receive the offering of
your psychoanalyst friend."

With his silvery hair, impeccably starched white coat,
and wire-framed spectacles hanging from a little chain
around his neck, Dr. Xiu, head of the department of
osteopathic surgery, is the very picture of medical
authority. His success in the late sixties with the first
reattachment of a severed finger brought him nation-
wide fame. Rumour has it that even today, at sixty years
of age, he still practices incessantly at home, reattaching
parts of dismembered rabbits in his wife's kitchen.

With a swarm of young residents and nurses in tow,
he makes his morning rounds through the dozen wards
on the eighth floor, including the one to which Little
Road was admitted yesterday. He gives a barely perceptible nod when introduced to Muo, the patient's adoptive father from France. After studying the X-rays he
delivers a swift, unequivocal diagnosis: a fracture of the
tibia, necessitating an operation to insert stabilising
metal pins. At least two months' convalescence will follow, along with potential loss of limb length, perhaps
even some degree of permanent lameness.

Little Road frowns, turns pale, then blushes. She
asks Dr. Xiu if he means that she will be a cripple for
life. Now more evasive, without meeting her gaze, he
hands her the X-rays. "Take a look for yourself, my
dear. It's not good news."

No sooner have Dr. Xiu and his retinue departed
than the air is filled with the condescension and pes-

simism of the other patients and their visiting relatives, and that of the bloodless nurse taking orders for lunch. The awful implications of Little Road's diagnosis begin to dawn on Muo.

He dashes into the corridor to catch up with Dr. Xiu.

"Oh, Doctor, you must help me, I beg you. I have already bought plane tickets for my daughter and myself. We have to be in Paris in two weeks' time. It's extremely urgent."

"This is a serious matter, sir. You who have come from France are no doubt far more knowledgeable than I regarding Flaubert's novel *Madame Bovary,* in which the heroine's husband rates as an excellent osteopath for having set his prospective father-in-law's broken leg to rights within forty days. Considerable progress has been made in our field since then. However, the elderly Frenchman's fracture was simple, with no complicating factors whatsoever. Your daughter's case is far more serious. The bone is broken in two—a compound fracture, in clinical parlance. All I can do is give you my personal assurance that the intervention will leave a minimum of scarring."

EVERY NIGHT THE MAYOR'S SON-IN-LAW heads to the Provincial Penitentiary no. 2 to sleep in a private cell.

The prison is a brick building in the shape of the Chinese character "ri" (*sun,* or *day*). The horizontal strokes at the top and bottom correspond to the south and north wings, respectively, of the blackened edifice. The south wing houses exclusively a printing plant operated by convicts, the north a cannery manned by prisoners awaiting trial. The vertical strokes, facing east and west, are the cells of the three thousand inmates. Each side is five storeys high. In the rectangular spaces between the factories and the cell blocks are the exercise yards. A transverse section at ground level is reserved for prisoners of privilege who, unlike the rest, have neither shaven heads nor only numbers as their identities.

Come ten o'clock this October evening, convict number 28-543, nicknamed "the Kalmuk," is sitting on his pallet in cell 518 on the top floor of the east wing, absorbed in the fabrication of a flying sock, of which each convict knows the secret.

The Kalmuk enjoys the privilege of working outside the prison two days a week, in one of the restaurants managed by the mayor's son-in-law.

With an illicit ballpoint pen he notes down the message his boss and friend has instructed him to transmit: "The mayor's son-in-law is looking for a doctor who can fix a broken leg in ten days."

He stuffs the scrap of paper down into the toe of the sock and adds a half-spent tube of toothpaste for ballast. Then he ties the top with string, drawing it shut like a purse. Finally, he attaches another piece of string, longer and thicker this time, after checking its strength with his teeth.

At the top of his voice, he sings a line from a revolutionary opera: "My husband's low wages have no effect on my ideology." It is the secret signal that announces the launch of a flying sock.

The prisoner on the lookout by the door gives the all-clear in the corridor. Holding the sock, the Kalmuk clambers onto the shoulders of another cellmate, the sturdiest of the lot, who shoves him up to the small window. The bars are too close together to allow more than a few fingers of the ordinary fellow to poke out. But after much deft twisting and turning, the Kalmuk succeeds in forcing his whole hand through and then, centimetre by centimetre, the rest of his forearm, at the end of which the sock dangles in the void.

With the skill of a puppeteer, he fingers the string, causing the weight to pendulate slowly in front of the barred windows of the fourth-floor cells directly below. Another hand comes out to seize the sock in midswing. The Kalmuk waits. Keeping his fingers quite still, he sings another revolutionary song:

> *The communist lover is truly amazing.*
> *Like a thermos flask,*
> *Cold on the outside,*
> *But scalding inside.*

The expert angler senses a catch; he feels the flying sock twitch at the end of the string, the signal that the message has been received. He reels the line back in, but when he looks inside he finds only his own note plus the tube of toothpaste. He ties the sock up again and casts it into the void once more, making it swing as precisely as a metronome before the windows of the third floor, before lowering it farther, to the next level, past one window after another, waiting for it to be seized again. Now and then the wind kicks up, making the sock jerk about like a dazed sparrow after it's crashed into a window. At times, too, the sock (which is nylon) catches on some hook in the bars or brickwork and resists all efforts to tug it free.

An hour elapses. When the Kalmuk finally reels his

sock back up, he discovers a different note inside: "Number 96-137, cell 251, knows someone and wants 100 yuan."

4. THE OLD OBSERVER

An X-ray photograph bows in the hand of a man known as the Old Observer as he holds it up to the light. It is a coarse hand, dark-skinned, gnarled and scratched, with crooked bony fingers like the roots of a little tree and sharp, thick fingernails, cut rough, perhaps with a sickle, the color of ash with mud (or something worse) under them.

Muo's gaze is riveted on the old man's deeply furrowed face, with its wispy white moustache between the thin lips and the flattened nose, pressed up against the pale silhouette of Little Road's shinbone, shimmering on the negative. He registers the faintest twitching of facial muscles, the slightest hint of a gleam in the eyes, as the two of them sit on a tree trunk in the muddy forecourt of the old man's abode, which is perched on a forested mountain two thousand metres high, far from the mountain path, in a clearing fringed with giant bamboo. Over the crude double doors a white-painted signboard proclaims: OBSERVATION POST OF PANDA DROPPINGS—BAMBOO FOREST.

As the old herbalist scrutinises the photograph showing the leg of the young aspiring ballerina, who—if her adoptive father's account is to be believed—is to take part in the national ballet competition in ten days' time, the X-ray whines like a saw in the breeze, the only sound but for the rustle of bamboo.

"What do you call the big bone that is broken in two?" Muo asks, anxiously testing the Old Observer's expertise.

"I don't know. What's the difference?"

"Please don't be difficult, sir. It took me fifteen hours on a country bus to get here. Don't you know what a tibia is?"

"No."

"An old prisonmate of yours, number nine-six-one-three-seven, claims that you once used a poultice to mend someone's broken shinbone after an accident in the printing workshop. This was ten years ago."

"I don't remember that."

"Nine-six-one-three-seven—that number doesn't ring a bell? Serving a life sentence? In return for fixing his leg you demanded that his family pay the school fees of your daughter, who was living with her mother in your home province."

"Sorry, I don't remember anything like that."

THE RAIN IS COMING DOWN in sheets when Muo, mad with frustration, leaves the Observation Post of Panda Droppings and makes his way down the mountain, back to the road to catch the bus that goes past once or twice a day. While waiting, he tries to stay dry under a jutting rock, but as it is getting late and he is soaked to the skin, he decides to seek refuge in a dormitory lodging the bachelor workforce of a bamboo-furniture factory nearby.

The medieval-style factory is not far from the Observation Post, and all the workers are acquainted with their solitary neighbour, the taciturn man bowed by hardship, who served five years in prison for attempting to cross the border into Hong Kong after the 1989 handover. (He spent all night swimming across the sea. The lights of Hong Kong were already in sight when they fished him out.)

According to the workers, his job is to patrol the forest, habitat of the region's last panda, one of barely a thousand surviving in the world. The animal, being even more solitary in its habits than the Old Observer, is rarely sighted, and the old man's contact with the creature consists entirely of collecting its droppings and sending them on to the regional centre, where they are analysed to assess the panda's need for nutritional or medical assistance.

The rain stops, but the drops sliding off the trees keep pattering on the corrugated iron roof. A mountain stream gurgles behind the dormitory. Inside, the workers play cards by the flickering light of spirit lamps in the smoke-filled air. Muo fills a dented copper kettle with water, which he puts on to boil over the crackling fire in the hearth, hollowed out of the earthen floor. Huddled on a wooden bench by the singing kettle, he dozes off. In a dream, he hears the name of Bei Le—a very ancient name with two sonorous syllables—being intoned in some palatial setting (the Forbidden City? the glass Palace of Justice in Chengdu?) while the enthroned emperor, robed in yellow, grants his morning audience to his ministers, generals, and courtiers, among them Bei Le, the country's leading expert on horses.

Having reached the qualifying age for retirement, Bei Le commends to the sovereign's attention one Mr. Ma as his potential successor at court.

"He is a genius, Your Imperial Majesty," Bei Le says. "He knows more about horses than I do. No man is better suited."

The emperor sends for this Mr. Ma, who is to present himself at the imperial stables with a view to picking out the best mount from among thousands of horses. The emperor is tyrannical, unpredictable, and given to violence. Mr. Ma (who in bearing and habits strongly resembles the Old Observer of Panda Droppings) understands that a misjudgement could be fatal. But after inspecting all the horses, his pick is unequivocal. The steed of his choice, when presented to the emperor and his courtiers, elicits peals of laughter: not only does the horse lack the telltale white forelock, the classic sign of purity and nobility of bloodlines, it is also an unprepossessing mare, scrawny and dun-coloured. The emperor summons old Bei Le and says, "How dare you play games with me, the supreme sovereign of the land? Your crime warrants death, the man you recommended can't even tell a stallion from a mare."

Before being executed, old Bei Le asks to see the mount selected by Mr. Ma. Setting eyes on the mare, he heaves a long sigh.

"Mr. Ma is truly a genius, your majesty. I do not reach even to his ankle in stature," he says, but the point is lost on the emperor, and with it the life of old Bei Le.

Two years later, when the tyrant has been killed in a

popular uprising, the mare is adopted by his successor, and sure enough it turns out to be the swiftest mount in the land, capable of covering a thousand *li* a day, like the winged horse of legend.

Muo wakes with a jolt. He has not yet finished recording the dream (faithfully as ever) in his exercise book when he comes to the realisation that the old emperor is none other than Judge Di, that Bei Le must be the mayor's son-in-law, and that Ma the supreme equine expert stands for none other than the Old Observer of Panda Droppings. When Muo presses himself, a final recollection of the dream comes to him: the new emperor, surrounded by guards in full armour, casts off his robes and a false beard, revealing himself to be Muo, while the winged horse steps out of the skin of a scrawny mare before transforming into the X-ray of Little Road's broken shinbone.

Mr. Ma has the power to see beyond mere appearances, Muo reflects, *so what can the Old Observer have been looking for in the X-ray of a bone, whose name he doesn't even know?*

At daybreak he climbs up to the observation post once more. He finds the old man with a hod on his back, on the verge of setting out on his daily collections.

"May I accompany you? Even the slightest chance to glimpse a panda in the wild would be an extraordinary opportunity."

"To take idiotic photos, I suppose?"

"No, I don't have a camera."

"I warn you that you'll be wasting your time."

Muo cannot remember where he read that men of action are always taciturn. In that respect, at any rate, the Old Observer of Panda Droppings must be a great man of action. When Muo talks, the old man seems pained. At first Muo takes this for contempt. But the deeper they penetrate into the bamboo forest, which is so dense that the sun is not to be seen and the old man must hack their way through the undergrowth, the more Muo understands the value of silence.

"If you are curious about pandas, you should be interested to know that they have ears, as we do," says the old man before turning silent again. His own ears, big and hairy, are in excellent working order, and suddenly he stops to listen in the direction of a pine wood nearby. They head off that way, and after twenty minutes' brisk walk arrive at the pines to discover on the boggy forest floor fresh footprints among the kaleidoscope of russet pine needles and cones smelling of damp and decay. The tracks are as large as a human palm, and have opposable thumbs. In the distinct marks, it is possible to distinguish the shape of the heel-pad and the claws.

"Could you really hear it from the other side of the mountain, more than a kilometre away?" Muo asks admiringly.

When the old man does not respond, Muo continues: "I'm nearly blind as it is, but thanks to you I have now discovered that I'm deaf as well."

Wordlessly, the Old Observer stoops to draw a tape from his hod and, squatting down, proceeds to measure the length and breadth of a footprint.

Muo breaks the silence: "I suppose that, lacking medical credentials, you are reluctant to prescribe treatment for visitors from the West, fearing you'll pay dearly for anything that might go wrong. But I assure you, I swear to you—and I will put it in writing—if your attempt to mend my daughter's leg should fail, however miserably, I will not hold it against you."

Pretending not to hear, the Old Observer extends the tape measure to note the precise distance between two footprints, inferring from the relative proximity that the panda was running. Then he draws himself upright and goes after the other marks on the muddy ground.

Muo follows at his heels, but the old man quickens his pace, as if to shake him off. He crosses streams, taking flying leaps from rock to rock with such agility that Muo wonders whether he has some Lolo blood. When he loses sight of the Old Observer from time to time, Muo must track the creature himself. Here and there its steps are crowded and confused, suggesting an animal dizzy with hunger—or could this mysterious, solitary panda have a sense of humor? Could it be leading the Old Observer on a merry chase? The traces suddenly change direction, forking its path in two, veering this way and that, before disappearing on the bank of a stream.

Muo eventually comes upon the old man, who is inspecting the trunk of a common birch tree. Around it the lianas have been disturbed, leaves have been crushed, and at the base of the trunk the smooth, silvery bark has been shredded and flaked off in places. The smell of aniseed fills the air.

Muo says, quite out of breath, "I just have one more thing to say to you, then I won't bother you anymore."

Without deigning to look at him, the Old Observer puts his nose close to the scratch marks and sniffs the pungent aroma of the sap with flared nostrils.

"I have a confession to make," Muo says before falling silent again, having second thoughts about divulging the truth: that having this broken bone mended could change the lives of several people, including himself. He holds his tongue, reflecting that even the mention of the word *judge* would, in the ears of this former convict, echo as torture, despair, iron, fire, and blood.

He takes another tack: "For the past ten years I have been studying psychoanalysis in France. Here's what I propose: if you can put the girl's leg to rights in ten days, I will teach you this new revolutionary science, with all its unequalled powers, from A to Z."

For the first time the old man turns his head, and throws Muo a quick glance of appraisal.

"It is a science invented by Freud, which lays bare the secret of the world," adds Muo.

"Which secret is that?"

"Sex."

"Say that again?"

"*Sex.*"

The old man bursts out in convulsive laughter, nearly collapsing at the foot of the birch tree.

"We should get Mr. Freud to come here," he gasps, pointing to the scuffed bark. "Then he could tell us why the panda rubs against this tree."

"Maybe it's hungry. Freud would say it's suffering from material frustration."

"Not at all, young man. All the panda wanted was to scrape off his balls."

Muo is stunned as he examines this evidence of self-castration, a behavior he has come across in biology books. The sun's rays project leopard spots on the silent, radiant, enchanted trunk. He is disappointed to note that, as usual, his expert interpretation is mistaken. He crumbles with self-reproach while the Old Observer presses on.

Since morning, they have seen swarms of butterflies of different species, each one more astonishing than the last, none of which have sparked even the slightest interest in the Old Observer, but an hour's hike from the unsettling tree of castration, the old man stops in his tracks, motioning to Muo to be utterly still: a tiny butterfly flits down the muddy, bamboo-lined path among the tufts of black centaurea and yellow tansy. With a satisfied grin, the old man declares, "We can go home early today."

On his guard, wary of what the old man might have up his sleeve, Muo tries to remember that he is a respectable and brilliant disciple of Freud, as the two follow in silence after the blue-black butterfly with grey stripes on its white wings. It advances slowly, zigzagging among the shrubs, toadstools, and grasses lining the dappled path, on which the mud is ankle-deep in places. Muo strains his eyes, following the little creature until its white and grey markings are lost against the ferns that grow over the pale, gnarled roots of bamboo and dark green lichens.

Suddenly the butterfly quickens, whirling and skimming in febrile flight, growing even more resplendent in the throes of some blissful intoxication. Is it the scent of some precious nectar? Of a nearby female? A Freudian gloss on this phenomenon occurs to Muo, but to his intense disappointment the insect swoops down into a ditch, where it settles on a heap of dung, its wings palpitating ecstatically.

"What good luck!" the old man exclaims, jumping into the ditch after the fragile creature. "Enjoy your meal, little one," he says as he gazes at his prize.

At this sight Muo is shaken to his core by a sudden recollection: eating, shitting, and fucking, the sly old prisoner Sun's trinity for living. For all Muo's tomes, his dictionaries, his notebooks, his emotions, his hopes and worries—could there in fact be fewer things in heaven and on Earth than are dreamt of in his master's philosophies? The spectre of futility hovers over everything Muo has done, from his peregrinations over the countryside on bike and by train, to his pursuits of love and of sex, to his dissimulations and fabulations, to every deed that followed from his idea of returning to China on a mission of salvation.

The dampness floating in the forest coats the dung with a brown varnish. Once the butterfly has gone, the Old Observer takes out his utensils and gathers up the panda droppings in a plastic bag. Muo watches him store everything in his hod.

Together they make their way back to the observation post, where the old man lays a mat of woven bamboo on the ground in front of his house. Spreading the panda turds on the mat so they can dry in the sun, he goes inside and returns with more plastic bags, each of them tagged with a date.

"My house is too damp, so I have to keep bringing my specimens out to dry," he explains. "The centre sends someone to fetch them only once every other week."

Spread out on the mat, neatly arranged in chronological order, is a fortnight's worth of the Old Observer's work, still somewhat pliant owing to the dampness of his house, with shreds of half-digested bamboo leaves visible in the lustrous masses. Suddenly there is a glimmer in the old man's eye; the man of action is aroused. He bursts out: "Would you be prepared to spend your life with a peasant woman?"

"I don't understand your question," says Muo.

"If I manage to set the dancing girl's broken leg to rights within ten days, will you marry my daughter?"

5. THE SEA CUCUMBER

Since his arrival in Peking for the conference of Chinese jurists and magistrates at The New Capital, a top-flight, four-star hotel, Judge Di has been uncharacteristically abstemious, not to say ascetic. On the advice of his sexologist, he follows a strict diet based on sea cucumber, in anticipation of the carnal delights that he is prepared upon his return to give that four-eyed psychoanalyst a second chance to furnish. (Though he stands to benefit most from this folly, Muo cannot but marvel at the judge's absurdly bad judgement, particularly considering that he was almost embalmed following his previous tryst. So underdeveloped must be Muo's own appreciation of the exquisite whiteness of a virgin's hand.)

To be deprived of the daily pleasure of unlimited food of unending variety represents a considerable torment to the judge, who even as a child was known for disgusting gluttony. Before each meal his mother would set aside an egg, a piece of meat, or a chicken leg to be fed later to the smallest of his sisters, whose stunted growth was aggravated by her inability to compete with her brother when meals were served. In those days the future judge's steely index finger—which would later win him fame and position—earned him the reputation of a virtuosic manipulator of chopsticks. (Plunging them into a pot, he was capable of seizing a pound of noodles in one go, leaving nothing for the others. As his family were of peasant stock, they did not go in for such refinements as serving dishes; his mother would transfer the pots and pans directly from the fire to the table for everyone to dip into. As soon as the spicy vapours began to rise from the greasy, blackened pot, the judge's siblings would wheel around to attack him before he could strike, but always in vain: he could take quite a trouncing before diving like a bird of prey for the choicest piece of meat.) As a grown man and elite executioner he retained this supremacy at mess in the barracks, where the soldiers squatted around a single iron pot to consume their coarse rations. In those days he would also take solitary walks to town, stopping always at The Donkey Pot. He would make straight for the kitchen, where a side of donkey was invariably stewing in a gigantic pan. The cook knew what was expected of him; without a word, he would take a prong and plunge it into the roast to extract a succulent chunk of sizzling, steaming, marbled meat. Using an oversized carving knife he would slice the meat into a bowl filled with stock, to which he'd add finely chopped chives, pepper, and salt. Then there would invariably ensue a

bit of theatre between the two men, as the cook posed
the ritual question: "Do I add some donkey's blood
today?"

If Judge Di nodded yes, it meant that he had shot at
least one condemned man that day, in which case the
cook would take the bowl through to the restaurant area,
where he would seat himself on a low stool to slice the
congealed blood into squares of red jelly, bobbing on
the surface of the stock. The judge adored—and indeed
still adores—the taste of those soft, bloody lumps melting in his mouth. Like a cannibal, he would devour the
meat, swallowing the gristle whole, cracking a rib with
his teeth and sucking out the marrow before noisily
slurping the soup. Some years later, when his life was all
sunshine (not thanks to the rays cast by the Great
Helmsman, despite the song sung by billions of his
countrymen for half a century—"The sky reddens in the
East. The sun rises. It is he, Mao, our president . . ."—
but rather to the sun rising in the West, the sun of
capitalism in the communist mode), he donned the
garments of magistracy. Since that time, wreathed in
the aura of power, money, and the indiscreet charms of
the bourgeoisie, he has been initiated into Western gas-
tronomy. With a white linen napkin tied around his
neck, amid the clatter of forks, knives, and spoons and
the strictly regulated changing of plates with each
course, he dines on *lapin chasseur, chou frisé à la duchesse,*
kidney in Madeira Sauce, creamed salmon . . . To him,
this exotic cuisine is a pageant worthy of the cinema, a
"good show" (he has a smattering of English and loves
that word, which he pronounces *"sow"* in his strong
regional drawl). He has discovered that the cuisine of
the West—in fact the whole civilisation—revolves around

the notion of *"sow."* Even going to war means a *"sow"* of force. This is contrary to Di's own spirit. Being in the business of passing irreversible sentences, he is a man of genuine deed, not of *"sow."* Back in his villa of an evening, the satisfaction at having destroyed a few more lives, and with them entire families, makes him feel young again. His step grows more assured, thundering as he climbs the stairs, so that at his approach his wife emerges from her quarters and, throwing herself at his feet, cries out in the long, drawn-out tones of a Chinese opera: "You have returned, Your Honour?"

(Chinese females, especially of a marriageable age, will surely agree: such formality between husband and wife is today atypical and uncalled for, especially in the intimacy of the home. It is well to note, however, that the phrasing of the question is ingenious. Here we have the key to the art of matrimony that has provided our families with a solid basis over thousands of years: never ask a question that might embarrass. In particular, never ask a man where he has been or what he has been up to. It is sufficient to establish the fact of his return in the interrogative form, thereby attesting not only to your solicitude regarding his welfare, but also to the miraculous good fortune that has brought him back to you, a beneficence so moving as to leave you unable to utter more than a few syllables. The same principle applies, more broadly, to social intercourse. When addressing someone over breakfast, do not ask what he is having, which might be cause for embarrassment if, for instance, the dish ordered betrays frugality or, worse, a want of means. Ask instead, "Are you eating?" and by this subtlety all will be well.)

One type of Western fare that Judge Di especially

enjoys is charcuterie. Sometimes, during breakfast at
the Holiday Inn, the best hotel in Chengdu, where the
buffet is set up in a rectangular garden, he gorges himself on sausage (his favourite), along with dressed ham,
breaded chops, smoked chicken breast, salami, and
black pudding. These are tasty appetisers, to be sure,
but hardly sufficient as a proper meal, especially when it
is a question of satisfying the acute hunger, both physical and moral, of a Grand Inquisitor. The moment of
condemnation is even more intense and thrilling than
the actual execution, which is merely the carrying out of
an order. Putting a man to death is a singular and
decidedly masculine sensation, but in the courtroom
the thrill of commanding life and death is enhanced
by the pleasures of cat-and-mouse, obviously a more
feminine pursuit, full of feigned innocence and
coquettishness. Spying a moment of potential release,
the mouse can't believe its luck; it trembles and cowers.
The cat remains obligingly aloof. The mouse makes a
run for the baseboard. The cat waits and watches, and
just as the mouse imagines itself free at last, the cat
pounces with his merciless claws. After such stimula-
tion, every organ, every muscle in his body, aches to be
recharged, just as some men, following sex, dive into
the refrigerator with bulimic ardour.

That is how Judge Di became a devotee of pork offal.
He likes to conclude a session at the tribunal or at the
mah-jongg table by feasting on the innards of a pig:
heart, lungs, stomach, kidneys, liver, entrails, tongue,
tail, ears, trotters, and brain. A live-in cook from
Shanghai, employed at the tribunal's expense, is on call
twenty-four hours a day to prepare a Shanghai delicacy
known as Tripe with Spirits, which requires stewing on

a low flame in a sauce of chopped ginger, osmunda flowers, star anise, cinnamon, grilled tofu, yellow wine, and a handful of the glutinous rice that is normally used as a fermenting agent. Now, in his Peking hotel room, that repast comes back to Judge Di in his dreams. His mouth, monotonously engaged with sea cucumber, waters at the thought of the earthenware pot sweating droplets outside while within bubble entrails of every shape and form, red, viscous, fatty, spongy, steeped in alcohol, and seasoned with herbs and fiery spices, salty-sweet, each morsel akin to a sliver of honeycomb complete with grubs working up the gravy.

The cucumber prescribed by the Peking sexologist offers none of the pleasures of this dish. An invertebrate mollusc related to the sea urchin and the starfish, the sea cucumber is hard to come by, expensive, and exotic; found mainly in the Indian Ocean and the western Pacific, it is collected from the coral reefs it inhabits by divers who go down beyond the reach of light to hunt for it, groping for this spiny marine creature confusingly named for a vegetable. Once out of water and set in the sun to dry, the sea cucumber, which is fronded with quivering feet, much like a centipede, shrivels into a viscid jelly. It has to be salted forthwith to preserve its shape and colour, after which it looks like a human penis ten to fifteen centimetres long—veined, ridged, and knobby. When cast into boiling water to cook, it inflates to reveal a glans at its tip.

The phallic aspect perhaps explains the sea cucumber's position of sublime isolation at the pinnacle of ancient Chinese pharmacopoeia. It was used at court to restore the energies expended by successive emperors on their thousands of concubines. Known as "marine manhood" during the Tang Dynasty, it is known in Chinese today as "ginseng of the sea." The democratic distribution of this seafood was very long in coming. During the dynastic period the emperor would offer tiny portions to ministers or generals to ensure their loyalty at times of political crisis or military conflict. Early in the twentieth century, after the collapse of the last dynasty, one He Gonggong, a eunuch-cum-cook (slandered by some as a eunuch-cum-hairdresser), opened a restaurant named Happy Virtue by the north gate of the Forbidden City. For the first time in the history of Chinese aphrodisiacs, the aroma of ginseng of the sea rose up over the palace wall and wafted across downtown Peking. But it took another hundred years and the advent of Chinese-style capitalism for the democratisation to reach today's levels, with ginseng of the sea of medium quality to be found quite typically at banquets of the newly rich.

The only shortcoming of this rare commodity, this fabulous remedy, is that it has no taste whatsoever, a fact that generations of imperial chefs have made strenuous efforts to alter with all manner of spices, but with no success. The sea cucumber is bland—disgustingly, nauseatingly so. Hence Judge Di's particular ill temper at his pre-copulative diet. Each morning, the restaurant across the road sends a waiter to his room bearing a chrome-plated serving dish, under the tightly sealed lid of which is a plentiful serving of rice-stock made with ginseng of the sea. The stock, which is continually topped off with water while simmering, is reduced for hours until it is impossible to distinguish a single grain of rice. But notwithstanding this recipe from one of Hong Kong's finest restaurants, the ginseng of the sea makes for a perfectly tasteless Chinese risotto. Come midday, the same waiter brings the same receptacle, this time with a serving of ginseng of the sea prepared with red oil or sliced sea cucumber with carrot gravy, one of the traditional imperial dishes first served to ordinary folk at He Gonggong's Happy Virtue Restaurant. But the flavour is, as ever it was for high and low alike, of nothing. In the evening, the receptacle is brought again, now with a ginseng-of-the-sea soup laced with savoury mushrooms and bamboo shoots. The bland sameness could make you weep.

At last, on the fourth day of his diet, Judge Di begins to feel some effect. He becomes aware of a faint stirring in his member, which has been stone cold and dormant since the incident at the morgue.

"I think I'll bring forward the date of my return to Chengdu," he tells himself gleefully.

6. THE ORIOLE

Hermetically sealed though they are in an emptied tin, a jam jar, and a flask—vessels as innocuous-seeming as cellars of salt, pepper and chili powder on a banquet table—when they make their appearance on Little Road's bedside table, the pastes concocted by the Old Observer of panda dung enrage the doctors and nurses of the Chengdu Hospital Department of Osteopathy. These believers in the exclusive primacy of the modern lancet inform the young patient and her father, orally and in writing, that a heavy fine and expulsion from the facility will result if they dare introduce again these dubious, unscientific, scandalous products of charlatanism, which will be confiscated forthwith.

With time running out for his scheme, Muo secures Little Road's discharge, and they move into The Cosmopolitan, a modest hotel in the southern suburbs. A quiet place with hardly any other guests, it is run by a peasant couple who, having struck it rich growing hothouse blooms, converted their old farmhouse into an eight-room hotel. The hallway features a shrine to the god of riches and a multitude of clocks indicating the time in far-flung cities: New York, Peking, Tokyo, London, Paris, Sydney, and Berlin. In the courtyard beyond the entrance is an impressive cage, not one of those wicker affairs that hang on a nail in the wall or a bamboo one suspended from the branch of a tree, but a metal cage in the shape of a pagoda, no less than two metres high and painted dark green. In it, an oriole roosts on the perch. As it does with all arrivals, the bird wakes up to sing a few notes of greeting to the two new guests: the girl hopping on one leg with the aid of crutches and her bespectacled companion, who, despite being weighted down with luggage, offers an arm of assistance. The girl haughtily waves him off, suggesting to the staff the appearance of a distraught young lady of noble birth with her nearsighted, clumsy old retainer at her heels.

Muo notes that she has changed over the past few days. Gone is the vivacious little film-dreamer; in her place he finds the irascible invalid. *Pain affects the mind,* he thinks. He questions the arbitrariness of Fortune, too: Why did she alone not escape the ordeal of the Blue Arrow, the attack of the Lolo, without a scratch? Now he must contend with a fellow conspirator who is erratic, volatile, and generally ill-tempered.

Her room, mercifully on the first floor, does little to moderate her mood; it is so dingy that the lightbulb hanging from the ceiling has to be kept on all day. The walls are infested with rising damp.

She is lying in bed with her left leg atop the covers when Muo enters with a basin of hot water, which he sets on the floor. Squatting down, he delicately rolls her trouser leg up to her knee. The limb is badly swollen and the skin has a morbid sheen, slightly phosphorescent, with dark blotches, something reminiscent of the Embalmer's customers.

"Worse than yesterday," she moans. "I can't stand it. My leg looks like an old map."

The bruises, fanning out and converging, going from blue to black, passing through every shade of violet, and assuming disparate shapes and degrees of roundness, do indeed bear some resemblance to a topographical atlas.

"Let's start with darkest Africa," he says.

He smiles again, hiding behind this pleasantry his dismay at the sight of this accusing, battered limb. He slips some cloth under the leg, soaks a compress in the basin of hot water, and dabs at the blotch in the centre of the world, a horrible expanse of black veined with purple, blue, and red in the shape of a sacrificed tortoise held aloft with its thin neck and triangular head dangling in the sea.

At the heart of this dark continent there is a visible dent with two sharp ridges: *Obviously a break in the tibia,* Muo tells himself. Fortunately, psychoanalytic training has blessed him with a good bedside manner, and so he resorts to prevarication.

"They say that the Old Observer's most spectacular achievement was with a disfigured hunter whose left cheekbone had been smashed in such a way that there was a deep hollow where the bump used to be. Not only did the old man repair the break, he also succeeded in remodelling the area into a jutting cheekbone."

"How did he manage that without operating?"

"By applying the same poultices he gave me for your leg, that's all. They're made with magnetic herbs that pull the bone shards together."

When he has finished cleaning the hideous limb he slides the penknife off his key ring and pries the lid off the can, releasing a fusty smell of damp and moss, mud and pestilence, which rapidly pervades the air.

"Ugh," says Little Road. "Smells like the bottom of the old well in my village."

The recycled can, which lost its unknown original contents, along with its label, long ago, is filled with a black, slightly blubbery ointment.

With the penknife he scoops the substance from the can and spreads it on the pad, really a piece of white cloth he has folded several times. Then, with a delicate touch, he applies the compress to Little Road's leg, securing it with gauze bandages.

That night, he is awakened by the sound of the young girl knocking on the partition between their rooms.

"Does it hurt?" he asks in the dark, putting his mouth so close to the wall that his lips brush the paint.

"Yes, it does, but not too much. Could you give that poor bird something to eat? It's hungry."

"Which bird, my lame princess?"

"The oriole in the cage."

He pricks up his ears and hears the scuttle of a rat along the rafters, a moth bumping against the window pane, the croaking of a frog, the honk of a car in the distance, and down in the yard, the cry of the oriole: metallic, shrill, agitated, like a scythe slicing the night air.

"You can tell it's a domestic oriole," Little Road says from the other side of the partition. "The wild ones don't sound like that."

"How do they sound?"

Her bird call sounds more like the high-pitched squawk of a fledgling sparrow, but Muo finds it amusing all the same. Wide awake now, he gets out of bed, puts some biscuits in his bag, and goes down to the courtyard. She was right; the oriole is famished. From its perch it swoops down like a golden arrow, splashing Muo with water from its trough. Clinging to the bars with its claws and lowering its wings, which are more splendidly feathered than its body, the oriole quivers with excitement as it pecks the crumbled biscuit from Muo's extended hand. It devours the last crumb without the least token of gratitude, then regains its perch, visibly fortified. It pays no further attention to its benefactor and sets about preening its feathers with a show of intense pride. Muo is disappointed and turns to leave. Suddenly he hears a sound like a mockery of a human voice rising from the cage. He wheels around to face the self-involved bird, which, for the next second or two, utters "words," various combinations of about a dozen distinct syllables, unintelligible but sharp and bright as diamonds.

In the morning Muo asks the proprietors about the oriole. The wife explains that its parents were orioles of a noble species kept by a Christian pastor. Other oriole-keepers flocked to his home with their own birds, bearing gifts of money and goods in the hope of being permitted to place their cages next to his so that their own birds might listen to his and learn to sing like the pastor's pair. But the pastor always refused. After he died, the oriole's parents did not survive for long. In the meantime, the orphan chick had grown up, and now, from time to time, it utters a phrase remembered from its mother and father, a phrase in Latin, apparently, something the pastor said at the close of each mass. Some say they are the last words of Jesus Christ.

Like his fellow psychoanalysts in the West, Muo has studied the Bible, but he can't remember what the last words uttered by Christ were. He goes to the trouble of making a note in a new exercise book, reminding himself to check the gospels, but with all there is to do it slips his mind.

DESPITE THE THICK PADDING, the smell of mud and decay persists in the lame princess's room for three days. Each time she wants to take a shower her loyal, nearsighted attendant kneels humbly by her bed to wrap her leg in a sheet of clear plastic, which he secures with big pink elastic bands, the smell of the poultice making his head spin.

On the fourth day, when he removes the soiled

bandages and washes the leg in preparation for the next poultice, he notes that the bruising has faded somewhat. Darkest Africa has lightened to a slate-grey, livid in places, and its surface area, like that of the other continents, has shrunk considerably. The inverted tortoise has lost its long neck, leaving just the triangular head, a small island in the ocean.

A wave of joyful excitement sweeps over the patient as Muo unscrews the lid of the jam jar containing the second remedy. The jar is old, the glass scratched and dull. The poultice is dark brown this time, and the smell, though no less objectionable, is far more complex, remarkable in fact for the diversity of notes: a chaotic blend of grease, opium, beeswax, incense, tree bark, roots, herbs, poisonous mushrooms, ink, ether, resin, and a hint of the dungheap. Spreading it on the fresh compress, Muo can make out fragments of leaves and mushroom stems.

"Is it true that your old shit-collector succeeded in fixing a broken cheekbone that had left a dent in the patient's face?"

"Yes. And you know what the key to his success was? The X-ray, he told me. He could tell there was still an invisible filament linking the extremities of the broken bone. His ointment succeeded in getting the bone to fuse by means of suction—that was the very word he used: *suction.*"

"Is it the same with my shinbone?"

"I think so, yes."

"Where did he learn all that stuff? Did he tell you?"

"When he was a boy he was apprenticed to an herbalist, who brought him into contact with a practitioner of traditional medicine in the same town. This traditional doctor was unsurpassed at curing cataracts by applying an acupuncture needle to just the right spot in the gums. He offered to share his secret with the young apprentice on the condition that he marry his daughter. The apprentice assented, thereby gaining possession of the lucrative secret cure. Years later, during the Cultural Revolution, he fled to the Emei Mountains where, while out collecting herbs one day, he fell into a ditch and broke a leg. A Buddhist monk put his leg to rights in ten days. They became friends, and the apprentice exchanged his acupuncture secret for the monk's bone-setting recipe."

TWO DAYS LATER, the mayor's son-in-law sounds the alarm: Judge Di wishes to bring forward the date of his return to Chengdu. Thank goodness the son-in-law's news reaches them, but it is only a short while before the judge reconsiders. The alarm is cancelled a few hours later, and everything settles down again.

THE STATE OF LITTLE ROAD'S LEG is improving by the hour.

"There's a sort of draught coming from my shin-bone; I can feel it in every pore," she says. "Just now I thought I felt a worm under the bandages, wriggling up from my ankle to my knee. And now it's going all the way down again."

The third and final poultice is applied on the sixth day, in keeping with the Old Observer's instructions.

Muo, now quite an expert nurse, cleans off the residue of the previous ointment, slips towels under the leg, and then opens the flask. (Little Road wants to pull out the stopper with her teeth, but Muo won't hear of it: "The old man told me it contains powdered peacock gall, which is essential but also toxic, not to say lethal. In olden days it was used by Mongolian and Manchurian nobles to commit suicide.")

Once the stopper has been carefully removed with the aid of the penknife, the flask exudes an acrid, savage smell, with a hint of gunpowder. This ointment is a dingy green, thicker and more viscous than the previous ones, and harder to spread on the compress.

"What is the poison called?" Little Road asks.

"Biliary vesicle of peacock."

"What a beautiful name. Everything about peacocks is beautiful, not that I know what a biliary vesicle is."

"It's a small, black, bladder-like sac in the liver. You must have come across it if you have ever dressed a chicken carcass."

"I love peacocks. They're like kings . . ."

"They say that death by peacock gall is gentle, sweet, and painless. Which reminds me of an ancient poem: 'Death in the shimmering sheaf of a giant peacock's tail.' "

A MAN'S FACE APPEARS: long, angular, glowering like a gun.

The light in the courtyard has been switched off. Muo can't make out the figure. *Maybe I need new glasses,* he says to himself. *Could be my eyesight has worsened again. If this goes on much longer I'll be blind by the time my disappearing act comes to an end.*

He hears the creak of leather shoes on the gravel—brand-new Italian shoes, to judge by the sound. *Souvenir of Peking, or a gift from one of his more fortunate victims?*

The shoes march up the stairs like a conquering army—not a swift ascent, but with a deliberate pause after each crashing step. There is a knock that awaits no answer before the door to Little Road's room opens with a long, yawning creak and from the other side of the partition Muo hears the voice of Judge Di, who speaks of himself in the third person.

"Judge Di to see you, miss."

"Please come in. Have a seat, Mr. Judge."

"No hidden mikes or cameras?"

(Footsteps pace the perimeter of the room, then approach the bed, apparently kneeling down to look underneath.)

"Do you know where Judge Di has just been? Peking. He wanted to return earlier, but was unable to." (The scrape of a chair as he takes a seat.) "The organisers of the conference prevailed upon him to address the assembly. All the jurists and magistrates of China were eager to hear all about how he broke a dangerous criminal case by posing as a corpse at the Chengdu morgue. A thrilling story, which is apparently to be adapted for television."

"Will you be playing yourself, sir?"

"Why not? If it's realism they're after . . . But what's this? You look a bit under the weather, miss."

"Yes, that's right. I'm not in the best of health. I have just had an operation."

"Just goes to show that Judge Di has a discerning eye. Nothing escapes him. What is your name?"

"Little Road."

"Not an attractive name. Today our fatherland is rich and prosperous; we have no more little roads. People advance proudly on the sunny highway of socialism. You must change your name. Judge Di will call you Great Road."

(Silence. She's quite right not to answer. The judge rises to his feet.)

"Come on, Great Road. Here, my jacket. Hang it in the wardrobe."

"There isn't one here. I'll hang it from the doorknob."

(For the first time, Little Road moves away from the partition, heading slowly toward the door.)

"What's all this? Tottering around like a little old woman with bound feet. Come here, you . . ."

(The judge is interrupted by a long groan from the girl.)

"Aha! So you like Judge Di, do you? Makes you swoon, does he?"

"Forgive me, it's not my fault . . . the Lolo . . ."

"Incredible! A Lolo maiden! Great Road of the Lolo—that'll be your name in full. I love seeing Lolo girls dance. They're so spirited, full of rhythm and joy. Go on, dance for me!"

"I can't."

"Don't be shy! Every Lolo girl can dance. Just hold out your arms. Come on now, we'll dance together, like sweethearts at the torch festival in your home province. What's that smell? Do you know you smell of gunpowder? Come, let's dance the 'Mountains of Gold in Peking.'"

(Hardly has he launched into the first bar of the revolutionary ditty when she is betrayed by the convalescent limb and collapses on the floor.)

"Don't be a foolish girl. Do you realise what you're doing? You're wasting the opportunity to dance with Judge Di. His patience is running out. Go and take a shower. Afterward, you may join him in bed."

(She scrambles to her feet, moaning pitifully. Her footsteps recede. The bed creaks under the collapse of the judge. Then there is a crash, followed by the cries of the girl, who has fallen again.)

"Stop playing games. Judge Di devises his own amusement."

"I'm not playing games. I broke my left leg in an accident."

"Well, I'll be damned! That bastard psychoanalyst had the balls to set me up with a cripple! How humiliating! Judge Di never sleeps with cripples!"

(He jumps up from the bed, spraying curses and abuse. Then the door slams so violently that the timbers shake. Finally he stomps away down the stairs, and Muo wakes from his dream.)

For a moment, in the haze of semi-sleep, he wonders whether it wasn't a reality. But he is reassured by the shrill cries of the oriole in its cage. He puts his ear to the partition and hears Little Road breathing regularly on the other side.

WHAT A THING OF BEAUTY! Muo reflects, studying the X-ray upon which the segments of tibia have finally fused into a single long, luminous stalk.

It had been early afternoon when he accompanied

Little Road to the hospital for her X-ray appointment.
Told that the results would not be ready for three hours,
he decided to wait. He gave Little Road two hundred
yuan and sent her off, saying, "Take a look in the shops
and buy yourself a present."

Now, leaving the hospital, the X-ray in hand, he is
scarcely conscious of his feet touching the ground. He
is floating, skimming the surface of the pavement.
He goes down People's Road, the city's main traffic
artery, then turns left to take the embankment of the
satiny Brocade River as far as the old South Bridge. He
smiles at everyone he sees—men, women, children, old
people, and even the dreaded policemen. He wishes
he could make them all stop and look at the X-ray,
which proves the Old Observer's great achievement,
this miracle that he has wrought.

"If I ever get married" (to whom? Volcano of the Old
Moon? the Embalmer? Little Road? At this euphoric
moment it hardly matters: I truly love all three—indeed
all four, if I count the daughter of the Old Observer,
whose acquaintance I have yet to make. If they would but
agree, and overlook my physical inadequacies, I would
happily marry them). But where was I? Ah, should I
ever get married, I will put this X-ray up on the wall in
the parlour. I will have it mounted and framed and lit
with a soft, diffuse glow for all to admire as a great work
of art."

It is the end of a lovely afternoon, and the sun is
veiled. A warm fog rises from the muddy, polluted
waters of the river. How it has frayed, the silky Brocade
River of his boyhood, once so limpid, such a wide
expanse of shimmering water that he could never swim

all the way across. What good times they used to have, he and his friends, sunning themselves like lizards on the half-submerged island in the stream. He is a different Muo today, not the nearsighted, awkward adolescent sworn to imaginary crusades. Even as a boy, in his recurrent, naïve, erotic dreams, he would see himself falling in love with one girl after another: a cousin, his teacher, the servant's daughter, a schoolmate—the list of his imaginary paramours never ended. Now, Fate has decreed that Judge Di should be the one to spur him on to resume his old quest, driving him to realise the old ideals concretely, with a proper balance of revolutionary romance and proletarian realism, as Mao would have wished. Nowadays, great leaps forward are par for the course in the communist world, but that hardly makes Muo's leap less great. Had Judge Di not required a virgin, Muo would probably have remained one himself, doomed to spend the rest of his life poring over his books of psychoanalysis in French translations, hypothetically living always at some remove, intellectual masturbation. Now, by the good fortune presented by his return home, he is in love with four real-life—and indeed quite estimable—women. Scanning the faces of those crossing his path on foot or on bicycle, he wonders whether any man in the whole of Chengdu has been so lucky. Not likely, he decides. You can tell by their expressions: normal people would find being in love with even two others stressful enough. Walking along, he ponders this thought, which has never occurred to him before.

"What a pity Volcano of the Old Moon is not in the same penitentiary as the mayor's son-in-law," he muses. (The Embalmer has been transferred elsewhere, too, but she is sometimes far from his thoughts, as Volcano of the Old Moon never is.) "Perhaps he knows someone in the women's prison who could launch a flying sock on my behalf. Some little cotton sock—blue, if I can have the choice, but any colour will do just as well—still warm from the anonymous owner's foot, threadbare at the heel and toe, in which I could put a note saying, 'Message for #1 479 437 in cell 5 005. Judge Di returns tomorrow. You'll be free the next day.' Or, dispensing with the wonderful ambiguity of words, I might draw a picture instead. A drawing of a girl reaching the highest point of the arc as she pole-vaults over a barbed-wire fence. When we were students she won three bronze medals at the inter-university games. I remember her training courses, the cloud of dust at her heels and calves as she ran, her sleek jump-suit emphasizing the curve of her hips and thighs, the long pole planted in the track. Each time, I expected her to remain aloft, evaporating into a puff of smoke or turning into a swallow."

This is an idyllic daydream to balance the terrible nightmare he's been having of late, every two or three days. It always begins the same: pitch darkness, the smell of stagnant water, and a voice groaning, "However constipated I may be, I'll never shit in a communal bucket." Then a stool drops with a splattering sound that fills the dark space. The voice belongs to the former director of the women's prison. There are three people in the cell: the director, one of the prison's doctors, and Muo. The reason for their incarceration is the pregnancy of convict number 1 479 437 of cell 5 005, who has been behind bars for the past two years, his beloved Volcano of the Old Moon. As they are the only three men to have had any contact with her in the past months, the perpetrator of this crime, unprecedented in the annals of the Chinese prison service, is surely among them. The director, who is inclined to confidences during his interminable defecations, has confessed that he almost fell in love with her because of her physical resemblance to Madame Tian, the great dancer of revolutionary ballet whom he idolized as a boy. He summoned the prisoner to his office, having made her dress up as the heroine of *The White-Haired Girl,* including the wig of white horsehair, the legacy of twenty years on a mountain in flight from a landowner with designs on her virginity. He put on a record of the ballet, but Volcano of the Old Moon wouldn't dance.

As to the prison doctor, who in the dream spent most of his time crying in a corner, his tale was simply another manifestation of the eternal phantasm of virginity. He had noticed number 1 479 437 during a gynecological examination. At thirty-six years of age, she was still a virgin, a rarity in present-day China and certainly unique among the inmates. At first, she was no more than a curiosity to him. But then, reading a new edition of an ancient book, he came across the secret recipe of the "red pill" developed by the alchemists of the Ming Dynasty to prolong the life of the emperor. The main ingredient was the menstrual blood of virgins. A clinical trial after eight centuries might be interesting, he thought. So he summoned the prisoner and, claiming to have discovered something untoward during his previous examination, instructed her to supply him with a sample of menstrual blood for additional tests. The sample never arrived on his desk, however, as the prisoner had been suffering from amenorrhea since the beginning of her sentence. Although he had done nothing wrong, the doctor was arrested one morning.

But despite their respective perversities, neither the doctor nor the prison director could have made the inmate pregnant, for the simple reason that they had both heeded the government's appeal twenty years earlier to support the one-family/one-child policy: both men being fathers already, each had presented himself at the local clinic for permanent sterilization—that is to say, ligation of the vas deferens. But then the eyes turn to Muo, who has never had a moment with his friend except in the visiting area, in the presence of other prisoners and their families, everyone under the strict surveillance of female wardens. The nightmare always ends with the jangle of keys, and the squeak of the door opening as the cell is raided by the firing squad with the red stars on their caps and the cold glint of gunmetal in their hands.

The first time he had the nightmare was during their first night at the Cosmopolitan. Muo awoke to a rush of blood filling his cheeks and, leaving his bed, went over to the window, where the pagoda-shaped cage stood in the courtyard below, just beyond the pool of yellow light cast by a streetlamp. It occurred to him that his unconscious was proposing in the language of dreams an indictment of Volcano of the Old Moon. In Freudian terms, it was a sign of "the beginning of the end of love." Why now? Was it the presence of the sleeping girl with the bandaged leg beyond the partition, over whom he hovered like a shadow day and night? Just then, an icy chill—no, a presentiment, a premonitory shiver—ran down his spine.

No one can truly comprehend a dream.

The soul of man abides by intermittence, as Proust observed in the French equivalent of *The Dream of the Red Chamber*. But not even artists, a breed apart, understand the meaning of dreams. They merely create them, live them, and end up as the dreams of others.

At the South Bridge, Muo the agnostic, polygamist in fantasy and polyglot in fact, decides to buy a gift for Little Road at the open-air market. Vendors shout bargain offers under the darkening sky; hungry chickens flap about in their cages; fish wriggle off their bed of ice and fall to the ground, openmouthed. Cinnamon. Star anise. Absinthe. Vermouth. Peppers. Exotic fruits. Genetically modified fruit from America. Vegetables from local farms. What manner of surprise could win Little Road's heart?

YOU MIGHT MISTAKE IT for a blob of black oil paint in water, or a tadpole. It is the biliary vesicle of a white-spotted snake. The salesman places it in a clear plastic bag filled with Chinese alcohol. The vesicle sinks to the bottom, where it curls and undulates yet keeps its shape thanks to the alcohol.

Muo does not intend it as a substitute for the peacock vesicle, which is incomparably more accurate and toxic. Rather, he is drawn to the specific merits of the snake vesicle, known throughout China as a highly efficacious

fortifying agent in the case of bone fractures. At the
same time, he is not unaware of the legendary powers of
this organ to inflate one's courage to kamikaze proportions. As agent of both kinds of fortification, the vesicle
of the white-spotted snake is considered superior to
that of the peacock.

But it will never be ingested by Little Road: within an
hour of its purchase, a blind beggar shambling along
the side of the road catches a whiff of alcohol. He sweeps
the point of his cane from side to side over the pavement until it finds a discarded plastic bag. The beggar
bends down, picks up the bag, and sniffs. The alcohol
has been spilt, but there is still something in the bag,
which he takes to a nearby shop selling food, drink, and
cigarettes, and where the proprietress has installed
domestic and international telephone lines in the hope
of making some extra money.

"That must belong to the man with the spectacles,"
she says, taking a quick glance at the bag. "He came in to
make a phone call. The battery of his mobile was dead
and he wanted to know the rate to phone a hotel in the
suburbs. I told him that the suburbs are the same rate as
the provinces—long-distance. He paid up. But maybe
he should have saved his money. Sounded like he got
some bad news. He turned pale, and kept saying, 'But
that's impossible . . . Impossible, sir!' I guess it wasn't
because he slammed down the phone and dashed out
into the street, and nearly got run over trying to hail a
passing taxi. But the taxi wasn't free. He walked in circles for a moment, before he stopped someone riding a
bicycle. He bought it on the spot, from the looks of
things. Must have paid a pretty penny, too, because the
cyclist didn't haggle and walked away all smiles. So this

little man with spectacles jumped on the bike and speeded away. That's when I realised he left this envelope by the phone," she said and produced the envelope from under the counter. "Nothing but an X-ray inside. When I saw him he was carrying that plastic bag in his hand. Must have dropped that, too, in all the hurry."

"Can you tell me please what's in the bag?" says the beggar. "It's been ages since I could see a thing."

"Let me have a look. What on Earth can that thing be? Wait, let me get my reading glasses. My own sight's not the best . . ."

"You're too modest. I can tell that you have an extraordinary nature."

"Huh, looks to me like the biliary vesicle of a snake."

"What luck!" says the blind man, and with that upends the bag and twists it to funnel the little organ into his mouth. He rolls it around with his tongue, savouring the taste.

"The real thing, nice and bitter."

The vesicle bursts between his yellow teeth, filling his mouth with dark juice. He is oblivious to the shopkeeper's remark that it has started to rain.

PEDALLING MADLY, Muo, with his glasses dripping wet, can barely see the front wheel as he plunges into puddles, splashing pedestrians and overtaking one ghostly cyclist after another in the grey of the downpour. He is racing to the station, where, according to the desk clerk of The Cosmopolitan, Little Road was headed when she left the hotel earlier that afternoon, now limping only slightly, the clerk was pleased to note.

"She was wearing a pair of dark glasses she'd just

bought, and had a six-pack of beer under her arm," he told Muo. "She said she was headed home to her parents and offered us forty yuan for the oriole, which the boss was happy to take. She opened the cage, reached inside with her hand, and watched it fly away. She didn't exactly get her money's worth, did she?" he'd added with a chuckle.

Muo hasn't even a moment to reflect on whether she'd given him any sign of her intention to flee. The train to his home province, on which he'd met her a fortnight ago, leaves at nine o'clock.

But as he races to the station against the clock, he can't help admiring Little Road for her strength of character.

"She won't likely get another chance to see Paris," he reflects, "not even at the price of her virginity."

His legs slow of their own accord. The rain lifts a little, as does the fog on his glasses. With a sudden decisiveness at two minutes until nine, he turns about-face, heading back in the direction he was coming from.

Tossing and turning all night long in his bed at The Cosmopolitan, he dares to muse that the heavens have intervened to save him from his polyamorous perversion. The wholesome love of a single good woman has prevailed.

At that moment he fancies he can hear the familiar cry of the oriole, free but still nearby, the orphaned bird of noble lineage once owned by a Christian pastor—distinct syllables, bright as diamonds.

What could its call be announcing? he wonders. *Could it be another return, that of the beneficent female who liberated it?* He could muse until the break of day on the oriole's mysterious song, except he suddenly remembers that tomorrow is the day of another return, Judge Di's, and that the appointed tryst is to take place in less than twenty-four hours.

Muo runs downstairs and into the courtyard, still dressed for bed. The pagoda-shaped cage looms even larger and lonelier, being now empty. After some moments of enlightened serenity a childish fit overtakes him, and he shakes the cage furiously, punching it, banging his head against the bars, and vainly trying to lift it, before settling for turning it over on its side. He takes a flying leap, as in a kung-fu film, and kicks it.

His cathartic fit of rage is cut short by a near dislocation in his right foot. Then Muo, the man of ripe age wreathed in the beatific smile of childhood regained, swings the door of the cage open and crawls inside.

"I'm a bird," he cries, convulsing with laughter.

His head knocks against the perch and his spectacles slide down off his nose and out of reach. He crouches and cowers, playing the captive game bird.

"Good practice for my future in a prison cell," he chuckles darkly. "Oh, my head is spinning. I feel sick. Why not just end it all tonight? If I had only followed the Embalmer's husband out of the window that evening, I would have spared myself all the subsequent humiliations, which have come to naught and which only more grief can follow." He wonders, if Little Road were to return and find him in the cage, would she set him free? "But she is on the train with her six-pack. Did she buy a ticket this time? Probably not. Petty fraud is the sport of the poor. But perhaps she hasn't left after all. Maybe she's gallivanting around town with some local boy or, being relatively able-bodied once more, perhaps she's found herself a job as a waitress or a cleaning lady. She could well be back. There are signs that tell me she is in love with me. Perhaps she loved me too much. Please come back, Little Road! What creature with wings of pearly glass may alight on the bars of this cage?"

Suddenly the words he has neglected for days to look up come flooding back—the last words of Christ on the cross, which the bird had been echoing: "It is finished."

How sorry he is that he can't, like the bird, say them in Latin. *Muo, you must learn Latin. Indeed, I shall have plenty of time for that very soon.*

THE NEXT DAY, he goes to his parents' flat to spend his last hours of freedom with them, before Judge Di has him rounded up. But by the time he arrives, at four in the afternoon, they are out shopping. Alone in the flat, he hears a knock on the door. He is doubtful at first; he could be hallucinating. But the knocking continues. Opening the door, he finds a girl on the landing—a country girl, by the looks of her. No doubt his mother has finally decided to hire some domestic help.

"It's too late now, perhaps tomorrow," he says, about to shut the door on her.

She blushes and hangs her head shyly, rubbing her right foot over her left calf.

"My father asked me tell you . . ."

"Your father?"

"Yes, the Old Observer."

Muo staggers as if before an exploded shell. All his life he will remember this uncanny moment. Embarrassed, he wants to ask her to come in, to take tea with him, but his tongue betrays his indomitable nature, and taking her by the hand with avuncular interest he hears himself ask: "Tell me, my dear, are you a virgin?"